The Thai Amulet

Berkley Prime Crime Books
by Lyn Hamilton

THE XIBALBA MURDERS
THE MALTESE GODDESS
THE MOCHE WARRIOR
THE CELTIC RIDDLE
THE AFRICAN QUEST
THE ETRUSCAN CHIMERA
THE THAI AMULET

Lyn Hamilton

BERKLEY PRIME CRIME, NEW YORK

This is a work of fiction. Names, characters, places, and incidents either are the product of the author's imagination or are used fictitiously, and any resemblance to actual persons, living or dead, business establishments, events, or locales is entirely coincidental.

THE THAI AMULET

A Berkley Prime Crime Book
Published by The Berkley Publishing Group,
a division of Penguin Putnam Inc.,
375 Hudson Street, New York, New York 10014.

Text design by Kristin del Rosario.

First edition: April 2003

Library of Congress Cataloging-in-Publication Data

Hamilton, Lyn.
The Thai amulet : an archaeological mystery / Lyn Hamilton.—1st. ed.
p. cm.
ISBN 0-425-19006-4 (alk. paper)
1. McClintoch, Lara (Fictitious character)—Fiction. 2. Antiquities—Collection and preservation—Fiction. 3. Women detectives—Thailand—Fiction. 4. Archaeological thefts—Fiction. 5. Missing persons—Fiction. 6. Antique dealers—Fiction. 7. Thailand—Fiction. I. Title.

PR9199.3.H323 T48 2003
813'.54—dc21

2002042690

PRINTED IN THE UNITED STATES OF AMERICA

10 9 8 7 6 5 4 3 2 1

For Carol and Roy

ACKNOWLEDGMENTS

As always I have many people to thank for their help with the research and writing of this book, including my sister Cheryl, Jane and Tim Marlatt, Jim Polk, Bella Pomer, and Natalee Rosenstein. For the details of court life in sixteenth-century Ayutthaya, I am indebted to the amazing translation of *The Royal Chronicles of Ayutthaya* by Richard D. Cushman, edited by David K. Wyatt.

CHARACTERS

IN THE PAST

Chairacha, king of Ayutthaya
Prince Thianracha, his brother
Lady Si Sudachan, royal concubine
Prince Yot Fa, son of Chairacha and the concubine
Prince Si Sin, younger brother of Yot Fa
Khun Worawongsa, court official
Chakkraphat, king of Ayutthaya

IN THE PRESENT

William Beauchamp, antique dealer
Natalie Beauchamp, William's wife
The Chaiwong family:
Thaksin, patriarch
Wongvipa, his wife
Sompom, Thaksin's first son by a previous marriage
Wannee, Sompom's wife
Nu, daughter of Sompom and Wannee
Chat, first son of Thaksin and Wongvipa
Dusit, second son
Prapapan, daughter
Yutai, family secretary

Wichai, family friend
Busakorn, Wichai's daughter
David Ferguson, U.S. consular official
Robert Fitzgerald, artist
Bent Rowland, literary agent
Tatiana Tucker, producer
Prasit, assistant manager, PPKK
Praneet, Will's neighbor

While the characters of the narrator and his mother in the ancient story are fictional, the other characters and the political events and intrigue in the ancient Thai capital of Ayutthaya described here are real. They took place between about 1534 and 1548. The same cannot be said for the present, where all events and people are figments of the author's imagination.

Prologue

Khun Worawongsa is *dead because of me. I did not strike the blow that killed him. The others saw to that. He died, though, because of what I said and to whom I said it. Sometimes, when the moon is full, illuminating the deepest recesses of my mind as it does the dark shadows of night, the specter of guilt overwhelms me. I do not mean that I was wrong to do what I did. I know what I saw and have no doubts as to his culpability.*

Three things, I think, contribute to the turmoil in my soul. The first is a dreadful sense that if I had been more observant, or rather, since I have promised myself I will be completely honest in recounting what happened, had I been less self-absorbed, the others might not have died. The second is the question of whether Khun Worawongsa was driven to the terrible deed by the person I consider to be truly evil, the one with the power to seduce even the most righteous among us, and was therefore entitled to some measure of compassion. The last is the realization of how much I have benefited from his death, so much more than I could reasonably expect from life, beyond, indeed, my wildest imagination: a royal appointment that brings with it wealth, but more than that, my place among King Chakkraphat's closest advisors, and most important, the hand of the most beautiful woman in the world.

Tomorrow, if what our scouts tell us is true, we will engage the enemy. We know that our bitter foe, King Tabinshwehti of Burma, hoping to profit from the political turmoil of the last many months, has swept through the mountain pass with a large army, even as we are attacked on our eastern flank by the Khmer king of Lawaek. We are besieged on all sides.

I am certain that, led by our good King Chakkraphat, our own courage strengthened by his example, we will most certainly prevail. But I may well fall in battle, if not tomorrow, then soon enough. It is for this reason that I chronicle the events leading to the murder of Khun Worawongsa and the others, and my role in his death.

Chapter 1

It is possible I am responsible for someone's death. I don't mean that the corpse found floating in the Chao Phyra River died by my hand. There were others all too willing and eager to do the deed. But sometimes, at the darkest part of night, when the world is so quiet it's impossible to still the demons of fear and guilt, I wonder if what happened was justified, even were all evidence of culpability laid out for everyone to see.

Looking back on it, I search for explanations for what I did and what I said, the point at which I lost all objectivity, where survival instincts took a backseat to revenge.

Mai pen rai, in Thai, means "It's nothing, it doesn't matter." It's an exotic and more cynical version of "Don't worry, be happy," a kind of collective shrug at the vagaries of life. Its spirit carries the average Thai through the average day of frustrations, setbacks, irritations, and even pleasures. But when William Beauchamp locked the door of his antique shop on the second floor of a building off Bangkok's Silom Road for the last time and then quietly disappeared off the face of the planet, I found that *mai pen rai* could be a thin yet almost impenetrable veneer over a seething mass of corruption, evil, and even murder. *Mai pen rai* means "It doesn't matter." The trouble was, it mattered for Natalie Beauchamp, and for me, perhaps, it mattered too much.

My transformation from antique dealer to murderer's accomplice, willing or otherwise, began, as I suppose so many things do, in the mundane, if not downright banal, tasks of a perfectly ordinary day.

"Have you ever wondered what happens to some people when they go to the Orient?" Clive Swain said that day, standing back to admire the display of Mexican patio furniture he'd just arranged. "Is it the heat? I mean you're there at least twice a year, Lara, and you come back more or less the same person. Tired and a little grumpy, maybe, but essentially unchanged."

"Is this relevant to something we're doing at this moment, Clive?" I said, sorting through invoices at the counter. "In fact, is it apropos of anything at all?"

"You remember Will Beauchamp, don't you?" he said.

"Of course I do," I said.

"Well, he's disappeared!"

"I see," I said. "Fellow antique dealer goes to Asia on a buying trip and sends a fax—a fax!—to his wife and child saying he's never coming back, and we call that disappeared, do we?" I closed the cash drawer with a little more force than was absolutely necessary.

"Ancient history," Clive said. "Two years at least. Now he's really disappeared. Poof, gone. You know, mail piling up behind the door, green slime in the refrigerator. That kind of disappeared. He's vanished." As he spoke, I caught sight of a streak of orange hurtling toward me and felt a familiar paw swatting my ankle.

"Speaking of vanished," I said, eyeing a strategically placed mirror in one corner of the shop, "you had better go and see what in the back room has got Diesel agitated. I believe vanished is what is about to happen to one of our little jade Buddhas in the alcove. Young woman in yellow blouse," I added.

"Well, she didn't get the Buddha," Clive said a few minutes later, as Diesel, McClintoch & Swain's Official Guard Cat, stood in the doorway growling at the retreating back of the would-be thief. "Nor anything else, I hope. Really, Lara, sometimes I think we should just move a table out to the street with a sign saying Free Stuff, Please Help Yourself. It would save us a lot of trouble, and we could just retire. Broke, of course. Nice work, by the way, Diesel," he said, tickling the cat's chin. "You will have your reward as soon as I get to the deli. Shrimp, I'm thinking. No—Black Forest ham! How about that?" The cat purred.

"I'm sure that's not good for him, Clive," I said. Both cat and ex-husband cocked their heads and looked at me. It surprised me that, given how long I'd known both of them, I'd never noticed until that moment how alike their expressions were nor how they both managed to avoid doing what I wanted them to.

"She's getting to be an old prune in her dotage, isn't she, Deez?" Clive said, stroking the cat. "We'll ignore her. But anyway, to get back to Will, apparently he hasn't been seen or heard from in months."

"Nonsense," I said. "Didn't we just get a postcard from

him? It was from Thailand, wasn't it? The one where he was promoting his merchandise, which he seemed positive we would want?

"The postcard you threw in the garbage all the while exclaiming, 'Over my dead body,' or words to that effect, you mean?"

"It is true," I said, "that there are few things that irk me as much as deadbeat dads who decamp for foreign parts leaving their families virtually destitute. But yes, that postcard."

"You never know what happens in other people's marriages," he said. "Take ours, for example."

"Let's not," I said.

"Let's not what?"

"Take our marriage, for example."

"Oh. Quite right. Water under the bridge and all that. So to get back to Beauchamp—"

"Do we have to? I can't say I much cared for the guy even before that fax business."

"Yes, we have to. I have it somewhere," he said, moving back into the little office behind the counter and rummaging about.

"What?" I said.

"The postcard, of course."

"You took it out of the trash?" I said incredulously.

"I thought you might reconsider," he said. "Those buying trips of yours are expensive, and they're hard work, and frankly, Will really knows, or maybe it's knew, I suppose—horrible thought, that—his stuff. Here it is!" he exclaimed. He peered at it intently. "The postmark is hard to make out, but I think it's almost a year ago."

"Time flies," I said.

"This may be the last anyone ever heard of him."

"Oh come on!"

"Three or four months, anyway. He probably got into bad company," Clive went on. "You know, in that red-light district, the Ping Pong, or whatever it's called."

"It's Pat Pong, Clive, as you very well know," I said.

"You're not going to bring up that little episode again, are you, Lara?" he said in an aggrieved tone. "After all, we've been divorced for almost five years now; we're both in nice relationships with other people. At least I am. You and Rob are happy together, aren't you, even if he's a policeman? Furthermore, you and I make very good business partners, much better than when we were married. Anyway, it's hardly the time for recriminations when poor old Will may be lying in a shallow grave, or rotting in an alley far from home, or something equally awful. Maybe he's a prisoner of some drug lord."

"Good grief, Clive," I said. "All I said was 'Pat Pong, as you very well know.' As for William Beauchamp, he's probably hiding because Natalie Beauchamp's lawyers finally tracked him down."

"I don't know. You are going to be in Thailand soon," he said, stroking his mustache and using that wheedling tone I remembered so well from our married years.

"So what?" I said. Neither the tone nor the gesture worked for him anymore, at least not where I was concerned.

"Well, it wouldn't hurt you to make inquiries. I mean, think of the poor woman. She's distraught, even if he did rather leave her in the lurch."

"You have got to be kidding," I said. "Absolutely not."

"You could just talk to her," he said.

"Who?"

"Natalie."

"Clive!"

"I suppose I did mention to her that you would be in Thailand."

"Have you forgotten that the Thai portion of this trip is the holiday part? That I plan to spend it with Jennifer and her boyfriend, whom I haven't seen in two months?"

"Right. Jennifer. I forgot you were doing the wicked stepmother thing. What's the boyfriend's name again?"

"Chat. And I'm not her stepmother, wicked or otherwise."

"Close enough, I'd say. You and Rob really should get a place together. Relationships have to progress, you know, or they stagnate. What kind of a name is Chat, anyway? No wonder I can't remember it."

"It's Thai. And I can't believe that you're lecturing me on relationships." The fact that Rob had asked me several times to get a place with him, and I had so far resisted, was something Clive didn't need to know.

"Thai, is it? I didn't know that. Well, I suppose it's no worse than Clive, when you get right down to it. Does he have a last name?

"Chaiwong," I said. "We're staying with his family, actually."

"Chaiwong," he said. "What does her father think about his daughter dating a guy named Chat Chaiwong?"

"Clive, you really are too awful. He said he thought Chat was a nice enough young man."

"Hardly a ringing endorsement, is it?"

"Actually where Rob and his daughter's boyfriends are concerned, it is. It's positively glowing, in fact."

"And what does the wicked stepmother think about him?"

"He seems very pleasant, and Jen likes him. Apparently he comes from a good family, to use that rather old-fashioned expression. He's a very responsible young man. He's a graduate student at UCLA, which is where Jen met him. Public administration. He wants to go back to Thailand and work in public service—get into politics maybe."

"He sounds like a barrel of laughs. At least he's smart, from the sound of it, just like Jennifer. Now here's an idea. Maybe they could both help you with your enquiries. It would be good for them. Give them a chance to meet the natives, as it were. Good for him if he wants to get into politics. Get to know his future constituents, that sort of thing."

"They've been backpacking through southeast Asia for two months. I'm sure they've met lots of natives, to use your vile and totally inappropriate expression."

"Whatever. I know how strongly you feel about the way Will just dumped his wife and kid, though. They must be in terrible straits—economically, emotionally. I would have thought you would want to help her track him down."

"Don't try to guilt me into this. It won't work."

"I don't understand you, Lara. You're always flailing about helping people you barely know. Why not lend a hand to someone you do?"

"That's the point. I don't know Natalie from Adam."

"You know all about her, even if you haven't met her in person, which, incidentally, is a deficiency that will be rectified almost immediately. She'll be at the Gala tonight."

"The Gala? You're talking about the Canadian Antique Dealers Association opening night Gala here, are you? The tickets are almost two hundred dollars each. She can't be in as bad economic straits as you're implying."

"You're starting to contradict yourself, Lara. Which side are you on? I mean, did he leave her destitute, or didn't he? Anyway, she's going as staff."

"You've contradicted yourself a few times during this conversation, Clive," I said. "You know, the stuff about you never know what happens in a marriage, etc. Whose staff?"

"Ours."

"Clive!" I exclaimed again. "I suppose she's attractive, is she?"

"That has nothing to do with it," he said.

"For you it always has something to do with it." I sighed.

"She is rather a looker," he said. "But that—"

"Hello, darlings," Moira Meller said, coming through the door and putting her arms around our shoulders. Moira is my best friend and Clive's life partner.

Clive shot me a warning glance before kissing Moira on the cheek. "The Gala. It won't kill you to talk to her."

"I suppose this means he's dead, does it?" Natalie Beauchamp said, pushing a battered bubble envelope across the table at me. Her tone was carefully neutral, but she spoiled the intended effect by chewing her lip and then hiccupping. A few feet away, Clive was extolling the virtues of a particularly lovely eighteenth-century writing desk to a young couple that most likely couldn't afford it but were desperate to own it anyway. In the aisle outside the McClintoch & Swain booth, the party was gradually winding down.

Opening night of the Canadian Antique Dealers Association Annual Fall Fair is a glittering affair, in a rather subdued Toronto sort of way. For $175 a ticket, the rich and fashionable, along with the wanna-bes, get to swill martinis, slurp oysters on the half shell, munch on various delectables from the city's finest caterers, and get first dibs on the antiques on display, all in a good cause, in this case the local symphony orchestra's endowment campaign. McClintoch & Swain was there as an exhibitor for the first time, and we were working hard at making a good impression.

Natalie hiccupped again. "Oh dear, how rude of me. I've only had one," she said, gesturing to the martini glass at her elbow. "Or maybe one and a half. But I don't get out much anymore. I'm feeling rather giddy. This has been lovely, by the way. Thank you for asking me to help out."

"Thanks for coming," I said. And indeed, despite my misgivings, she had been a real asset. She was, as I had suspected, an attractive woman, fortyish, slim with dark hair, very pale skin, and blue eyes, with a hint of a French accent and a French woman's sense of style. Her plain black suit was made distinctive by an elegantly draped silk-fringed scarf held in place by a diamond pin. She was a little too thin, perhaps, and she looked exhausted, but she was charming and, as it turned out, really quite knowledgeable about antiques.

"Let's see what we have here," I said, carefully emptying the contents of the envelope onto the table. "What is all this stuff?" It looked more like a child's play box than something an antique dealer would have considered special, if indeed that was how Will Beauchamp had regarded it. There were letters, newspaper clippings, a few pieces of terra-cotta wrapped in tissue, some of them broken, and a photograph of a monk.

"You should probably start with the pink one," she said, pointing to an envelope in a startling shade of rose. Inside was one sheet of similarly pink paper with a typed message.

"Dear Mrs. Natalie,"

it began.

"Regarding your Mr. William. I have been store in Silom Road. I have got informed from Mr. Narong Mr. William not there. I have been apartment, but I couldn't found him also. Got informed from Mrs. Praneet, live beside, Mr. William wasn't arriving long time. Mr. William ask me if not coming long time send Mrs. Natalie. I have also send mail from apartment. So sorry.

Best regards, Your friend, Prasit S, Ass't Manager, PPKK."

"It's a bit obscure," she said.

"I get the general idea," I said. "Do you know what PPKK is?"

"No," she said. "It sounds rather rude, doesn't it?" She smiled a little. "I suppose the PP could be pink paper, or even purple prose. Have a look at that one next."

She pointed to a second envelope, this one on creamy vellum, addressed to William Beauchamp, Esq., at a different address but referencing the Silom Road location, which while certainly clearer, was considerably less pleasant in tone.

"Sir,"

the letter opened.

"We regret to inform you that in respect to monies owing our client for the premises currently occupied by Fairfield Antiques, and the contract signed by you, William Beauchamp,

the contents of said premises have been seized, and unless restitution in the amount of 500,000 baht is paid to us in trust by November 1, these same contents will be placed at auction in the River City Complex at ten A.M. *of the clock on November 5 of this year."*

The letterhead was obviously that of a law firm, the signature illegible.

"That one is pretty clear, isn't it? I don't suppose you know how much five hundred thousand baht is," Natalie said. "I keep meaning to find out. I've been thinking that if it isn't too much, maybe I could borrow the money somehow, then sell the shop in Bangkok as a going concern."

"It's something over $10,000 U.S.," I said.

"Good grief," she said. "I guess that's it, then."

"We shouldn't assume anything," I said. "Maybe he's just the manager. We don't know he owns it."

"I think we do," she said. "Fairfield—it's a translation of Beauchamp. *Beau,* in French, is 'pretty or good or fair,' and *champ* is 'field.' So, Fairfield Antiques."

"Yes, I see," I said. "I suppose that's right. Is there anything on the keys that would indicate what they're for?"

"I'm afraid not," she said. "But have a look at the newspaper clippings, why don't you?"

I unfolded them carefully. They were yellow, almost brown with age, and rather fragile, not surprising, given that they were dated January 1952. The headlines, however, were clear enough. "Mrs. Ford Found Guilty!" *The Bangkok Herald* trumpeted. Then, in smaller letters: "Execution Date to Be Set Next Week." A second, from the same paper, but a week later, was even more lurid: "The Murderous Mrs. Ford to Meet Her Maker March 1," it said. Apparently they liked alliteration at the *Bangkok Herald* in those days.

"I'll spare you the effort of reading them right now," Natalie said. "The short version is that a long time ago, someone by the name of Helen Ford killed her husband and then hacked him in pieces and buried him in various locations around her neighborhood. She may also have killed one of her children, the body has never been found. All rather gothic, I'm afraid. I wouldn't have thought Will would have been interested in such garbage, but apparently he was."

"Does the name Helen Ford mean anything to you?"

"Nothing. This is the first I've ever heard of it. Do you have any idea what that pottery stuff is?" she said, pointing to the heap on the table.

I looked at the terra-cotta pieces carefully. There were two unbroken. They were both a little under four inches high, maybe three inches wide, flat along the bottom, but curving up like an arch to a peak at the top, and only about a third of an inch thick, sort of like a thick wafer. A Buddha figure, seated on a throne, appeared in relief on the surface of one. On the other was a Buddha in another classic position, this one with one hand held palm out in front of him. I picked up the broken pieces and fitted them together to form a third, about the same size, with a standing Buddha image on it.

"I think these are amulets," I said.

"Amulets!" she said. "Are they worth anything? I'm sorry. I didn't mean that the way it sounds. I'm not entirely mercenary. I just can't image what Will would be doing with amulets, and why he would ask the assistant manager of PPKK, whatever that is, to send them to me, especially broken ones."

"They could have been broken in the mail," I said.

"No," she said. "The pieces were individually wrapped."

"Oh," I said. It was the best I could do at the moment. "Still, if you look at the postcard Will sent soliciting our business," I said, showing it to her, "you can see he had some amulets on offer, along with the carvings and Buddha images. Amulets are only worth something, though, to those who believe in their powers. I'm told people pay a lot for amulets they consider particularly potent, or rather, I should say, people make large donations for them. You're actually not supposed to buy and sell amulets. People merely rent them permanently or make a donation for which they receive them in return. Most of them go for very small donations, however. Frankly, the only way you'd make money from this amulet would be if you knew who had blessed it, which monk, I mean, and he'd have to be an important one, and also what the amulet was for."

"I see. Maybe this is the monk who blessed them," she said, pointing to the photograph.

"Maybe," I said, turning it over. "Unfortunately it doesn't say who it is."

"It's all rather baffling, isn't it? Why would Will ask someone to mail me fifty-year-old newspaper clippings and some broken bits of amulet if he went missing for a long time? That's what the pink letter means, doesn't it? That Will asked this Prasit person—is Prasit a man or a woman, by the way?"

"Man, I think," I said. "There's a Thai wood-carver I deal with whose name is Prasit."

"Well, why would Will ask this fellow Prasit to send me junk like this if he didn't show up for awhile?"

"I don't know, Natalie," I said. "I'm sorry. I don't mean

to be unkind, but I just can't think what I can do for you here."

We both sat there for a minute, saying nothing. She was a little teary-eyed, and stared at a point somewhere over my head before speaking. "It's sort of sweet, isn't it, the way Prasit addresses me? Mrs. Natalie. It reminds me of my childhood. My French relatives called me Mademoiselle Natalie. Is that the polite term of address in Thailand?"

"Yes," I replied. "The use of surnames is relatively new in Thailand. Everyone uses first names. I had a hard time getting used to Ms. Lara at first, and calling people by their first names all the time."

"And Mr. William," she said, as if I hadn't spoken. "It seems rather familiar but also respectful at the same time. It's rather sweet," she repeated. "You know, I keep wondering if there was something I could have done. If I'd got on a plane and gone to see him the minute that horrible fax arrived, maybe everything would be different. But I was so devastated by it, paralyzed really, I didn't seem to be able to do anything except show everybody the fax, as if perhaps they'd tell me I'd read it all wrong or something, or that it was really a ransom note for kidnapped William. I don't think I was being very rational. All I did was cause myself deep personal humiliation. Everybody knew he'd left me in such a horrible way. You knew, I'm sure, even if we hadn't met before this evening. Didn't you?"

"Well, yes," I said. "It is a rather tight little community, antiques I mean."

"And not above some juicy gossip, I'll bet," she said.

"I think there were lots of people on your side," I replied. "Even though we'd never met, I was one of them."

"That's just it," she said. "Maybe it was a cry for help on

Will's part. After all, he'd hardly be the first man to have a midlife crisis, and maybe my telling everybody what he'd done just made it impossible for him to change his mind and come back after he'd had a bit of a break. I can understand he couldn't take it any longer, that it was just too hard. God knows I've felt that way."

"What was it he couldn't take anymore?" I said. I wasn't inclined to have any generous feelings toward the man, but I supposed letting her talk was the least I could do under the circumstances.

"You don't know?" she said, reaching for her drink. "Caitlin, our little girl, is developmentally challenged—that's politically correct speak for brain damaged," she added, pausing to drain the glass. "She was just perfect when she was born, but a few days later she started to have convulsions. Nobody has ever given me a really satisfactory explanation for what went wrong. Not that it would change anything, but I'd just like to know. And it's hard to think about having another child when you don't know what happened the first time; although maybe if we had . . . but we didn't.

"Caitlin's six now, and about as bright as she's going to get. She can't even dress herself, and I pretty much put all my energy into looking after her. I see now that I neglected our marriage. But he adored her, you know, despite everything, and I thought he loved me, too. He called us his girls. I keep thinking that maybe if I'd gone to see him right away, he would have come back. We could have worked something out." She paused for a minute and then gave me a rueful smile. "I wonder how many times I've said maybe in the last few minutes. Ten? Twenty? There are an awful lot of maybes in all of this, aren't there?"

"Too many," I said. "You make it sound as if it's all your fault, that if you had just done something or other, it wouldn't have happened. I think you should stop doing that to yourself. As you said, he would hardly be the first man to have a midlife crisis, and it would have nothing to do with you."

"I just wish I could convince myself of that. You know what bugged me most about the fax? That it came from Thailand. We went to Thailand on our honeymoon ten years ago, and the fact that he chose the same place to end our marriage may have seemed like symmetry to him, but it looked just plain cruel to me.

"Afterward, I tried to keep the store here going, you know," she said. "I took Caitlin with me every day. But you can't do both, and I couldn't afford any help. What with all Caitlin's expenses, we only just managed it when there were two of us. I finally sold the business to the first person that came along. We've been living off what we got for it, but it will be gone soon. I've sold all the jewelry, except this pin: fifth anniversary present from Will. Silly of me to keep it, but I haven't been able to part with it for some reason. The time has come I'll have to, though, and then I just don't know what I'll do. Sell the house, I guess. I shouldn't drink, should I." It was a statement, not a question. "These martinis are making me maudlin. Or maybe I'm just plain tired. I haven't had a holiday since Will left really, except for a week this past summer. Friends lent me their cabin in the woods and took Caitlin for a few days. There was no electricity, no water, nobody around, and it was absolutely heaven. But Caitlin was just miserable while I was away. So I guess that's it for holidays."

I opened my mouth to utter something appropriate but

realized there was nothing I could possibly say that would fix anything. "But you did speak to him at some point, I presume," I said finally.

She started chewing on her lip again. "I intended to," she said.

"But . . ." I said.

"I know you're going to think I'm awful. I decided that if he didn't have the guts to tell me to my face he was leaving, then I wasn't going to speak to him either. When I finally pulled myself together, in a manner of speaking, I did what most spurned women do, I guess. I cut up his ties, wrecked his golf clubs, then cleared every last piece of his stuff out and sent it to a charity. Then I got a lawyer and filed for divorce. The lawyer has been dealing with it ever since. I always meant to talk to him eventually. I kept thinking he would phone. I was damned if I was going to do it first. I practiced what I would say when we spoke. I planned to call him, but only when I was absolutely sure I wouldn't break down and embarrass myself when he said hello. The longer you put off speaking to someone, though, the harder it is to do it. After two years, you don't just phone up and say, 'Hey, how are you doing?' At least I couldn't."

"Then how do you know he's been missing for months?"

"I suppose I don't exactly. My lawyer told me he sent off a document to Will for signature at least three months ago, and didn't get the papers back. So he tried again, this time by courier. The courier tried for several days to deliver it and eventually sent it back as undeliverable. Steven—that's my lawyer—thought Will was just avoiding us; we were asking for a reasonably substantial settlement, and so he didn't think anything much of it.

"He remembered he had an old chum from law school

living in Bangkok, so he asked him to send someone over to see what they could find. The friend reported back that the shop was dark, there was mail piled up behind the glass door, and according to the shopkeepers in the vicinity, it had been for many weeks. None could remember having seen Will for some time, at least that's what they told Steven's friend. They could be covering for William, I suppose, but why would they? The chum tried the home address, too, and didn't get an answer there either. The woman next door—maybe she was Ms. Praneet—said she couldn't recall when she had last seen William, but it had been some time.

"Then this package arrived. I didn't know what to make of it, but I did call the office that's listed in that lawyer's letter about the auction to see if it was for real. I couldn't make out the signature, but eventually I got to talk to someone. All he did was repeat what was in the letter—at least I think that's what he said. It's hard to do these things over the telephone when you don't speak the language. I mean, when you're there, in person, you can kind of wave your arms around and get yourself understood eventually. I didn't find him at all helpful, but maybe it was just a misunderstanding. I was able to ascertain, though, that the rent hadn't been paid in three months before they sent the letter, and as you can see, it's dated almost a month ago."

"Was the letter still sealed when you got it?"

"Yes," she said. "I think that's what made me realize something might have happened to Will, that this wasn't just some horrible prank."

"Have you made official enquiries?" I said. "The police? The Canadian Embassy?"

"I called the U.S. Consulate here in Toronto. Will's an

American, and although he lived here for twenty years, he never took out citizenship. One of the consular officers said they would send something off to Bangkok, but I haven't heard anything since."

We both sat looking at the pathetic pile of Will's stuff for a minute or two. "This really is all that came in the bubble envelope?" I asked.

"There was a letter from my lawyer about the divorce postdated over three months ago. I didn't think I needed to bring that. It was unopened, too, by the way. Will never saw it. I don't think you answered my original question," she said. "Do you think Will is dead?"

"I don't know," I said vaguely. What I wanted to say was that I thought that Will had simply chosen to disappear again. After all, the package might contain some strange things, but it was what wasn't in it that struck me. Things like a passport, a driver's license, credit cards, the kinds of items that would make you think he was dead if they were there, but the absence of which just made you think he'd made a run for it. I kept these thoughts to myself. To voice them seemed unkind.

"There is life insurance," she said. "He never changed the beneficiary, so I'm it. And he seems to have kept up the payments, at least until four months ago. It isn't a huge amount, but it would certainly help a great deal. The point is, for me to get it, he has to be dead. Really dead, with some kind of certificate that says so. I know in cases where people disappear, the death certificate is eventually issued, but it's something like seven years, and I can't wait that long. So either I find him alive and see what we can work out, or I prove him dead and collect the insurance. I'm sure that sounds callous, but I'm not in a position to be anything else.

"You asked me if this is all that was in the package. I suppose I should tell you there was one more letter." She hesitated. "It's for me. I don't really want to show it to anyone. It seems so personal. But it's the one that really made me think something awful has happened, although it doesn't actually say so, not in so many words."

The letter was well handled, the fold almost transparent, and some of the ink was smudged.

"Dear Natalie,"

it said.

"I'm sorry. I know how inadequate this is, but if you get this, then probably it is all I will ever be able to say. Tell Caitlin I love her. I have always loved both my girls, no matter what it looked like."

It was signed simply *W.*

I handed it back to her and watched as she carefully tucked it back in her purse. "I know this is an imposition," she said. "But would you consider making a couple of phone calls or something when you're there?"

Chapter 2

I **remember vividly** *the first time I saw The Royal Palace of Ayutthaya. My dear mother told me often how I stood, transfixed by the sight of the soaring buildings, the gold, the exquisite carving, the splendor of it all. It was the most beautiful and astonishing sight of my young life, and I confess I have never lost the feeling of awe that I felt at that moment. The city has the power to overwhelm me still.*

Now that I have been forced to some introspection, I see that my enchantment blinded me to the raw ambition, the poisonous intrigue that rested so close to the heart of the palace. The signs were there, even then, and certainly later, but as a boy in a place so very different from anything he had known until that moment, I lacked the ability to read them.

It is a fact of life that being in the antique business puts you in touch with wealth, and those who possess it. While scouring the world to find the perfect objets d'art to grace the showroom of McClintoch & Swain, I've been in homes that are palaces, yachts the size of the average house. I have met people with more money than most of us can even imagine. By and large, with the exception of a few pangs of envy from time to time, I like to think I keep my feet firmly planted in reality, and I am always glad to get home to my little house in Cabbagetown with its tiny garden, and my store, even if, at 3,000 square feet, it would fit into the living room of some of the mansions I've visited. I have never, however, seen anything like the residence of the Chaiwong family. Nor am I likely to forget it, or them.

I was met at the airport by a car and driver and quickly whisked away from the masses of humanity that one finds in international airports: the travelers; their friends; the totes selling transportation, hotels, visits to "special" shopping places with the best of prices. In the car was an English-language newspaper, the *Bangkok Herald*, a damp towel, neatly packaged in plastic, for my hands and face, and a bottle of ice-cold water.

"I hope you will enjoy the journey to Ayutthaya," the driver said. "Please rest, and if there is anything you need, you will tell me."

"I'm fine, thank you," I said, sinking back into the leather seat. I would have liked to enjoy the sights, but there wasn't much to see. We took a major highway, heading north from Bangkok, and as it was ten o'clock at night, all was in darkness. After thirty-some hours of traveling, it wasn't long before I dozed off in the cool comfort of the backseat.

I awakened to the sound of the driver's voice speaking quietly into his car phone. He saw me in the mirror and said, "Only five minutes more. I have alerted the household of your arrival."

We pulled up in front of what looked to be an office tower or perhaps a hotel, ten stories of attractive enough white stucco at the summit of a slight incline on a circular driveway. Two stone elephants about three feet high marked the entranceway, which was also lined with orchids. In my jet-lagged state, I couldn't figure out why I would be at such a place, but I didn't have time to wonder for long, because within seconds of my stepping out of the car under the portico, I caught sight of a familiar blond head hurtling toward me.

"I am so glad to see you," Jennifer said, hugging me tight. A shy young man hung back a few feet.

"Hello, Chat," I said, giving him a peck on the cheek. "It's nice to see you again, too."

He blushed. I would have to remember that public displays of affection were frowned upon in Thailand, and now that he was back home, my greetings should be less effusive. "Hello, Aunt Lara," he said. "I am very happy to welcome you to my home."

A very efficient-looking man in a crisp beige suit came forward, his palms pressed flat together and up to touch his forehead in the traditional Thai greeting, the *wei.* I find it difficult sometimes to tell people's ages in foreign countries like Thailand. My usual reference points are gone. But I would put him in his late thirties, with rather owlish glasses over high cheekbones and a quite distinctive somewhat flattened nose. "I am Yutai," he said. "Secretary to Khun Wongvipa. I am most pleased to meet you. You are most welcome to the residence of the Chaiwong family. The family has retired for the evening, except for Mr. Chat here, but

I will see you to your room. The family hopes you will sleep well, rest tomorrow, and that you will join them for dinner tomorrow evening."

I turned back to the car, but my bags had already disappeared. "Your suitcase will be brought to your room," Yutai said. "Please," he said, gesturing toward the entrance, an enormous carved wood double door, which swung open as if by magic, but in fact was opened by two young men in uniform. A gold sign beside the door said Ayutthaya Trading and Property.

"Wait until you see this place," Jennifer whispered.

I found myself in a marble lobby. The ceiling was wood, painted in the most extraordinary colors of gold and coral and blue. Ahead were two elevators, and beyond that, glass doors through which I could see banks of computers and office cubicles.

"Those are the offices," Jennifer said. "Ayutthaya Trading. The offices are on the first six floors; the family lives on the top four. We go this way."

A separate lobby with another two elevators was off to one side. Yutai beckoned me into one, and using a key, pressed Nine. "The guest floor," Jennifer explained. "There's just you and me, and we have the whole wing to ourselves. I'm really glad you're here. It was a little daunting all by myself."

"Khun Wongvipa would like you to have the gold room, if it is to your liking," Yutai said, as the elevator door opened to an entranceway the size of my living room. The walls were stenciled in gold, figures of some kind of deities as guardians, perhaps. Extraordinary carved wood doors led off the foyer on either side.

"This way," Yutai said, sliding out of his shoes before

turning left. I stopped gawking long enough to follow him. Jennifer, beside me, giggled.

The gold room was just that. It was paneled in teak, but then gold leaf had been rubbed into the wood to give it a rather sensuous sheen. There was a canopy bed in black lacquer, already turned down. In addition to the bed there was a sofa, a coffee table, an armchair with a reading light, and a desk. There was a platter of fresh fruit on the coffee table and a large bouquet of orchids on the desk. Heavy silk curtains were pulled against the darkness. "Your dressing room," Yutai said, leading me into another paneled room with rows of hangers and a bench where my suitcase already rested. Beyond that was a huge bathroom with tub, glass shower stall, two sinks, and a toilet and bidet. Fluffy white towels and a bathrobe awaited me. A spray of orchids graced the space between the sinks. I thought I'd died and gone to heaven.

"And now I will leave you, if there is nothing else I can do for you," Yutai said. I assured him there wasn't. "I have arranged for jasmine tea to be sent up. It will be here in a minute or two. Extension forty-three," he said, pointing at the phone beside the bed. "Call me at any time, day or night, if there is something you require, or, if you wish, you can come to my quarters, which are on this floor on the other side of the foyer. In the morning when you wish breakfast, dial forty-two. The cook will have whatever you like sent up. There is a small kitchen, again on the other side of the foyer, which you are most welcome to use. There is bottled water and some light food in the refrigerator. Dinner is at eight P.M. tomorrow evening on the tenth floor. This key activates the elevator. In the meantime, the car and driver are at your disposal if you wish to do some sight-seeing while you are here."

"I, too, will leave you," Chat said. "I look forward to seeing you tomorrow and hearing about your journey, Aunt Lara. Also telling you about ours," he said, smiling at Jennifer.

"Isn't this something else?" Jennifer said as their footsteps faded. "Rather grand, wouldn't you say? Especially after the dump we stayed in on the beach near Phuket."

"This would be rather grand after Buckingham Palace," I said. "So where is your room?"

"I'm just down the hall. The silver room, my dear. Do join me, won't you?" she said, affecting a veddy British accent. "Oops, here's the tea." A pleasant woman in bare feet knelt by the coffee table and set down a tray, then poured tea into exquisite little celadon porcelain cups, before backing out of the room.

"Who is Khun Wongvipa?" I said.

"Chat's mother," she said. "The woman I have been incorrectly referring to as Mrs. Chaiwong. You'll meet her tomorrow. I don't know what you'll think of her. I find her kind of scary. His dad seems nice, but he's really old. Everybody calls him Khun Thaksin. I call him sir."

"What do you mean by old? Marginally older than your father and I?"

"Even older than you and Dad. Like ninety or something. Well, eighty anyway. His first wife died, and he married Chat's mother. Chat has a half brother, the first wife's son—I haven't met him—and a younger brother named Dusit, and a little sister, who is a bit of a brat, called Prapapan. Her nickname is Fatty, if you can believe it. I have no idea why. She's actually rather tiny."

"What do they call you? Miss Jennifer?"

"Yes," she said. "It's just as well. They'd have trouble with Miss Luczka. It comes out sort of Roocha."

"I love this room, this suite, I should say," I said, walking over to a carved chest. "I think this is quite old, and rather fine. It's a manuscript cabinet, did you know that? It's used to store religious manuscripts, or would have been at one time. The gold and black lacquer is wonderful. Probably mid- to late eighteenth century."

"I'd like to talk to you about this," she said. "Not tonight. I know you're tired. But this place is all rather overwhelming."

"And look at these gold boxes. Gold nielloware. Did you know these were once made exclusively for royalty?"

"If you think this floor is something," Jennifer said. "Wait until you see where they hang out. I swear they own half of Bangkok. I exaggerate, of course, but only slightly."

"And those doors when we came in. Did you see the carving? Exquisite! I think they're temple doors, real ones, I mean, off a real temple."

"I had no idea Chat came from this kind of home. He has a nice enough apartment off campus, and yes, he drives a BMW, but this is way beyond well off, you know. I find it all a bit much."

"Do you know what this is?" I said, picking up a small bowl on the desk. "It's called Bencharong, which means "five colors" in Sanskrit. This kind of ceramic was made in China for Thai—at the time it would have been Siamese—royalty. It's lovely, isn't it?"

"I feel as if they're sizing me up all the time, and I'm sure I don't measure up. I don't think he wanted his family to meet me, but they insisted."

"Look at these lamps. The bases represent deities. They're called kinaree. See, they're half human, half bird. What did you say?" I said, pausing for a moment in my catalogue of the treasures.

"I don't know," she said.

"Yes, you do: something about not measuring up. Of course you do," I said. "They may have lots of money, but they're lucky their son likes someone like you. So there!"

"I guess," she said. "Now you better get some sleep. It's almost midnight. We'll get all caught up tomorrow. Shall we have breakfast together?"

"Yes," I said. "Please wake me when you want to eat. We have a little project while we're here, by the way."

"I love a project," she said. "What is it?"

"We have to find an antique dealer by the name of William Beauchamp," I said.

"That shouldn't be too hard," she said. "Where's his store? I'm sure Chat will know where it is."

"I know where the store is," I said. "At least I have an address. But he hasn't been seen in months. I'll tell you all about it in the morning."

"I like it!" she said. "A little detective work, just like Dad. I can't tomorrow, though. Khun Wongvipa wants me to go somewhere with her. I figured you'd need the day off, given how long it takes to get here. Sleep well."

I had a shower and gratefully crawled into the big bed. I was asleep almost instantly and awoke some time later, I'm not sure when, to the sound of footsteps padding down the hallway. I was reasonably sure they went into Jennifer's room, and I was almost certain it was Chat. I wondered what her father would think if he heard about that. And then I wondered where Will Beauchamp was.

I was in Bangkok early thanks to a combination of a twelve-hour time change that got me up at the crack of dawn and a car and driver who dropped me off at the Sky-train and promised to pick me up again at five.

I love Bangkok. Sometimes it's hard to explain why, even to myself. The traffic is horrendous, the air even more so, the poverty relentless, the sex trade highly visible and unpleasant. Still, when the sun touches the golden spires of The Grand Palace or reflects off the glass mosaics on the temple facades, making them sparkle as if wreathed in a million tiny, multicolored lights, when I smell for a moment, even in the city, the heady scent of jasmine and frangipane, or catch a glimpse of the rhythm of daily life on the *klongs*, then I am seduced once more. It is as if I have arrived for the first time, to be overwhelmed by the sights and smells, drugged by the heat, confused by sights so foreign. But it is also as if I've been there all my life, that somehow it is where I belong. For a few moments, I just stood there, taking it all in.

As Clive had pointed out, more than once since we'd had our first conversation on the subject, I held wildly divergent views on Will. Part of me thought he'd be easy to find. All I had to do was wait for an hour or two outside his home, and he was bound to come crawling out. The other part held that he was off on some beach somewhere, a drink with an umbrella in it in one hand, suntan lotion in the other. Both these scenarios were based on a single premise, however: that he was trying to avoid paying a dime to his wife and daughter.

I had no trouble finding Fairfield Antiques. It was located on a *soi,* or lane, off Silom Road, in an old mansion that had been converted into the Bangkok version of a shopping plaza. The area was once the center of town from the point of view of foreigners, or *farang* as they are called. It is near the river, off what was then referred to as New Road, now by its Thai name of Charoen Krung, a street built in the mid–nineteenth century to accommodate the carriages of foreign diplomats, and many of the embassies were nearby. The neighborhood then centered, and perhaps still does, on the exotic Oriental Hotel, which played host to writers like Joseph Conrad, Somerset Maugham, and Graham Greene, and where the expatriate community liked to gather and socialize.

The mansion, which may well at one time have housed an embassy or perhaps an adventurer who had made his fortune in the East, was now a maze of tiny shops, most of them purporting to sell antiques. I say purporting, because my experience is that some of the best fakes in the world can be found in Bangkok, an alarming proportion, indeed, of what is an offer. Worse yet, a disturbing number of those left over after the fakes are factored out have been ripped illegally from temple sites, in other words, stolen. A quick look around confirmed my opinion. It is one of the reasons that my buying trips to Asia often bypass Thailand, and when I do go there, it is to find interesting articles—carved doors, windows, furniture, other decorative pieces—that McClintoch & Swain offers as reproductions to our clients who like the look but don't insist upon or can't afford the genuine antique article.

Fairfield Antiques was there, on the second floor. At least the sign was, in English, and presumably in Thai. The display window was covered with brown kraft paper, however, and the door was securely locked and fastened with a padlock and chain. A few advertising flyers had been partially stuffed through the mail slot, but there was nothing of any interest in them, at least the ones I could read. A notice taped to the door, again in two languages, indicated exactly what the lawyer's letter had, that the contents had been seized by the landlord—in this case the landlord was mentioned, a firm called Ayutthaya Trading and Property as it turned out; I don't know why I was surprised, given Jennifer had told me they owned the proverbial half of Bangkok—and would be auctioned at the River City auction facility on the weekend.

I peered through a tear in the paper. It was dark inside, although a window on the far side did shed some light, enough that I could see the place was completely empty.

I did a canvass of some of the stores surrounding Fairfield's. All said they hadn't seen Will for some time. One young woman, who perhaps had not been employed long, had no idea whom I was talking about. It was in a tailor's shop that I made some headway, although not much.

"Mr. William, yes," the proprietor said. "I know Mr. William. You like to buy Thai silk?"

"I'm not sure," I said, reluctant to bring the conversation to a close before I learned anything."

"This color very good for you," she said, pulling a jacket in a gorgeous sapphire blue off a rack.

"It's lovely," I said. "Now, about Mr. William. Have you seen him recently?"

"No recently," she said. "I think this color more better," she added, this time showing me a mustard yellow jacket. "You very white. With skirt, very good. Same color or maybe black silk. Good for your parties."

"It's too small, I'm afraid," I said. I towered over this woman and most of the Thai women I met. Nothing in this shop would fit me. But a tape measure was produced with lightning speed.

"You come back tomorrow," she said. "I have for you. Perfect fitting."

An assistant, a pretty teenage girl, miraculously appeared from the back and started writing down my measurements as the diminutive woman called them out. Fortunately, I couldn't understand them—she was speaking in Thai—so I didn't have to sink into a deep depression at the mention of my waist size.

"I think we make jacket a little longer for you," she said. "Covers, you know," she said, patting her hips. "Not so much extra you pay."

"But about Mr. William," I said, doggedly determined to get something out of this. "When do you think you saw him last?"

"Two, maybe three months," she said. "How you like skirt? I think at the knee, on top, is good for you. To show your legs, yes?" She pushed up my pant leg and peered at my calves. "Leg is okay," she said.

"Do you know Mr. Narong?" I asked, referring to the name Mr. PPKK, as I was coming to think of him, had mentioned. The girl who was helping out tittered.

"Of course," the tailor said, also smiling. "Is my husband. He will make for you the clothes. Not here now. I think you need also silk pants. Black is very good. Also blouse for under jacket. Maybe two. One yellow like jacket, one black. With sleeves, I think. The arms you know," she said lifting up her arm and pulling at the fleshy part of her upper arm. "For older women not so good to show. Very versatile for you."

"I'm not sure I need all this," I said. "Maybe just the jacket."

"Thai silk best in the world," she said, severely. "Why you not buy more? You will be most beautiful in your country. Now you stand here," she said, pointing to a raised platform. "I measure for your pants and I tell you about Mr. William. You wear shoes like this always?"

I sighed and silently cursed Clive for about the thousandth time since he'd first mentioned Will Beauchamp's disappearance.

"Very sad man, Mr. William," she said. "Turn please." I turned.

"I think he want to go home," she said. "At first he find Bangkok very nice, but after he misses very much his home, I think. Why he not go home I don't know."

"What happened to the business?" I said. I was already in a mental debate about whether or not to tell Natalie about this most recent revelation. "Fairfield Antiques. Do you know why it's closed?"

"Mr. William has very good antiques," she said. "Not like some of the others," she added, waving her arm in the general direction of the other shops. "Maybe not so many people know the difference between his antiques and the others. I don't know. One evening I see him lock the door. He stops here to say good night as always. I never see again. Soon the others came. Turn again please."

"What others?" I said.

"From Ayutthaya Trading. They own this plaza. They ask many questions, then they take away all Mr. William's lovely antiques.

"What kind of questions did the people sent by Ayutthaya Trading ask?" I said. My, but dinner that evening was promising to be useful.

"Just like you," she said. "When did you see him? Things like that."

"How long after you last saw him did they come?"

"Maybe one month, maybe more."

"Do you know a Mr. Prasit?" I asked.

"Many Mr. Prasit," she said.

"The Mr. Prasit who is assistant manager of PPKK," I said. I felt like an idiot saying that.

"What is this PPKK?" she said.

"I was hoping you would know," I said.

"No," she said. She spoke to her assistant in Thai, but the girl shook her head.

"My daughter not know also," she said. The girl said something to her mother.

"My daughter tells me there was a young man came here asking for Mr. William. He spoke to my husband. My husband knows nothing of Mr. William also, so the young man left. Maybe he is Mr. Prasit."

"Perhaps," I said. "Has anybody else asked about Mr. William?"

"No," she said. "You like blouses, yes?"

"I guess so," I said.

"I am mistaken. There was a woman like you."

"You mean a *farang?"* I said.

"Yes," she said. "Not so nice as you, though. She not buy Thai silk."

"What did she look like?"

"A *farang,"* the woman replied.

"Hair color," I said. "Like mine?"

"Maybe," she said. "But more," she added, indicating a spot just below my shoulder blades.

"Eyes?" I said.

"Like you," she said. "*Farang* eyes." I meant what color, but it seemed hopeless to pursue this.

"Was she taller than me?"

"Yes," she said. "I think also slimmer. I didn't measure, but I know. Twenty years in business."

"Did she tell you her name?"

"No," she said. "She came here only one time. She do the same as you—try to look into store." She put her hands up to shield her eyes and pretended to be peering at something. "Nothing there to see."

"Nobody else?"

"No," she said. "What time you come back tomorrow for fitting? Same time?"

"Okay," I said. Why argue? A rather tall man in a very fine dark suit entered the store, and the three of them began a heated discussion.

"Mr. Narong. My husband," the woman said. "He says there was one other who asked for Mr. William. Thai girl. Very pretty. No name also. Now," she said, whipping out a calculator and showing me the tally. "Very good price, yes?" I stared at it for a moment, thinking what a fool I was. It was awfully pretty though, I thought, fingering the bolt of fabric, the color so rich and the texture, with its hint of roughness, so pleasant against my hand. I could picture myself wearing it at the next CADA Gala, even if it was a year away. Maybe I would bring Jennifer in and get something made for her, too.

"Okay," she said, taking my hesitation for reluctance.

"For you, special, as friend to Mr. William, another ten percent. You pay half now," she said. I paid.

Having forked over about a hundred and fifty dollars, with the same amount to come, for a "versatile" outfit and very little information, I went on my way. Will's house was my next stop. It was as easy to find as the shop, and for the same reason. I had the address from the lawyer's letter in Natalie's packet. My vision of Will hiding out at home, embellished over the thirty hours or so of traveling to reach Bangkok, was one of a house on a *klong*, or canal, complete with teak floors and walls, exquisite art—he was, after all, an antique dealer who specialized in Asia—and a terribly young and beautiful Thai woman, a sort of Madama Butterfly who catered to his every whim, at his side. At some point in my jet-lagged reverie, there had even been a baby gently rocking in a cradle nearby. Or maybe it was a grass hut on a beach in the south I was thinking of, open to the ocean breezes, à la Paul Gauguin in Tahiti. Or something like that.

What it wasn't, was the six-story concrete apartment building I found myself standing in front of, checking the address several times to make sure I'd made no mistake. The building was supremely unattractive, sitting stolidly on its footings in a neighborhood that had lovely temples, markets, and gardens, and poor but at least interesting houses on stilts.

Next to it was a shell of a building, similar in design. It looked as if construction had halted in an instant, and the workers had dropped their tools and walked away, which is probably exactly what had happened a few years earlier when the white-hot Asian economy had abruptly hit the brakes. There were steel rods exposed in several places, including the top, and no glass in any windows. A couple of the units had some sheets hung up, some squatters presumably having taken up residence. It was a very depressing sight, a blight really. My shattered visions, totally without foundation and inappropriate as they had been, had been considerably more romantic than the reality.

The building did, however, boast a view of the river, which is not inconsequential. The Chao Phyra is a fascinating waterway. The heart of the city, it functions as a major roadway. On it, rice barges ply their trade alongside speeding longtail boats that serve as water taxis, and ferries that work much like buses, stopping every few hundred yards at jetties along the river's banks. From the river one can see beautiful temples, spires of gold and tile, thousands of little businesses, and even tiny houses almost falling into the water. Will's building towered over a group of these houses where children played in the water, while their mothers cooked and cleaned. If he lived on the river side of the building, Will would have a rather splendid view.

I went into the building foyer and found a letterbox with Will's name on it, and, lo and behold, an apartment number. Obviously they were not as obsessed about security as we are. Even the front door was unlocked.

Will's apartment was on the top floor, arrived at on a creaking elevator, off a dreary hallway that may have been somebody's idea of American modern. I pounded on the door but received no answer. I listened for a time, just standing in the hallway, but I had no sense there was anyone moving about inside.

Having interpreted the letter from Mr. PPKK—the part about Mrs. Praneet live beside—as the apartment next door, I knocked on the door to each side of Beauchamp's as well.

There was no answer at either one. The place was as still as a tomb. No doors opened in response to all the pounding I was doing, nor did anyone come in or out. It was almost as if no one lived there.

I bought a bottle of water in a little greengrocers just down the lane, with a clear view of the apartment building, and they offered me a chair in the shade outside. It was the time of day when the heat, noticeable but bearable to this point, suddenly becomes oppressive. It's as if everything, the streets, the buildings, even the chair I was sitting on, has soaked up the heat in the early hours, and then starts to radiate it back into the air. The humidity seemed to have reached saturation point. I must have dozed off, a combination of jet lag and heat, because I had a rather grotesque dream in which Natalie Beauchamp cried, as a man in a referee's striped uniform blew his whistle in a most annoying way, and Will sank beneath the waters of a lagoon. It was a watery kind of dream, perhaps because it had started raining while I was still asleep. I awoke to find the shop proprietor staring at me as if I was some kind of lunatic, as drops began to seep through the awning onto my head.

On the street, the gutters, such as they were, rushed with water as the rain came down in sheets.

As I pulled myself together, I heard several sharp blasts of a whistle, and a ferry pulled up to a pier a hundred yards or so away. That at least explained the referee, the ferry conductor, if that's the right term, signaling its arrival and departure. A stream of people disembarked and dashed through the rain, several of them running into the building I was supposed to be watching. Not one of them, however, bore the slightest resemblance to Will.

Given that at least two ferries had come and gone while

I dozed away, if my dream was anything to go by, it seemed pretty clear I wasn't in any shape for a stakeout, and having learned next to nothing so far, except that another *farang* had also been inquiring about William, I decided I needed some official help. I made my way to the American Embassy on Wireless Road and asked to speak to a consular officer about a missing American.

I can certainly understand why everyone visiting the embassy would be carefully screened before being permitted in, but after being treated like a terrorist and made to wait for an hour and a half before seeing anyone, I was in rather bad mood by the time I was finally ushered into a small office.

"I'm David Ferguson," the man said, standing up to shake my hand. He was an attractive man, very tall and thin, with dark hair peppered with gray. "How may I be of assistance?"

"I am looking for an American citizen who has been living in Bangkok for some time, but who has been missing for about three months."

"Name?" he said.

"William Beauchamp," I replied.

"Not Will Beauchamp, the antique dealer?"

"Yes," I said. "You know him?"

"I do," he said. "Good fellow. I didn't know he was missing. Was a report ever filed?"

"His wife reported it to the U.S. Consulate in Toronto," I said. "They told her it would be passed along to Bangkok."

"I'll be back in a minute," he said, rising from his seat and then heading down the hall. It was considerably more than a minute, but he did return with a document in his hand. "Found this in the pile," he said. "We would have got to it eventually. It's just we have all these congressmen and senators asking us to look at their constituents' files first. Okay, fill me in."

I told him what I knew, which wasn't much.

"He was still here July fourth," he said. "I saw him at a party he threw to mark the occasion. I think that's how I actually met him, last year, at a party at his apartment. A lot of us Americans throw parties on the Fourth of July. That and Thanksgiving. Lots of drinks and nostalgia, and sometimes even fireworks. There's always a party here, of course, but people just go from place to place pretty much the whole day."

"I've been to his apartment," I said.

"Fabulous, isn't it?" he said.

"You think so?" I said.

"I do," he said. "Not much on the outside, but inside—I'd kill for that place."

"I only saw the outside," I said. "And the hallway."

"Too bad," he said. "Great view of the river, and he had really wonderful stuff there. He made me start getting serious about finding myself a decent place to live. I was quite envious of his place when I first saw it. I'd been posted here for a couple of years, and was still living in a bachelor apartment that looked as if I was still in college. Hot plate, bed with an Indian cotton throw, nothing on the walls, except a poster of the Stones. You get the idea. And here's this guy Will who has made the place really nice. He had a balcony with a great view, small and there wasn't much room on it because he had two huge pots filled with those flowers, whatever they are, that girls strap on their wrists for the school dance—purple things."

"Orchids?" I said.

"Right. Orchids. But the view! And his furniture! He'd

really got into Thai style. Every piece looked like a treasure to me. I don't know antiques at all, but he had a stone Buddha head that looked pretty authentic. And he had framed paintings, Jataka tales, if you know what those are: stories about the Buddha in previous lives. The walls were covered with paintings and carvings. It was a guy kind of place, though. The furniture was solid, not that flimsy stuff that often passes as valuable as long as you don't want to sit on it. He had a real dining room table, carved jade, with lots of chairs. No standing up at the kitchen counter to eat for our Will. The only thing I didn't take to was a painting he kept in the bedroom. It was of a beautiful woman, but it had those eyes, you know, the kind that follow you around the room. I mean who wants someone watching everything you do in your bedroom even if it is only a painting? Otherwise, I was quite envious of everything and in fact set out almost immediately to find myself a decent home. Even the coffee table was something—it's one of those jobs that has a glass top but a drawer underneath where you can put stuff, and see them through the top, if you know what I mean. He had these terra-cotta amulets, several of them, all different, arranged there."

"Sort of like this?" I said, reaching into my bag and handing him the amulet Natalie had given me.

"Exactly like that," he said, looking at it carefully. "How did you get this one?"

I told him.

"Weird," he said.

I couldn't disagree.

"Did his wife report this to the local police here?"

"No," I said. "I think she thought you would do that. I don't mean you personally. . . ."

"And I don't take it personally. We would have eventually, as I said."

"Did he have a companion, a lady friend?"

"I don't know," he said. "We didn't know each other very well. We got together for drinks a couple of times, in addition to the July fourth events. We didn't talk about our personal lives, though. But as for girls, a lot of guys who come to Thailand . . . how should I put this?"

"Rent one for the weekend?" I said.

"I'd have preferred 'play the field.' But there is no question that it's a great place for an unattached guy."

"Except he wasn't unattached," I said.

"Oh," he said. "I see. I'm not attached. Not anymore, anyway. Are you?"

"Yes, I am, and I don't forget it just because I'm in Thailand," I said rather primly. I couldn't believe my schoolmarmish tone. Maybe Clive was right. I was turning into an old prune in my dotage.

"Ooooo-kay," he said. "Let's go."

"Where?"

"Back to the apartment," he said. "You see, once you get our attention, we get right down to work. Do you have a rental car?"

"Are you kidding? Drive in this traffic?"

He laughed. "Are you prepared to risk coming with me?"

"I guess," I said.

"Well, here we are," he said about an hour later. "You can loosen your death grip on the armrest now. We could have done it in about a third the time if we'd taken the ferry, but I just like to prove I can drive in Bangkok."

"You're a brave and possibly foolhardy man," I said.

The heat made me gasp as I got out of the air-conditioned car, and my sunglasses fogged over instantly. Ferguson repeated my door knocking of earlier that day and then said, "Wait here," before disappearing down the stairs. He returned a few minutes later with a man introduced to me as Mr. Poon, the building superintendent.

"Mr. Poon here has informed me, several times, in fact, that he is unable to let us into the apartment. However, he has been persuaded for a small monetary consideration . . ."

I looked over at Mr. Poon.

"It's all right," Ferguson went on. "He doesn't speak English. He has been persuaded to open the door and let us look in from the hallway."

Mr. Poon turned out to be one of those people for whom even the smallest task is an effort. He fussed around with the keys, decided he had the wrong ones, went away for what seemed a long time, and fussed again on his return, trying first one key, then another.

"I'm starting to feel like Howard Carter waiting for his workers to break through into what was to be King Tut's tomb." I whispered. "Sorry. That was a poor choice of metaphor."

Ferguson laughed. "Let's not rush to conclusions," he said. "Here we go." Poon turned the key at last, and the door swung open.

I was surprised how quiet it was in the apartment. Outside there was the sound of traffic, the boats on the river, the din of a large city. Inside, the place had an airless quality to it, along with a certain dankness, like a summer home that's been abandoned all winter, closed and silent. "I'm going in," I said.

"I'm right behind you," Ferguson said, as Poon started to

protest. "I'll claim diplomatic immunity for us both."

It was, as Ferguson had said, a lovely apartment. The orchids on the balcony had definitely seen better days, but the view was fabulous, as were the furniture and the art. The teak dining room table was all that Ferguson had said it was, and the Jataka paintings were really lovely.

"Does it look to you as if some amulets are missing?" I said, pointing to the display beneath the glass coffee table top. "There are some spaces. It doesn't look symmetrical somehow."

"I think you're right," he said. "I can't recall exactly."

"I wonder if they're the ones he sent Natalie," I said.

"Could be."

"Kitchen next," I said. The kitchen, off the dining area was spotless, with not so much as a crumb on the counter or the floor. I opened a couple of cupboards. Nothing out of the ordinary there. Ferguson had a look in a small pantry, and shrugged. We both eyed the refrigerator. "Women's work," he said, pointing to it.

I opened it carefully. "Yuck," I said as the odor of rotting food reached me. "Green slime and sour milk," I said, closing it firmly.

This way," he said, gesturing down a short hall. Mr. Poon followed us, jabbering away. There was a bathroom at the end of it, spotlessly clean, towels folded and hung just so, medicine cabinet filled with perfectly normal stuff.

"That's the bedroom," Ferguson said, pointing to a closed door.

"Your turn," I said.

"Thanks," he said. He put his hand on the door handle and paused for a second. Then, giving me a mock terrified expression, he pushed the door open and peered inside. "I think it's okay," he said.

The bed was neatly made. I opened a couple of drawers. Will Beauchamp was a meticulous man. His socks and underwear were sorted by color and carefully folded. The only thing in the room that wasn't just so was the closet, the door having been left open. Inside, though, shoes lined up nicely and there were a couple of suits and carefully ironed shirts and jeans all in a row.

"Hmmm," Ferguson said.

"Yes?" I said.

"Well he's certainly not here."

"No."

"Neither is the painting," he added. "The one with the eyes that follow you. You can see the mark on the wall. A couple of missing amulets, no painting. Other than that, everything is as I remember it. What do you figure this means?"

"I don't know. My theory all along has been that he is hiding out from Natalie and her lawyers. I guess the question is, if that's what you're doing, would you take all your stuff with you, or, for that matter, clean out the refrigerator before you left?"

"Maybe he just couldn't pay the rent here either, and was clearing out before the landlord caught up to him," Ferguson speculated. He said something to Mr. Poon, and the man replied.

"I'm wrong on that score. The rent is paid up until the end of the year, and Poon had no idea Beauchamp was gone," Ferguson said. "Well, I guess we might as well be going. There isn't much to learn here, I'm afraid. I'll drop you off at the Skytrain station."

And then I made one of those unconscious gestures we train ourselves to do, like turning off the lights when we leave a room, or giving the door handle one more turn, just to be sure, after we've locked it. Without much thinking about it, I closed the closet door.

A splatter of dark reddish brown droplets, now dry, speckled the wall behind the door. We both looked at it in silence for a moment of two. "I suppose it could be tomato sauce or red curry paste," I said finally.

"In the bedroom?" Ferguson said. "I think it's time we called the police, don't you?"

Chapter 3

I should begin with an explanation of how I, son of a rather minor court official, should come to play a role in the political affairs of the royal court of Ayutthaya. It is because my mother was appointed wet nurse to Prince Yot Fa, son of King Chairacha by the royal concubine Lady Si Sudachan. The lady, who had not a drop of motherly love in her, as her consequent actions make clear, had no interest in the nurturing of her child.

That role fell to my mother, whose loss of a daughter, my only sister, when the baby was three days old, made her an excellent candidate for the position. She lavished the love for her lost child on the little prince.

I was six years old at the time and can recall my fierce jealousy of the child I saw as a rival for my mother's affection. In time though, I came to love Yot Fa as a younger brother. He was a melancholy child, a worry for his father, and everyone was pleased that I took the boy under my wing. For me it meant the run of the inner palace, the finest of food and clothing, and an education way beyond my station. I began to take on the swagger of a prince, to imagine that somehow I had been switched at birth. My mother scolded me for putting on airs, but she, too, was happy that we were so close, that I, unlike others, could make Yot Fa laugh.

Six years later, a second son was born to the king and the concubine, the Prince Si Sin, but I believe that the two princes were never as close as Yot Fa and I were, and certainly my affection for Yot Fa did not extend to his little brother, despite my mother's obvious adoration of both princes. I found Si Sin—I'm not sure how to put this—untrustworthy, perhaps, or even somewhat devious as he grew older—although I'm not sure one should ascribe such traits to a child. Perhaps it was the rather churlish disdain older children have for those much younger, but I felt Si Sin was his mother's son, unlike Yot Fa, who was much more like his father, the king.

As I grew older, I came to admire King Chairacha, if it is not too presumptuous for someone like me to say so about divinity. I was well aware, as was everyone in the palace, that he gained the throne by putting to death his nephew, the young King Ratsada. Despite that, I found him to be a wise and even-handed ruler, and diligent in his efforts to improve our seafaring capability and our army by improving the river channel and bringing in the Portuguese to instruct us in the use of firearms. He was also a religious man, building Chi Chiang Sai Monastery and placing there an image of Lord Buddha and a holy relic soon after he became king. I have often wondered since, though, if the horrible act that brought him the kingship lay at the heart of the difficulties that plagued his reign, as if the spirits, angered by the deed, wreaked their revenge. Certainly there were many evil omens that indicated all was not well in the kingdom. But perhaps I imagine this.

It is difficult for me to describe Lady Si Sudachan, in part because of what was to happen later, but also, if I am to be honest, the fascination she held for me. I was afraid of her certainly. She was not a woman to be taken lightly, often cold and distant, always quick to anger, even faster to seek revenge for any insult, intentional or otherwise. She was also—I don't know—seductive? I was much too young to appreciate the sexual side of her appeal, of course, but I sensed something. As much as I feared her, I also found myself wanting to be near her, to do something, anything, which would cause her to see me in a favorable light, to smile in a certain way she had, to glimpse a flicker of interest or even amusement in her eyes.

In a way, I suppose, we were two of a kind, both commoners who found themselves in the inner palace, both barely tolerated by the queens and consorts, all of them, unlike us, of royal blood.

Jennifer looked absolutely beautiful at dinner that evening. In a bright blue silk dress, her blond hair piled up on her head, she had a quality about her—I'm not sure what the word is: luminescence, perhaps?—that made her the subject of many admiring glances. I felt a pride in her I cannot quite explain. She was not, after all, my daughter, just my partner's. I could claim no hand in her upbringing. Watching her, so poised, I wanted everything to be perfect for her.

She'd spent the day shopping with Khun Wongvipa and arrived in my room a few minutes before we were due to go upstairs for some help with her hair.

"Do I look all right?" she said.

"No," I said. "You look wonderful. I ordered a mustard gold suit today. I wish I had it to wear this evening."

"Will they think I look all right?" she said, with a slight emphasis on "they."

"If they don't," I said, "then you and I are going to have

to come to terms with the fact that there is something seriously wrong with your boyfriend's family."

She giggled. "It's all a bit overwhelming, isn't it? All this gold and everything. Look at these, will you?" she added, leaning her head toward me and gesturing to a pair of small but not insubstantial gold earrings set with tiny sapphires. "These are a gift from Chat's mother. Not a loan, a gift," she repeated.

"They're lovely," I said. "But you don't have to accept them if you're not comfortable."

"I couldn't imagine saying no in the first place, and now I can't imagine giving them back," she said. "Chat would be hurt. His mother would be hurt. She scares me a little. I can't really tell you why."

"Can't wait to meet her," I said.

She smiled. "I am so glad you are here," she said. "I don't know what I'd do if you weren't. I think I'd get lost, somehow, sucked into this family and all this wealth."

"That wouldn't happen to you," I said, feeling my way through this new intimacy between us. "You have a very firm grasp on reality and a very good sense of what is important in life. Your father has done a good job raising you. While he and I disagree on a lot of things in life, one thing we agree on is you. I wish he were here to see how beautiful you look."

"You'll get to meet the rest of the family, too," she said. "Dusit, that's Chat's brother, and his dad, Khun Thaksin. I hope he's here. He's been in Chiang Mai on business the last couple of days and is supposed to be back."

"I look forward to meeting them all."

"You know what I like most about Chat?" she said. "It's his belief that one determined individual can really make a difference. He thinks he can change things for the better in Thailand, do something about the poverty and things like that. He's quite different from the rest of them."

"That's wonderful," I said. "That's all that matters."

"I don't know if that's the only thing," she said. "He's also kind of cute, don't you think?"

"Very cute," I said. "I believe I heard Mr. Cute last night creeping down the hall to your room?"

She blushed. "Dad won't be pleased, will he? He couldn't possibly think that we traveled together for three months without . . . you know."

"Actually, he probably could. I'll talk to him," I said. I was tempted to say that given the state of her father's current relationship with me, he could hardly be judgmental, but it didn't seem appropriate somehow, disloyal to him and perhaps not setting the right tone in my discussions with her. "Time to go. Let's see how many of them we can intimidate between the two of us."

"I'm so glad you're here," she repeated, taking a deep breath. "Let's go."

To say that the Chaiwong family was wealthy was an understatement. They lived high above the troubles of everyday life, the poverty, the disease, the hopelessness of many a Thai's situation, floating instead in a cocoon spun of golden threads. They lived ten stories above the Chao Phyra, where the lights of the barges could be seen below, and off in the distance, a *chedi,* or spire, of some ancient temple, was lit against the darkness.

Khun Wongvipa was waiting to greet us as we stepped off the elevator onto the tenth floor. "You are most welcome to our home," she said, shaking my hand, Western style. "I hope you've found your accommodation comfortable."

"It is absolutely wonderful," I said. "Thank you."

"Doesn't Jennifer look lovely?" she said, and Jen smiled shyly. She looked for a moment as if she was going to curtsy, but mercifully didn't. I could immediately see why she felt the way she did about Chat's mother. Khun Wongvipa looked too perfect, for one thing. Her dark hair was immaculately coiffed at chin length, her skin was almost impossibly smooth, and, for a woman in her mid-forties, and the mother of three children, she looked to be in remarkably good shape, slim, almost tiny. If she had a flaw it was that her face was almost expressionless, which might explain the lack of any perceptible wrinkles. She did smile, of course, but her eyes did not smile with her. She was dressed in a spectacular green and gold silk dress, a modern version of the traditional *phasin,* with its long tube skirt, deep hem in contrasting fabric, and short jacket. "Please," she said, indicating we follow her.

"What a lovely home you have," I exclaimed, as she led us into the living room, and I meant it. It could so easily have been overdone, but the room was huge, and it was decorated with impeccable taste. Furthermore, I loved the mixture of periods and styles. A lot of my clients want a particular look right down to the last detail: Victorian, Tuscan farmhouse, Provence, Georgian, whatever. I am, of course, always glad to sell it to them. But for myself, perhaps because I travel so much and like so many different things, I prefer a rather more eclectic mix of objects.

The living room was an antique dealer's dream. There were priceless objets almost everywhere you looked: stone carvings, Khmer-style wood carvings, antique textiles, and silver. There was more of the gold nielloware I'd seen in my bedroom; mother-of-pearl inlay on half the furniture; exquisite coromandel screens; gilded lacquer furniture; Chinese Shang bronzes along with artifacts from India, Cambodia, and Laos. Surprisingly, a lot of the furniture was European in design but covered in silk. There were a pair of wing chairs in a lovely pale green silk, a couple of Queen Anne side chairs, and in a corner, that most Western of instruments, a grand piano.

While most of the art was Asian, there were two oil portraits, the kind you'd expect in an oak-paneled hall of some baron's estate: the family ancestors on display, over a lacquered side chest.

"Thank you," Wongvipa said. "I'm honored that someone who knows so much about antiques and antiquities would be so kind in her comments about our home."

"My wife has done all the decorating herself," a man said, coming forward to greet us. "It is her aesthetic alone that has made this place what it is. I am Thaksin," he said, "and it is a pleasure indeed to meet Miss Jennifer's stepmother." There it was, that odious word again, the one Clive kept taunting me with. It wasn't the *step* part I objected to, it was the word *mother.* I wasn't her mother, I was her father's partner, that's all.

Khun Thaksin was not as old as Jennifer had implied, but he was, I'd say, at least seventy-five. His obvious status in the room would indicate that I should *wei,* but I'm never sure if it's appropriate. There is something often referred to as the foreigner's *wei,* a sort of halfhearted effort where the palms are brought up just below the chin, but there are so many conventions associated to whom and when one should *wei,* I usually just stand there wondering what to do with my hands. My discomfort was over in a second, though, because he reached out and shook my hand, then signaled for a waiter to bring me a glass of wine.

"This is Prapapan," he said, as a girl of about five or six dashed by. "We call her Oun. In English that would be Fatty," he added. "That is because she was so tiny when she was born that we worried about her. We named her Fatty so she would grow big and strong. As you can see," he said, as the little girl stuffed a handful of peanuts into her mouth, "we succeeded. That's enough now, Oun," he said indulgently. "I consider myself most fortunate at my age to have a little daughter," he said to me.

Chat was there, in a dark suit, white shirt, and tie. A lovesick puppy expression came over his face the moment he cast eyes on Jennifer. Rather than standing beside her, he remained where he could just look at her. It was rather sweet. He caught sight of me watching him and blushed.

"This is our son, Dusit," Khun Wongvipa said, presenting a young man of about seventeen or eighteen. Dusit was rather pouty, if not borderline surly, but at a glance from his father, he spoke a few polite words of welcome and then went back to playing something on his handheld computer.

Yutai, the family secretary, came over to say hello and to ask about my day, before I was introduced to another couple, Sompom and his wife, Wannee, a rather large woman in a silk sari, and their daughter, Nu. A young woman named Busakorn was introduced as a friend of the family. She was rather plain, it must be said, but she looked very nice in a red and gold version of the *phasin,* much like Wongvipa's. She was accompanied by her father, Khun Wichai, a rather handsome man who I gathered was a business associate of Thaksin's. All, even little Fatty, spoke English, to my great relief.

Dinner was at a table set for twelve, but which could easily have accommodated twice that number. The table was low, Asian-style, but with an artfully concealed depression beneath, which allowed us to sit Western style, something for which my middle-aged bones were most grateful. We sat on gold silk cushions, with *mon kwang,* or pyramid-shaped cushions, also in gold silk, as arm- and backrests. An antique silk runner in red and gold ran the length of the table, on which were placed banana leaves, each topped with a single red lotus blossom, with orchids and gardenias strewn about the bases. Sprigs of jasmine had been twisted in little chains, which served as napkin rings. The places were set with brass rather than silver flatwear, gold-rimmed crystal, and china in a lovely red, green, and gold Benchar-ong. The rim was decorated with a stylized lotus blossom, really lovely, and it was all I could do not to turn one of the plates over to read the manufacturer in hopes of finding some to import for McClintoch & Swain.

"I see you are admiring the china," Yutai, to my left, said. "It is designed by Khun Wongvipa herself. The pattern is called Chaiwong, and for the use of the family only." So much for the shop, but I did think Khun Wongvipa and I just might be able to do business if this was the sort of thing she came up with. "She also did the floral arrangements herself this afternoon."

"Khun Wongvipa is obviously an extraordinarily talented person," I said. I was quite envious really, of everything: her obvious talents, her home, her antiques, her life of wealth although obviously not leisure. So enchanted was I by every-thing I saw, it took me a minute or two to notice that Khun Wongvipa and Busakorn matched the table. I'm all for the perfect table setting, but this, if deliberate, and I was reasonably sure it was, was over the top, and there was something vaguely unsettling about it. Busakorn was seated in an honored position at Khun Thaksin's right, and next to Chat, while Jennifer was down the length of the table from her beau, seated between Sompom and Wannee. Wichai, Busakorn's father, had the other position of honor, to Wongvipa's right. Jennifer seemed to have recovered from her earlier stage fright, however, and was talking in an animated fashion to Sompom. I was seated to Thaksin's left, and while Busakorn sat across the table from me, she rarely spoke to me. Indeed, she rarely seemed to speak at all.

Yutai sat on my left. "How long have you worked for the family?" I asked him, as my opening conversational gambit, prosaic though it might have been.

"Eight years," he said. "I worked as a clerk at Ayutthaya Trading at first, but Khun Wongvipa discovered me, I suppose you might say, and offered me the office manager's position at Ayutthaya, and then later the position here. Khun Wongvipa is most generous and kind, as are the others, and I feel I am treated almost as one of the family."

"I don't suppose the name William Beauchamp means anything to you," I said.

There was a perceptible pause before he answered. "I do not believe so," he replied. "Should it?"

"Not really, I suppose. It's just that he rented space from Ayutthaya Trading, but when I went to his shop, it was closed. He is a fellow antique dealer from Toronto, and I was hoping to drop in to see him while I was here. I was wondering if there was any chance you would know where he'd moved."

"I don't believe the name is familiar. Ayutthaya Trading has so many properties, I'm afraid. But perhaps tomorrow I could look in the files and see what I could find. The name is not familiar to me."

"Who are you looking for?" Khun Thaksin, at the head of the table to my right, asked. He seemed a little hard of hearing and cupped his ear in my direction.

"William Beauchamp," I said, a little more loudly than I might otherwise. Heads turned in my direction. I wasn't sure, but the name seemed to be a source of interest.

"Certainly," Khun Thaksin said. "We know Mr. William. He has been in our home. You remember him, Yutai."

"That was a long time ago," Khun Wongvipa said, down the length of the table, before Yutai was required to reply.

"I suppose it was," Thaksin said. "But he was here. Pleasant fellow. I can't recall why he was here. Do you?" he said, looking at his wife.

"I think he was interested in some of our antiques," she said.

"That's right," he said. "Antique dealer, wasn't he?"

"I suppose he was," Wongvipa said. "Now, I hope everyone will enjoy the meal."

"I hope you like Thai food," Thaksin said. I was sorely disappointed to have the conversation turn away from Beauchamp, but politesse was required. Indeed, I do like Thai food, and the meal was a rare culinary experience. "In this part of Thailand we really have two types of cuisine," Yutai, who apparently had taken on the responsibility for my education in all things Thai, said. "One is what I suppose you would call the cooking for the everyday. The other is what we call palace cooking, I suppose, or perhaps royal cuisine would be a better name for it. It is much more elaborate and at one time would have been made only for the royal court. Now we have it on special occasions. This evening

Khun Wongvipa has planned a royal meal in your honor."

Dish after dish flowed from somewhere mysterious. There was soup, chicken and coconut scented delicately with lemongrass. There was a spicy green papaya salad, a really elaborate dish called *mee grop* made with very thin and crispy rice noodles served with shrimp, some lovely little pancakes stuffed with pork that are called *kai yaht sai,* grilled whole fish flavored with lemongrass and basil, a couple of curries, vegetables of all sorts, mounds of steaming, fragrant rice, and much more. Each platter was decorated with exquisitely carved fruits and vegetables. I wondered if Wongvipa had carved the melons into roses herself, and if she'd consider showing me how to do it. It would certainly add a certain élan to the meals I served at home.

"Jennifer was telling me you have been in Chiang Mai the last few days," I said to Khun Thaksin in an attempt to make small talk. "I've heard it is a most interesting city, with a great deal of history."

"It is, but I suppose when one is there on business, one doesn't appreciate the surroundings," he said. "Even at my age there is a requirement to deal with business problems, putting out fires, I believe would be your expression. Unfortunately, there have been a number of fires in our Chiang Mai office of late. A problem with a supplier. Khun Wichai has been helping me resolve the problem. I notice, though, you have been looking at the prang of Wat Chai Watthanaram," he said, changing the subject and gesturing to the window. "It looks rather splendid against the night sky doesn't it?"

"Is that what it is?" I said. "I wondered."

"It is a world heritage site now," Thaksin said. "But once Ayutthaya was a powerful kingdom that ruled over much of what is now Thailand, and also part of Cambodia. It was founded in the thirteenth century and ruled until it was defeated and destroyed, burned to the ground, by the Burmese in 1767. We have still not forgotten, nor forgiven, them for that. I suppose coming from such a young country you find that extraordinary, holding a grudge for centuries. I think we Thais see the reign of Ayutthaya as a golden age, really. You must go and see it. It is in ruins but still evocative, I think, of that time. You can sense the great power that it once held."

"Perhaps," Chat said, turning from his conversation with Busakorn, "we ignore the fact that it was a time of almost constant warfare, terrible disease, slavery, autocratic rulers who believed they were god, who marched the common people back and forth across the country as the spoils of war, to say nothing of the fact that during that golden age, as you call it, women's status, once considered equal in the Sukhothai period, deteriorated to the point they were barely considered human."

"Please," Wongvipa said. "No politics during dinner."

"My idealistic son," Thaksin said. "And so serious. Sometimes I worry about him, that he will be hurt by life's disappointments."

"Chat is quite right," Sompom said. "In many respects it was not the best of times. However, to offset that, we should remember it was also a golden age for the arts. Music, dance, the decorative arts, all flourished, supported by the royal court. Some of the most beautiful temples and palaces in all the world were constructed during that time."

"My team won our cricket match," Dusit said.

"Dusit is an excellent sportsman," Wongvipa said, smiling indulgently at her younger son. Fatty started throwing little balls of sticky rice at her brother.

"My other idealistic son," Thaksin said.

"Dusit?" I said. That young man didn't strike me as idealistic at all. *Spoiled* was the word that immediately sprang to mind.

"Sompom," Thaksin said. "My eldest. He is a professor at Chulalongkorn University. I wanted him to take over the business, but he has chosen the academic life and the arts over more material goals. He is something of an expert, apparently, in a form of dance we call Khon. It probably developed in the royal court of Ayutthaya, but was lost when the Burmese burned the city. The National Theater puts on Khon performances from time to time. You should take one in if you get the chance. Rather esoteric, I'm afraid, but interesting nonetheless."

I looked at Sompom, who had touches of gray at his temples and a daughter, Nu, who was maybe thirty-five.

"So Wongvipa is . . ." I said, then stopped. When in a foreign country, don't ask too many personal questions would be a good general rule.

"My first wife died many years ago," Thaksin said answering my unfinished question. "I am fortunate to have a second family. I met Wongvipa shortly after I lost my first wife."

"Khun Wongvipa worked in the office of Ayutthaya Trading," Sompom's wife, Wannee, said. "Packing boxes, I believe. That is where my father-in-law met her." I heard a rather sharp intake of breath from Yutai, beside me, and a brief hint of displeasure crossed Wongvipa's face. I thought I saw the faintest hint of a smile flit across Khun Wichai's face, but I couldn't swear to it, and when I looked a second later it was gone. Thaksin, however, seemed to have missed the remark entirely.

"We will have tea and coffee in the living room," Wongvipa said. Her tone had an edge to it. We all climbed out of our seats.

"I know Mr. William," Nu said very quietly as the beverages were served. "I do not know where he has gone, but I would be very happy to talk to you about him." She looked as if she was going to give me her business card, but stopped. I looked up to see Khun Wongvipa coming toward us. "I was just offering to show Ms. Lara around the ruins of Ayutthaya," Nu said before she moved quickly away to sit by her mother.

"That will not be necessary, Nu," Wongvipa said. "We will see to it that Ms. Lara is shown the sights. Yutai is well steeped in our history and would be delighted to show her around. Now, I see you looking at some of the objects in the room. Is there anything I can tell you about them?" she said, leading me away from Nu.

"I think everything is so beautiful," I said, making appreciative noises as Wongvipa pointed out a few of her possessions to me. "Who are the people in the portraits?" I asked, peering more closely at them. "Family? That's Khun Thaksin, is it not?" I asked pointing to a portrait of two relatively young men, dressed in very formal Thai clothes. Both men were dressed in high-collared white jackets, what we might call Nehru style, dark, short pants I suppose we would call pantaloons, and what the Thai call *chong kaben,* white kneesocks and black shoes. Both wore brightly colored sashes, chunky silver rings and bracelets, and one of them, who reminded me of Chat, held a sword.

The portrait was very detailed and quite extraordinary.

Thaksin looked rather determined and serious, the other young man rather more relaxed, distracted might be a better word. The artist had captured with his careful brushstrokes something very fundamental, I thought, about his two subjects.

"Yes," she said. "My husband, many years ago, of course, and his brother, Virat. Virat unfortunately died shortly after this was painted. It was a great tragedy for the family."

"And this?" I asked, pointing to the second portrait. It showed a woman in a rather luxe dress of gold-printed silk. It was a combination of Thai fabrics and Western dress and looked unbelievably opulent. The woman was standing with one hand resting on the shoulder of a young boy, who was dressed like a little Siamese prince in heavily embroidered fabric and a gold, pointed headdress.

"That, if you can believe it, is Sompom," Wongvipa said. "With his mother. My husband's first wife," she added, in case I'd forgotten. "Rather grand, isn't it?" She abruptly turned away and went back to the group.

"Rather unusual portraits, aren't they?" Khun Wichai said, coming up behind me and studying them closely. "A moment in time, and a certain social status captured forever."

"They are very interesting," I agreed. My companion was taller than the average Thai, and he had lovely almond-colored eyes, which seemed to take some amusement from everything he saw.

"I hope you'll enjoy your stay in Thailand," he said graciously.

"Thank you," I said. "I'm sure I will." I found myself wanting to talk to him more, but it was clear Wongvipa had other plans. She was signaling me to rejoin the group.

As I turned to do so, I had a sense the woman in the portrait was watching me. *I wonder,* I thought, and went back to check for a signature. It was there, Robert Fitzgerald, signed with something of a flourish.

"Do you know anything about the artist?" I asked our hostess. "This Robert Fitzgerald. Is he well known in Bangkok? The paintings are really exceptional."

"I know nothing, I'm afraid," Wongvipa said. "The paintings have been in the family for years. My husband likes them." Something in her tone told me she did not.

"I was interested to read the paper you sent me, your thesis, Chat," Thaksin was saying as we returned to sit with the others. "On the possibilities for true democracy in southeast Asia. I am interested in your theories about . . ."

Dusit sat down at the piano and started playing, not particularly well, but loudly.

"I have a gift for you," Wongvipa said, handing me a beautifully wrapped parcel.

"And I have one for you," I said, "And some little things for the family." I had arrived with some packages, which I'd placed on a side table. When I'd seen my surroundings, I'd felt that it would not be possible to give anything to this family that they didn't already have, but I soldiered gamely on. I had brought a pair of lovely old sterling silver candlesticks for Wongvipa, which rather paled in comparison to all the lovely silver she had, but they were unusual and, as I'm always telling my customers, you can always use more candlesticks. She seemed pleased, but perhaps she was just being gracious. Fatty declared the maple sugar candy to be excellent, and Thaksin asked a number of questions about the piece of Inuit soapstone I'd chosen for him. They were all rather perplexed by the cranberry preserves and the Ontario ice wine, but you can't win them all.

My gift was quite lovely. A padded silk box contained four unusual, cone-shaped silver pieces, with a beautiful repoussé design, and each of them different. "They are betel nut containers," Wongvipa said. "Not very old, I'm afraid, only two hundred years or so. I find them very useful as napkin holders."

"What a creative idea," I said. "I love them." I did, too. I like original uses for old things a lot, but I was getting hard pressed to come up with new superlatives for everything I'd seen that evening.

"And here is another small gift," Wongvipa said. "I have one for you and another for Jennifer."

I opened the package to find a terra-cotta amulet. I just didn't know what to think about that, nor could I think of anything appropriate to say. I just sat staring at it for a moment, thinking about Will Beauchamp's apartment and the missing amulets.

"They are for good health, speaking of which, you must be exhausted," Wongvipa said. "After all that traveling. Please do not feel you have to stay if you are tired."

"You know, if you don't mind, I think I will retire for the evening," I said, and after an exchange of pleasantries with everyone there and profuse thanks all around, I went to my room. Still, sleep wouldn't come. I blamed it on jet lag, but I knew it was more than that, even if I couldn't articulate it right at that moment. Perhaps there was something unsettling about the family. Jennifer certainly thought so. It was hard to think what it might be. Dusit was a rather tiresome young man, obviously jealous of his older sibling, but there was hardly anything earth-shattering about that, nor the fact that the matriarch was a paragon whose only fault that I could see was that she was something of a control freak. Wannee, Sompom's wife, was jealous of her, but it would be hard not to be. Maybe, I thought, as a vision of splatters of red crossed my mind, my sleeplessness had nothing to do with the family but instead with the possibility that Will Beauchamp was dead.

Regardless of the reason for my disquiet, I couldn't get to sleep for hours. Sometime very late I decided to see if there was some nice herbal tea in the kitchen, something preferably with the word *sleep* in its name. I tried to be exceptionally quiet, so as not to disturb Jennifer. The light was on in the kitchen, and I could hear low voices. It was Yutai and Khun Wongvipa. Yutai's tie and jacket were gone, and his shirtsleeves were rolled up. He looked much more casual and relaxed than I'd seen him heretofore. Wongvipa was in a silk blouse and slim black pants. As I watched from the dark of the hallway, Wongvipa reached up and took Yutai's glasses off. It was a gesture so intimate, somehow, I was stunned. I turned back as quietly as I could, but in my haste to get away, stumbled on the edge of a carpet. The voices stopped abruptly, and I heard footsteps moving to the doorway. I was reasonably sure they saw me retreating quickly down the hall.

Chapter 4

The king, certainly, *had much more than a serious little boy to worry about. The Burmese, long a weakened state with no power to threaten us, had suddenly grown strong under the leadership of King Tabinshwehti of Toungoo, who captured the Mon state of Pegu, acquiring all its people and wealth.*

When Prince Yot Fa was only two years old, King Chairacha was forced to raise a large army and march against the Burmese, when the evil Tabinshwehti attacked a müang, Chiang Krai, which sent tribute to Ayutthaya, and was thus entitled to our protection. A brilliant tactician and soldier, the king dealt firmly with his enemies, driving them from our region, and for a time, Ayutthaya enjoyed peace.

But it was not to last for long.

"I wonder if I might have a few minutes of your time?" Khun Wongvipa said to me the next day. "A private word, if you don't mind."

"Certainly," I replied. A twinge of apprehension tugged at the back of my mind.

"I would appreciate your advice on a subject of some delicacy," she said. I sincerely hoped I didn't know what it was.

"My husband, you see, is not really supportive."

No kidding, I thought.

"Would you mind accompanying me to the fourth floor?"

"Not at all," I said. I did, after all, have to be nice to my host and Jennifer's beau's mother, although what the fourth floor had to do with the subject was a mystery, and there was absolutely no way I wanted to discuss her love life. We emerged from the elevator into a bright, airy space with a wonderful view of the river. A desk and workstation had been set up, along with two drafting boards, and two young men were working away at drawings. There were bolts of fabric everywhere and some very fine reproductions of old Thai carvings and furniture.

"This is the home of what I call Ayutthaya Design," she said. "It has nothing to do with Ayutthaya Trading. I have started my own little business. My husband thinks it is a silly notion of mine. He doesn't understand why, given we obviously don't need another business, I would do such a thing. Before I met my husband, I was poor, and I worked very hard. Even in the early days of our marriage, I worked in the company. But then I had children, and the business did exceptionally well without me. Still, I would like to have something of my own. I cannot help but feel you will understand. Jennifer has told me about your shop, which sounds quite wonderful, and even though I am sure it is easier for North American women than it is for Thai, you must still have had many challenges. I really could use your advice as to whether you think there might be a market for my lines in North America, and if so, how I might go about getting started there. I'm hoping you could help me, if it is not too much of an imposition."

"Of course I understand," I said. "And I'm flattered you would ask me." And relieved, too, that it was such an innocuous subject. "I know very little about business in Thailand, but I will help in any way I can. I loved the china last night, by the way. Yutai told me you designed it. I am terribly impressed."

"You flatter me, I think," she said, but she looked pleased. "It isn't a new design, really, just an updating of a very ancient one."

"I think that's a real talent," I said.

She made a self-deprecating shrug. "I only make what I like myself. Now let me show you what I'm thinking about. And please, be absolutely honest with me. I need to know if this will work, so don't feel you have to be polite."

"I will tell you exactly what I think," I said. This is something Clive and others have told me I do rather too often, but it made me smile to hear her say it. If anything, I have found Thai people to be way too polite.

We spent a very pleasant hour or so talking about business in general and discussing her plans. She had designed a china pattern similar but not identical to the Chaiwong pattern I'd seen the night before, a flatware pattern to go with it, and an interesting line of bamboo and rattan furniture. She also had, she told me, a warehouse full of both antiques and reproductions, a few of which she had brought in to show me. There were some lovely sterling silver pieces, including some reproductions of the betel nut containers she'd given me, some puppet heads on stands that were quite striking, lovely silk cushions, some made from old textiles, and a line of terra-cotta products, including the kinaree lamp bases that were in my room, and some attractive Buddha statues. Everything was high quality and chosen or designed with impeccable taste.

In the end we agreed that she would send me details on prices and so on when she was ready to go, and in the meantime that I would make inquiries on her behalf. I told her I'd be interested in carrying the flatware and china, although in relatively small quantities, and would try to find her a suitable importer. I thought I might even consider doing it myself, starting my own little business on the side, but didn't say as much.

"You have been most kind and helpful," she said, smiling at me. "I knew I had found a kindred spirit the moment I met you."

"I've enjoyed this immensely," I said, and much to my own surprise, I had. Not once during that hour or so did so much as the most oblique allusion to the previous night's activities cross her lips or mine.

"Here, please," she said. "A gift." She handed me a lovely terra-cotta Buddha about twelve inches high. "To take to your home."

"You mustn't," I said. "I'm only too happy to help." She looked hurt. "You don't need to give me anything. You have already showered me with gifts, and I am glad to be able to help you."

"Please," she said again. "I would like you to have this." It seemed churlish to refuse further. It occurred to me that it looked familiar, similar if not identical to the Buddha images on the postcard Will Beauchamp had sent months ago asking for our business.

"Do you mind if I ask your help with something?" I said.

"Of course not," she said.

"I'm a friend of Will Beauchamp's wife," I said. "He was the antique dealer mentioned briefly at dinner last night."

"Yes," she said. "I know him. Not well, but we met several times, and he visited our home." There was something in her tone, the same note I'd heard last night on the same subject, a hint of disapproval, perhaps. I wasn't sure what nerve I was touching, but I felt I had to continue asking questions.

"Do you have any idea where he might be?"

"I assume he's in Bangkok. He had a shop there. I haven't seen him in several months, however."

"His shop is closed," I said, watching her carefully.

"I didn't know that," she said.

"Actually Ayutthaya Trading seized the contents for non-payment of rent and is going to auction off everything."

"I didn't know that either," she said. "I have no real dealings with Ayutthaya Trading. I am sorry about your friend, though."

"I'm wondering if he left a forwarding address, or any hint at all where he might now be," I said. "Would it be possible for someone to have a look? His wife is desperate to know where he is, and I told her I would look. There would be a file on him at Ayutthaya Trading somewhere, wouldn't there?"

"I expect so," she said. "I'll ask my husband."

"Thank you," I said.

"It would be my pleasure to help you in return for your kindness," she said. "It is interesting to hear what you say about William. Perhaps this explains something. You have been honest with me, and I should return the favor. He was here, in my studio, on more than one occasion. I showed him what I have shown you, and he, too, offered to help me, just as you have. He said he had all kinds of contacts in Canada and the U.S. he'd get in touch with. But I never heard from him. I was a little disappointed. He seemed very nice, but then nothing. I suppose when you mentioned him last night and then again today, I was still influenced by what I saw as rudeness. I know you won't be like that."

"I'll certainly try not," I said.

"I know you won't, and I am telling you this only because I want to explain my rather dim view of him. Perhaps I was wrong."

"He has disappointed a lot of people. I'm sorry to hear you are one of them," I said.

"Mai pen rai," she said, as we parted company. "It doesn't matter."

"It's not blood," Ferguson whispered, sliding into the seat beside me. "I assume that's good news."

"I guess it is. So what is it?" I whispered back. As we spoke, an auctioneer was trying to whip up enthusiasm for a particularly uninspired painting of the Thai countryside.

"Good question. They didn't say. I expect once they'd determined it wasn't blood, everybody pretty much lost interest. Any chance we could talk outside? I'm afraid I'll wave my arms around in here and be the proud purchaser of an extraordinarily expensive treasure. Or is there something coming up soon you want to bid on?"

"There's something I'm interested in, but it's not coming up for awhile. How about a coffee?"

* * *

"You know," Ferguson said as we looked around. "I've lived in Bangkok for three years, and I've never been here. This is really something."

It is. The River City Shopping Complex is four floors, atrium-style, around a central indoor courtyard, right on the edge of the Chao Phyra. It is filled with very fancy shops, many of them antique dealers. The third and fourth floors house some of the most gorgeous Asian antiques and antiquities I have ever seen. Just being there made my pulse race. I knew I could do serious damage at the auction if I put my mind to it. I was trying not to.

The auction was to take place in what is referred to as the exhibition center, a glassed-in space on the top floor. From where we were standing with our coffees, leaning against the railing overlooking the atrium below, the auction was well in view through the floor-to-ceiling glass windows, so I could keep one eye on the proceedings.

"So where does this latest information get us?" he said.

"I don't know," I said. "I had several scenarios in mind when I got here. My personal favorite is the one in which I find Will the day I arrive, he tells me he really wants to go home but has been afraid to call his wife, then Natalie welcomes him with open arms."

"I can see you're a romantic at heart, but presumably that one has to go. Was there a scenario B?"

"I think B is the one that Natalie was working herself up to, which is that I get enough information to have Will declared legally dead so she can collect the insurance. If that had been blood, I would have had a start on that one. Then there's C, of course, which may be the option I'm left with."

"Which is?"

"That's the one where I track him down and give Natalie and her lawyers enough information to nail his ass."

"I see. I must remember to try to stay on your good side. I have some additional information that may or may not help clarify your thinking," he said. "Will had, still has, in fact, 500,635 baht in his account with the Krung Thai Bank."

"Isn't that more than he owed Ayutthaya Trading?"

"It is."

"And could you check the activity on the account?"

"I could, and did. Regular deposits and withdrawals, usually on a Thursday. Nothing spectacular, but reasonably regular was our Will. Last deposit and withdrawal July third, except for his rent checks for the apartment that cleared on the first of every month. Presumably he had left a year's worth with the building manager or owner."

"I've been thinking about the amount owing his landlord at the store. Now that I've seen the place, I'm wondering about it. I don't know rents in Bangkok, but on the assumption that he owed rent for three months before Ayutthaya moved in on him, that lease is fairly steep."

"I thought so, too. I checked into that as well. I talked to Ayutthaya's lawyers. Apparently Will borrowed a reasonably substantial sum from Ayutthaya to get started—to acquire merchandise for the store. The monthly sum was rent plus loan repayment, which was based on a percentage of sales, and to my eyes at least, once again there was nothing particularly unusual about it."

"I suppose he could have oodles of money somewhere and was able to leave that much in his account as a clever ruse, to make it look as if something bad happened to him, I mean. That seems to be a little farfetched, though. He left

Toronto with whatever he had in his suitcase. His wife had the store and the house."

"But she still couldn't manage?"

"I think there's a pretty sizable mortgage on the house, and she couldn't run the shop. The daughter has some problems that require twenty-four hour care. Did he strike you as well off?"

"Not particularly. Certainly by Bangkok standards he lived reasonably well, on the river and everything. But the building is no luxury condo. He had nice furniture, but not a lot of it, as you saw. There was the art, of course. You'd have a better idea what he had to pay for that. There are still bargains here if you know where to look, and he should have been an expert."

"You said you got together for drinks from time to time. What did you talk about?"

"Not much really. I've been thinking about him since you arrived in my office. We met from time to time, I got invited to his place a couple of times—the most recent was that Fourth of July party—but we didn't talk about anything important. I didn't even know he was married. He was certainly chatting up the young, unattached women at his own party. We talked sports, weather, guy stuff and not particularly revealing. I had the impression he partied pretty hard, but it was an impression only. I didn't run into him that often at social events. I saw him a couple of times at the Royal Bangkok Sports Club. I don't know if he was a guest or a member.

"The only thing even remotely out of the ordinary was that he claimed to be writing a book. Not that that in and of itself is all that extraordinary. There are lots of us Westerners planning or trying to write about their experiences in exotic Thailand. He must have been more serious than most about it, though, because he had an agent. Met the guy at the party. Rawlings, something like that. Unusual first name, but I can't remember it. It will come back to me. Anyway, one of those nights in the bars of Bangkok, Will told me that he was almost finished with it. He wouldn't tell me what it's about, but said it would blow the lid off Bangkok society, or words to that effect. Corruption in high places or something, I suppose. He was convinced he'd be able to retire on the proceeds. Not much to go on, is it?"

"No. He seems to have been a model citizen in many ways, or at least a typical bachelor even if he wasn't one. He goes to work every day, pays the rent, has a reasonably nice apartment, which is paid for until the end of the year, he meets friends for drinks, he holds a party every now and then, goes to a number of others, chats up young women, and in his spare time, like millions of would-be authors, he attempts to write a book. One day he just stops. He lets his landlord take over the store and leaves all his possessions behind. Anything else you can tell me?"

"No. Well yes, one thing. We check airline records, of course, to see if he has left the country. It will take a few days to check that out. However, so far we have discovered he made regular trips to Chiang Mai in northern Thailand last spring. That wouldn't be unusual, by the way. Lots of dealers go to Chiang Mai to find antiques."

"Not much to go on, is there?" I said.

"Unfortunately not," he said.

"Surely in this day and age you can't just disappear," I said. "Without someone noticing."

"Apparently you can."

"I don't think so. No matter what the scenario, someone knows where he is," I said.

We stood in silence for a minute or two, digesting that thought. "We seem to be at a dead end here, don't we?" Ferguson said. "We'll keep checking, of course, and if you come up with anything, let me know. The police are no longer terribly interested, with no clear evidence of a crime. I'm not sure what more we can do."

"I can't think of much, either," I admitted.

"Let's stay in touch," Ferguson said. "I'll let you know what I hear, if anything, and you do the same. Did you say you were planning to buy something here, by the way?" he said, indicating the auction.

"Maybe," I said. "I did go to the preview yesterday, and there's a very interesting sword there—sixteenth century, they say, and I believe them—with a carved bone handle and a silver repoussé scabbard. I went to an Internet café and scanned the photo and description from the catalog and sent it to a fellow I know who has a fantastic military collection to see if he'd like me to get it for him. I've already inquired about an export permit, and I think it shouldn't be a problem, so if the price is right, I'll try to get it for him. And I may see if there is something I could get for Natalie. I'm not sure what would be appropriate, particularly under the circumstances, but perhaps something from his shop. Some Bencharong dishes, maybe, would be nice. Just in case I'm wrong and he's dead, that is."

"I'm surprised how boring this auction thing is," he said. "I expected vicious battles, screams of disappointment from the loser, tasteless hoots of satisfaction from the victor. People don't even call out their bids, just kind of signal some way. All terribly civilized, unfortunately. Half the time I can't tell who got the thing."

"This one has been rather sedate so far," I conceded. "It can get pretty exciting, though, even if you're not bidding but other people are fighting it out for something. We'll have to see how it goes. Do you see those two portraits on easels over against the far wall, the two rather pompous looking men?"

"Yes," he said.

"They came from Will's store."

"Did they?"

"Anything strike you about them?"

"Not really."

"They don't remind you of anything?"

"Should they?"

"They're by an artist by the name of Robert Fitzgerald. The Chaiwong family has two portraits by the same man. I was wondering if you thought Fitzgerald might have done the portrait that's missing from Will's apartment."

"Could be, I suppose," he said. "Can't say I'm an expert on art, though. They're about the same size. That's as far as I could go. So, are you enjoying this?" he asked, changing the subject. "The auction?"

"Actually it was making me slightly nauseous, all those antiquities being sold to private buyers," I said. "I'd be willing to bet at least one of the heads in an earlier lot came off a temple at Angkor Wat."

"In Cambodia, you mean? Museums could buy them, couldn't they?"

"They can't afford to, and even if they could, most won't touch stolen antiquities. It's one of the little paradoxes of this business. Stolen artifacts come on the market, the museums won't buy them, and they fall into private hands never to be seen again. How's that for a little speech?" I added.

"Impassioned to be sure," he said. "If you like, I could give you mine. It's about Americans who travel abroad having to respect the customs of the country they're in, which in Thailand means no shorts, sleeveless tops, and sandals in the temples, nor public displays of affection, among other things. I think I'll stop there."

"I think that's fair, one speech for another. You said you'd only been here three years. Have you been posted a lot of other places?"

"I've been in Asia for almost twenty years," he said. "I was born here, in fact, in Thailand. My mother died when I was very young, and my aunt raised me in the States. It was interesting to come here again. I do have some memories of the place, and the Thai language came back pretty quickly. I'm due to retire in a couple of years, and I'm thinking I may just stay here. I feel very much at home, if that's possible for a white guy like me. Is it time you were going back in?"

"Probably. I don't suppose you would happen to know that young woman, the Caucasian woman in the red suit in the back row?"

"She looks familiar, but I'd have to say no, I don't. I wouldn't mind if I did, though. Nice-looking woman. I'd never thought of an auction as a place to meet women, but maybe I've been missing something good. Why do you ask?"

"She was here yesterday, too."

"Surely that's what previews are for," Ferguson said. "To give people a chance to check out the merchandise before it goes on the auction block."

"I'm just checking out potential competition. I'd say she's new to auctions. She's very focused on the sword, almost exclusively so. Yesterday she was looking it over very carefully, ignoring everything else. She was completely engrossed in it. She even reached out to touch it. The security guard stopped her. A veteran wouldn't spend that much time looking at what they really wanted, or if they did spend that kind of time on an object, it would be because they actually wanted something else. You wouldn't want to give the competition, in this case me, any ideas. That sword is going to be very expensive, but my client can afford it. I'm just wondering whether she can afford it, too. Whoever she is, she hasn't bid on anything so far. It will be interesting to see what she does when the sword comes up."

"Maybe auctions are like flying a 747 to Europe," he said. "You know, several hours of boredom followed by a few minutes of excitement as you try to land the thing, in this case outbid someone for something you want. I can't wait to see you battle it out for the sword—in a refined way, of course. Should we go in?"

It did get rather exciting, for a few minutes at least. The young woman did, indeed, want the sword, and at first she and I were in it with three others. Then there were just the two of us. At several hundred dollars, I relaxed. I could tell by the way she kept shuffling in her seat and looking over her shoulder in my general direction, that she wasn't going to be able to keep up forever. Soon her shoulders slumped, and the sword was mine. She left a few minutes later.

"Congratulations," enthused Ferguson. "That was rather more fun once I had a personal interest in it. I'd better get back to the office, though. Are you staying?"

"Yes," I said. "There are a couple of other things I might be interested in. I'll see how it goes."

It was another hour, at least, before I was ready to leave. I paid for the sword and a couple of other purchases and had them wrapped up. I thought I'd send them off to a shipper if I found a lot more for the store, but would just pack them in my luggage if I didn't.

I'd kept the Chaiwong family's car and driver with me that day, so that I wouldn't be standing out in ninety-five-degree weather trying to hail a cab. The driver had told me he would wait for me in the parking garage attached to the shopping complex, so I went through the doors between the well-lit shopping area into the dimly lit garage.

I couldn't see the driver, so I started to walk along the aisle thinking he might be napping in his car, or had parked on a lower level. As I walked, I heard footsteps coming up fast behind me, and I clutched my purse tightly as someone grabbed my arm. I opened my mouth to yell for help, but then I heard a woman's voice.

"Sorry, sorry to startle you," she said. It was the young woman in the red suit. I glowered at her.

"We have to talk," she said.

"No, we don't," I said. She had scared me, and I wasn't feeling too kindly disposed.

"My card," she said, undeterred. Tatiana Tucker, Producer, it said. There was no address, except for E-mail and a cell phone number.

"Producer of what?" I said.

"Films, of course," she replied, looking offended. "Film, video, TV movie of the week."

"Oh," I said. "Well, what can I do for you? If you're thinking I'll sell you the sword cheap, I won't. I'm sorry there weren't two of them so we could both have one, but that's life."

"I'm sure we could work something out," she said. "Perhaps we could borrow it from you, or, if you insist, rent it."

"For what?"

"A film!" she said, as if I was stupid. I just turned and walked away from her.

"I'm sorry," she said again, catching up to me. I caught sight of my driver and signaled to him. He nodded and went bounding off to get the car. "I'm not doing this right, am I?" she said. I could see on closer examination that she was younger than I had at first thought, barely older than Jennifer, probably, despite her confident air and tons of makeup. And Jennifer, too, at university in California, had been bitten by the movie bug and was talking about a career of some kind there. Rob had been horrified, of course.

"You're talking to the wrong person, I'm afraid," I said, softening at the thought of Jen. "I'm just a dealer, and I've purchased this for a client. If you'd like me to ask him if he'd be interested in lending or renting it, then send me the details." I handed her my card.

She stared at it for a moment. "I guess that's it then. I'll have to come up with something else. This is not my day."

"Could I give you a lift somewhere?" I asked her as my car pulled up. "It's air-conditioned," I added. She was looking rather hot in that red suit.

"I was just going back to work," she said. "I could probably walk."

We both looked down at her red suede high heels. "I'd take me up on my offer if I were you," I said.

"So much for power dressing," she said, smiling for the first time. "I accept." She gave directions to my driver in what I took to be passable Thai, because he nodded and pulled away.

"I work for a travel agency," she said. 'It's not too far, although in this traffic, it will take awhile."

"I thought you were in films," I said.

"So far, that's really just a dream," she said. "I'm sure that the project I'm working on will change all that."

"Have you been in Thailand long?"

"A couple of years. I came out here to work on a film, actually. That's what I did in the States. I fell in love with Thailand, everything about it, even the heat. So when the time came to go back, I quit and got the job with the travel agency. I manage two of their offices. It's not the best job ever, but it's not bad, and it allows me to stay here awhile longer."

"So what is this film about?" I asked. "The one you need the sword for."

"I can't tell you that," she said. "It's all very hush-hush."

"I see," I said. "It will be difficult for me to convince my client to lend you this if I can't tell him what it's about. I'm sorry to have to say that a card with Tatiana Tucker, Producer, on it is not very reassuring in terms of lending an exceptionally valuable antique."

"You really would talk to him?"

"Sure. I have no idea what he'd think of the idea, but yes, of course I would as him. So is this a historical drama of some sort? Sixteenth-century Siam or something like that?"

"Sixteenth century!" she exclaimed. "Who cares what happened that long ago?"

"I do," I said. "Perhaps I delude myself, but I can't help feeling there are others like me."

"I'm sorry," she said. "I've offended you again." She

looked about as if she thought someone might be hiding in the trunk with a listening device, or that the driver might be a spy. "Helen Ford," she whispered.

"What?" I said.

"Helen Ford," she repeated. "You probably never heard of her, but you will."

"Isn't she the one who . . . ?" I paused, searching through my memory to the newspaper clippings Will had sent Natalie.

"Chopped her husband into little bits? That's her. Don't you think it's a fabulous idea? I've pitched it to a major studio, and they're interested, but they need more before they make a final decision. Docudramas are huge right now. I'm thinking I might even be able to find her."

"But she's dead," I said. "She was executed March 1, 1952."

"No, she wasn't. There was an appeal, and the sentence was commuted. She was supposed to serve life in prison, but I think she was only there a couple of years, maybe three, and then she just disappeared. I think this is really interesting, don't you? I mean normally when a *farang* is charged with something and found guilty, they are simply deported to their home country to deal with, particularly when the crime is against another *farang*, if you see what I mean. But the whole expat community was up in arms about this crime, and it really was horrendous. So how did she get off, and where did she go?"

"Back to the States?" I said.

"Maybe, but there is no record of her doing that."

"That was fifty years ago. She could be long gone."

"Yes, but if she's alive, she's only seventy-eight. That's not impossible."

"So what gave you this idea?" I said.

"I went to an Independence Day party," she said. "At the apartment of an antique dealer, just like you. He told me all about her, or at least I managed to extract the information out of him after a few drinks and a lot of eyelash batting. He was writing a book. He gave me a copy of the first chapter. He had an agent and everything, Rowland, some name like that. The agent was at the party, but I didn't like him. Will said that what was really interesting was not the murder but the fact that she'd been able to just disappear. He said somebody must know where she went, even if they hadn't talked in fifty years, and he had a pretty good idea who might know, even if she wasn't saying. I told him it would make a fabulous documentary, and he agreed. I sent an E-mail proposal off to a couple of studios right away, and got a semipositive reply. I was hoping Will—that's his name—would be a consultant and help me out a bit, but I haven't been able to get in touch with him since. I don't want you to think I was just stealing his idea, or anything."

"Will Beauchamp," I said.

"You know him? No kidding!"

"I know him. He's gone missing, I'm afraid."

"Oh dear," she said. "What do you mean by missing?"

"No one seems to have seen him since the July fourth party."

"No kidding? I'm really not having much luck here, am I? He had a portrait of her, Ford, I mean. It was really eerie, kind of scary even. It was going to be a real feature of the film. I was going to get someone to scan the image and then computer age her, to see what she might look like now. I don't suppose you know where that picture might be."

"I have no idea," I said.

"I remembered the artist's name: Robert Fitzgerald. Will told me that he was the painter of choice in those days when the rich and famous wanted their portrait done. I phoned Fitzgerald, asked if he happened to have another, or a photograph of it, but he didn't. I was hoping it would be part of the auction, but no such luck."

"The artist is still alive after all this time?"

"Sure, although now that you mention it, he didn't sound all that old. He knew which portrait I was talking about. I told him I'd seen it at Will Beauchamp's place, and he didn't argue with me or anything. But he said it was an original and there were no photos and no copies. I didn't tell him who I thought it was, though."

"So you haven't seen Beauchamp since July fourth either?" I asked.

"No. I've tried. We exchanged phone numbers. He gave me two, one for his store and one for his home, but I haven't been able to reach him at either. I thought he was kind of interested in me, if you get what I'm saying. As a potential lady friend, I mean. I was surprised not to hear from him. I wasn't really interested in him that way, though, although I'll admit I flirted a bit. He was kind of old. Oops, I've done it again, haven't I?"

"I'm sure he was too old for you. He was also married, with a child."

"Eew," she said. "He didn't tell me that."

"He was trying to forget it," I said. "Is this it?" I said, pointing to the street as the car pulled over and the driver turned to look at us. "Give me your work number, too. We'll talk again soon. You might like to join my sort of stepdaughter and her boyfriend and me for dinner one evening."

"Wow," she said. "That would be great. Thanks. I really hope I'll hear from you."

"You will," I said. "Is there any chance you might let me read the first chapter of Will's book? I would like to find him, and maybe that would help. I realize this is grasping at straws."

"Oh, I don't know," she said. "He gave it to me in confidence. Let me think about that, okay? You aren't with a rival studio or anything, are you?"

"No, I promise, and I also promise to try and get you the sword once you're ready to film. By the way, why would you need a sixteenth-century sword in a film about Helen Ford?"

She looked at me as if I was really dim-witted. "Will was almost certain he had the sword that she used to chop up her husband," she said. "I'm assuming this is the one."

"Sorry to bother you, David. I know we just parted company a few hours ago, but I really have to show you something," I said. "Can I meet you somewhere just for a few minutes before I head back to Ayutthaya?"

"Is it in connection with the Beauchamp business?"

"It is."

"Then, sure," Ferguson said. "Why don't we start the cocktail hour a little early?"

"Thanks," I said.

"Have you ordered yet?" he said a few minutes later.

"No. I just got here." *Here* was the lobby lounge of Bangkok's Regent Hotel, a most cool and beautiful spot filled with flowers and graced with a wonderful mural depicting scenes from the life of Prince Rama and ceilings hand painted in gold and cream, green, blue, and coral. A young woman in a *phasin* hovered nearby.

"For the lady?" Ferguson said, looking at me.

"A glass of Chardonnay," I said.

"And a single malt scotch on the rocks," he said. The woman brought her hands, palms together, up to her nose and bowed her head in a *wei* before backing away to get our order.

"This is nice," I said. Upstairs on the mezzanine overlooking the lobby, a quartet was playing lovely afternoon tea–type music. The noise and heat of Bangkok could be neither heard nor felt, and Natalie Beauchamp's problems seemed very far away. I could have stayed there forever.

"Thought you'd like it. Now, what have you got?"

"You know that portrait you talked about in Will's apartment, the one with eyes that followed you?"

"Sure," he said.

"I don't suppose the woman in the portrait would bear any resemblance to this one," I said, pulling a newspaper clipping out of my bag and pointing to a photo.

"No question in my mind. They are one and the same. I'm as certain as I can be without having the portrait in front of me," he said. "Who is she, and how would you come to have this?"

"It's a portrait of someone by the name of Helen Ford. She was an American, convicted here in the early fifties for hacking her husband to pieces and possibly killing her child."

"You're kidding! Will Beauchamp had a painting of an axe murderer in his bedroom?" he exclaimed.

"I'm not, and he did, if this is the same person."

"Whew," he whistled. "I thought it was bad enough the

way she stared at you. Funny, isn't it? I found that portrait disturbing, but I didn't know why. Now that I know who she is, I'm wondering if you can sense these things, just looking at a picture. I'd like to think Will didn't know about her grim past."

"Actually, he did. He sent the clippings from the *Bangkok Herald* of that time to his wife as part of the package of junk I told you about. That's why I have them. I spoke to the young woman who was my competition for the sword, and—"

"You didn't happen to get her name, did you?" he said.

"Tatiana Tucker, film producer," I said. "She was at the Fourth of July party at Will's place."

"Right. That's why she looked familiar," he said. "If I remember correctly, Will was all over her. Did you get her phone number?"

"I did, and I'll ask her if she's interested in meeting you. She would confirm that Will was interested in her, yes. She managed to extract from him the information that he was writing a book about Helen Ford and that he had a portrait of her. I really just needed your unbiased confirmation."

"I can confirm it, but I wish I couldn't. An axe murderer! Over his bed! He looked like a perfectly normal guy," Ferguson said. "I think I need another scotch," he added, signaling for the waiter.

"I'm sure it's not as bad as it sounds," I said. "Will may simply have picked the portrait up at a sale somewhere, because he was captivated by it as a work of art, and then started researching to find out who she was. That kind of research would hardly be unusual, or even particularly difficult, for someone in his business."

"If you say so," he said. "You couldn't just give me that phone number? I'm a nice guy."

"I know you are. I'll talk to her. I have to warn you, though, that she thought Will Beauchamp was an old geezer."

"Oh. Scratch that one, then. Forget I mentioned it. What has this Helen Ford business got to do with Beauchamp's disappearance, do you think?"

"No idea. It's all I've got, though."

"Be careful," he said.

Chapter 5

Peace in Ayutthaya *came to an end the year that I reached the age of the ceremonial cutting of the topknot, that is, thirteen years of age, and was forced to move from the inner palace. The king generously saw to it that I had a position as a page in the outer court. Nonetheless, it was a wrenching time for me and for my mother who stayed on to care for Si Sin, only three at the time. I craved the prestige of being a part of the life of the inner palace, hated my life as a servant, and missed Yot Fa greatly. I believe it is fair to say, no matter how self-serving it may sound, that he missed me as well. We found ways to meet outside the palace, using my mother as messenger, and made secret excursions to the elephant kraal, or even more exciting, down to the harbor where ships from faraway lands berth, bringing with them exotic goods from afar. We loved to watch the rice barges ply the three rivers that embrace our good city, and to visit the bustling markets in the port.*

While my unhappiness with my personal situation consumed me, there were much more important events taking place that would affect me more deeply, even if I did not appreciate that at the time. It had become apparent that the Burmese regarded their defeat by our King Chairacha as a temporary setback only and were consolidating their power through the amalgamation of Pegu and Toungoo.

If that were not enough, the kingdom of Lan Na to the north was disintegrating, and the king's advisors told him that it was only a matter of time before Lan Na fell to the evil Shans, or even, perhaps to Lan Sang. Neither alternative was good for the fortunes of Ayutthaya.

Thus, only seven years after he had routed the Burmese, and when Yot Fa was nine years old, King Chairacha was forced once again to go to war. I was old enough for military service, but Yot Fa was not to be separated from me and begged his father to leave me at home, a request the king granted.

At the head of a huge army, the king moved aggressively northward, planning to take Chiang Mai. That city, however, was not to fall, and our king, while he had inflicted heavy losses on our enemy, was forced to retreat back to Ayutthaya.

Other problems plagued our kingdom, the worst being a terrible fire that swept through the city. It took many days to extinguish the flames, and in the end, over a hundred thousand buildings were destroyed.

Even then, the news had only grown worse. Setthathirat, king of Lan Na, whose ambitions for power and land could only be at the expense of Ayutthaya, was mustering his forces with hostile intent, and reinforcements from Lan Sang were moving to join him.

King Chairacha, still exhausted, and perhaps demoralized by his inability to take Chiang Mai, although he certainly gave no such indication to Yot Fa, who I am sure would have told me, once again led an army north. At first the news was good. Our army took Lamphun and then advanced again on Chiang Mai.

In the royal palace, life went on much as before. Lady Si Sudachan continued to live her selfish life as a royal favorite, and Yot Fa and I entertained ourselves while we waited for what we were certain would be news of a great victory.

It was then, I am told, a terrible event occurred. When our armies came to Chiang Mai, blood was seen to fall on the doors of all the buildings, even the monasteries, in the city and the villages beyond. It was the most evil of omens, and the king left Chiang Mai immediately to begin the long march back to Ayutthaya.

As unfortunate as this outcome was, when we heard the news that the king and the army were retreating, we thought that the king would simply make another, surely successful, attempt when the weather permitted. This was, the young prince and I decided, a temporary setback. We were wrong.

Now that I had what I suppose one could call a lead in the search for Will Beauchamp, no matter how bizarre, I found my home base of Ayutthaya rather restricting. It meant at least three hours in the car every day traveling between there and Bangkok, and it didn't allow me any time in the evening to hang out at Will's apartment building waiting for the elusive Mrs. Praneet "live beside."

Still, as much as I felt I would rather stay in Bangkok, I couldn't think of a polite reason for moving, other than the pressure of work, which was, in a way, true. I wasn't going to find Will Beauchamp lolling about in the lap of luxury in Ayutthaya.

As it turned out, I needn't have worried about excuses. At dinner that evening, Wongvipa took me aside for a moment or two. "I've checked into William Beauchamp," she said, handing me a piece of paper. "The only information in the file is his home address, which I have written down here, and the name of his bank. Perhaps they could help in some way. I'm sorry there isn't anything more."

"It's very good of you to do this," I said. "I hope it wasn't too much trouble."

"Not at all," she said. "I simply asked Yutai to look into it. And now I have some other news. Unfortunately, there is a rather persistent problem with my husband's business, and we are all going to Chiang Mai tomorrow so that he can deal with it. We would be delighted if you would accompany us. We have a summer home there, and there is room for both you and Jennifer. I have already spoken to Jennifer—I hope you don't mind—and she said she would like to come. I hope you will, too. My husband will be working, of course, but Chat and I could show you around Chiang Mai."

"If you don't mind," I said. "I will decline your lovely invitation. I have work to do in Bangkok, for the shop, and I think I really must get to it."

"You can stay here, then," she said. Once again, I said no. "Then you must allow us to make arrangements for you in Bangkok. You are our guest, and I must insist."

The next morning, after a quick good-bye to Jennifer, who seemed most unhappy about my decamping and leaving her alone with the family, and during which she exacted a promise that I would call her every day, the Chaiwongs' chauffeur whisked me and my luggage into Bangkok. I regretted leaving them more than I thought I would, not just because I would miss Jennifer, but because I had come to see there was much to admire in Wongvipa, and I had begun to feel more at home in Ayutthaya.

The family had rather generously booked me into the Regent Hotel—the same one I'd found so simpatico the day before—and at their expense, too. I was not entirely comfortable with this, but given I had made no other arrangements, I checked in. The hotel was the public equivalent of the Chaiwong family home. My room was smaller, of course, but tastefully appointed, with a nice view over a beautiful swimming pool.

I still had the sword with me, something I wasn't too happy about, even if I didn't believe for a moment the tale Tatiana had told me. It was difficult to carry, I certainly wasn't going to be allowed to take it onto any aircraft, and frankly, it gave me the creeps. I was certain, from her description of the party, that Will had told Tatiana about the sword as part of an attempted seduction. He'd been drinking quite a bit, according to Tatiana, and Ferguson had said he liked to party. Having heard she was a would-be film producer, the temptation to tell her about his book must have proved too much, even if he had refused to tell casual friends like David Ferguson. A few more drinks, an embellishment or two on the story, and he probably figured she was his.

Still, the Helen Ford angle was an interesting one, if he really was writing a book about it. I suppose people have been killed to stop publication of books, although legal injunctions against publication are so much more civilized than murder. It was worth an hour or two of my time, I decided. I left a message for David Ferguson about my change of address, and another, a voice mail, for Tatiana Tucker at the travel agency, telling her where I could be reached and reminding her that I would be very interested in reading the first chapter of Will's book—in order to convince my customer to lend the sword to the production, of course. I also, as promised, told her that my companion at the auction was single and interested in meeting her. Then I was off on the trail of Will Beauchamp, and if that helped, and I wasn't sure it would, Helen Ford.

Will Beauchamp's agent worked out of a small office near Siam Square shopping plaza. Bent Rowland, Talent Scout, Investment Advisor, and Literary Agent, the sign on the door said. A man of many talents was our Mr. Rowland. Finding him had not been as difficult as I feared, and once I'd mentioned Will's name, I had no trouble getting an appointment; which is to say, I lied and said Will had suggested I give him a call.

"Yes, I represent William Beauchamp," Rowland said, patting his hair. He was one of those men who try to cover up baldness by growing their hair long on one side and combing it over the bare patch. "I'm shopping his book around right now, as a matter of fact." He had stuffed a half-eaten hamburger into his desk when I walked in, and the room smelled of French fries.

"Have you been in regular contact with Will?" I said.

"Of course," he said, making a feeble attempt to straighten up the chaos that was his desk. "I check from time to time to see how the manuscript is coming along."

"So have you seen him lately?" I said. "I've tried to reach him a couple of times without success. I was hoping to see him while I'm here."

"I believe the last time we were in direct contact was a party at his place on July fourth. The book was almost finished then, and I had hoped to hear from him by now, but the muse works in strange and wonderful ways. But of course," he added. "You know that."

"I do?" I said.

"That is why you are here, is it not? Please, don't be shy. You don't have to be embarrassed. Your baby is safe with me."

"My baby?" I said. There it was, that stepmother business again. But how could he know?

"Your book," he said, taking out a large handkerchief and mopping his brow. A window air conditioner was chugging away valiantly but was clearly not up to the task. The air in the room was warm and stale. "I am very busy. So many authors, so little time. But I do promise to give it my undivided attention. There is a fee. I'm sure Will told you."

"I've forgotten how much," I said.

"Thirty thousand baht, or, if you prefer to pay in U.S. dollars, $500 will do it, a discount for fellow countrymen. A bit steep, I know, but for that you get an expert opinion on the viability of your manuscript. I have to tell you I have a knack for this, just born with it. Nothing I can claim credit for, really, but I have made it my business to have my fingers on the pulse of the publishing industry both here in Thailand and abroad. Will's book, for example, I will be taking to Singapore, given the subject matter. Publishers here won't want to touch it. Their fingers might get burned. Positively incendiary! Of course I can't tell you what it's about."

"Helen Ford," I said. "Will told me all about it."

"I told him not to talk about this to anyone," he said, frowning. "It's the kind of book that will arouse a fair amount of resentment in certain circles. However, what's done is done. To get back to your book and my fees: If I accept the manuscript, I will move aggressively to find a publisher. I get thirty percent of all earnings."

"Isn't that a bit higher than average?" I said.

"It is," he agreed. "But my services are worth more than average."

"So how would this work?" I said. "I mean what did Will give you? Did he send you chapters as he went along, or—?

"Before we get to that, tell me about your book. Fiction? Nonfiction?"

Inwardly I sighed. I just wanted to get out of there, it was all so depressing. There was the odor of failure in the room, or worse, deceit, and I could not figure out why Will had signed up with this man, nor why he would ever invite him to a party. "It's fiction, but based on a true story," I said. "It's about an antique dealer who comes to Bangkok and loses his moral compass, enticed by the exotic lifestyle here. He abandons his wife and disabled child, lives the good life for awhile, and then disappears," I said, trying to watch closely for any reaction from Rowland.

"Hmmm," he said, swiveling in his seat to look out the window. It had a rather dreary view of an alley, but he seemed transfixed by it. His face was hidden from my view. "I like it. I really do. But let's work with your concept for a minute. I have one word for you: Fantasy. It's hot right now. You'll have to trust me on this. Could you set it in a more, I don't know, mythical spot—that's the word I'm looking for—an island, perhaps, that doesn't appear on any map. It has to be fantasy but relevant in the broader context, if you see what I mean. Just a minute," he said, tapping his head. "An idea is coming to me. Your man is shipwrecked on this island nobody knows about—you'd have to create this whole world, you know. He falls under the spell of the gorgeous women who inhabit the place, blah blah blah, forgets his wife and child. I don't like the idea of the disabled child, by the way. Too sad. It distracts from the plot, unless . . ." He tapped his head again. "I've got it! The child has some special ability, a sixth sense of some kind, about where his father is, and then . . . I'm sure you'll think of something."

"Love it," I said. I could see his face now only in profile, and could not tell if the man was merely an idiot or if he was lying through his teeth, as I was. I felt as if my usual instincts for such things had been dulled by the heat, that I was a stranger in a strange land without the usual moral reference points to guide me. At last he turned and smiled. "I'll get working on it right away," I said. "But what will you need to decide? I can't quite recall what Will said he had to give you."

"A few chapters and an outline will be all I require to make my decision," he said. "That's what I got from Will. He'd been to a few other agents, of course, but only I could see the potential. Given you haven't been published before—you haven't been published before, have you?"

"No."

"Then give me whatever you have, along with a check for my fee, and I'll have a look at it. In the meantime, think about that fantasy idea of mine."

"I don't suppose you could give me an idea of what an outline might look like," I said. "Will's maybe. I intended to ask him for a copy of it, but unfortunately, I can't seem to reach him."

"That would not be appropriate," Rowland said. For a second I caught a glimpse of something in his eyes, suspicion surely, but also perhaps guile.

"Would you happen to know any of Will's friends?" I asked. "I really would like to get in touch with him."

"I can't say as I do," he said. "Now, your manuscript?

Perhaps you would let me have a quick peek at it?"

"Sorry," I said. "I didn't bring it. Too embarrassed, I'm afraid."

"That is something you will have to overcome, with my help," he said, clasping his hands in front of him and attempting to look sincere. He had the expression of someone trying to sell salvation on television. "I know how it is for authors, working away in solitude on their manuscripts with no one to confide in, but—"

"Speaking of solitude," I said. "I'm finding it really hard to find the space I need to write. There are always interruptions. Will told me he had a place he went to for peace and quiet so he could write. I don't suppose you know where that is. I could really use a little solitude."

"No," he said. "I don't believe he mentioned it." Well, it had been worth a try. "Now to get back to your work—"

"You've given me a great idea about that island and everything," I said, interrupting him. "I'll get right back to work and send it in to you. Could I have your mailing address?"

He handed me a greasy card and smiled at me in the most unpleasant way.

"Thank you," I said. "You'll be hearing from me as soon as I get a few chapters done."

I hurled myself down the stairs and out into the street as fast as I could. Even gas fumes and heat like a furnace were an improvement over the office and person of Bent Rowland. The worst of it was that I'd suffered needlessly. I now knew nothing more than I did when I went in, other than, of course, that fantasy was really hot.

I went back to the cool and the calm of the Regent and called Jennifer.

After describing the family home in Chiang Mai in glowing terms, she lowered her voice. "I'm not sure exactly what is going on here," she whispered. "But I really wish I'd stayed in Bangkok with you. Chat won't tell me anything, but I know it has something to do with the business, Ayutthaya Trading, I mean. Khun Thaksin, Wongvipa, and Yutai have been locked in Chat's dad's study for hours with Khun Wichai. You remember him from dinner, right? I can't hear what they're saying, but they do raise their voices from time to time. They're in a snit about something. I'm thinking maybe I could just buy an airline ticket for Bangkok and come and stay with you. Is there room?"

"There's room for a small army in my junior suite at the Regent," I said. "It's gorgeous, and I'd be delighted to have your company. Do you want me to arrange for the ticket?"

"No," she replied. "I'll see how the rest of the day goes and let you know tomorrow."

No sooner had I put the phone down than it rang again. "Hi," David Ferguson said. "I have what may be bad news. I don't know. At our insistence, the police had a more thorough look at Beauchamp's apartment. They found blood, I'm afraid, in the grout in the bathtub. Whose blood, we don't know."

"Surely one could make some assumptions about whose blood it is: the most recent tenant in the apartment, for starters," I said.

"Assumptions, yes. Hard evidence, no."

"Can't they test for DNA or something?"

"And compare it to what?"

"Oh," I said slowly. "I see. You'd want to have some DNA from Will directly for a positive identification, and you can't because he isn't to be found."

"Exactly."

"Surely they could find a trace of it in his home—in Toronto, I mean. Mind you, now that I say that, he's been away a long time, and it sounded to me as if Natalie, his wife, practically had the place fumigated when he left."

"Even if we could, what would it prove?" Ferguson said. "That he bled? You know what they're always telling us, that more accidents happen at home than anywhere else. How often does a guy cut himself shaving, after all? I seem to make a habit of it."

"I just wish I knew whether I was looking for a live man or a dead one," I said.

"I'd say dead," Ferguson said. "Although I have no idea why, other than that he's been gone so long, without anyone seeing him. If I could have found evidence that he'd left the country, then I'd say he disappeared on purpose, but we've heard from almost all the airlines now, and there's no indication of that."

"But what could have happened to him?"

"Many things, obviously. We know he went to Chiang Mai regularly. Maybe he went walking in the hills, got lost, and wandered around till he dropped. Or he had an accident, got trampled by an elephant—"

"Surely this is getting a little farfetched," I said.

"This is not your average small town in America," Ferguson said. "There is wildlife in the jungles, and the border with Burma isn't always the safest place. There are drug smugglers, bandits, you name it, and the occasional skirmish between the two countries to top it off. I'm not saying this is what happened. I'm just saying that things do happen here, and not just in the jungle. Thailand has a crime rate, including violent crime, that is rather higher than one would like."

"This all sounds so awful," I said. "Here I've been cursing

him as a runaway parent, and he may have been lying in pain in the jungle for days before he died."

"I shouldn't be scaring you like this, but I think we have to come to terms with the fact that he may well be dead. That's all I'm saying."

"I guess," I said. "I'm still saying someone has to know where he went. If he went hiking in the hills, then where did he stay? He must have had a base of some kind, although, now that I say that, I realize he could have been backpacking, and just left the hotel or hostel or whatever, and never come back. No one would have been expecting him to. What a disheartening thought, that you could disappear and no one would know or care."

"Perhaps I could change the subject to something rather happier," Ferguson said.

"Please do," I replied.

"I want you to come to a special party. Now that you're staying in Bangkok, I won't take no for an answer. I'm having a housewarming party of sorts. I suppose I should say it's a moving in party. I've got myself a house—that's a big step for me—and I have to move in the day after tomorrow. The place is still a mess, but the priest says tomorrow is the day. You may not know that there are lucky and unlucky days to move into a house. In fact, there are lucky and unlucky days for everything here. Very complex calculations are called for to determine the most auspicious day for this, even more complicated than the calculations about where to put the spirit house. You missed that particular event. It took place before you got here."

"I'd love to come," I said.

"You would? Really? That's great." He sounded surprised by my quick acceptance. "The day after tomorrow is move in day, and ready or not, that's what I'm doing. The party will be a very casual affair, given the state of the place. If your niece—Jennifer, isn't it?—wants to come, she's welcome, too. My aunt and her best friend are coming all the way from Nebraska for the occasion. They're sweet old dears. My aunt brought me up when my mother died. I think you'll like them, although they both, my aunt especially, get a little muddled from time to time. I'm really happy they were able to get here."

"What can I bring?" I said. "In fact, what does one bring to a moving in party in Thailand?"

"Just bring yourself. The ceremony—I'm having a priest bless the place—will be late in the afternoon, and the party will go until everyone gives up and goes home. I don't suppose you'd consider being my date for the occasion, would you?" I must have hesitated for a second too long. "No, I guess not," he said. "Especially if Jennifer comes, that wouldn't be appropriate, would it? You'll still come, won't you, even if I've just committed a faux pas?"

"I'll be there," I said. "In the meantime, I have a favor to ask of you."

"Ask away," he said.

"I need an address for an artist by the name of Robert Fitzgerald."

"You never give up, do you?" he said.

Robert Fitzgerald, artiste, lived in a tree. Literally. A tree *house,* of course, but still. I almost missed it, looking, as I was, for something a little closer to the ground. I'd have missed it completely had it not been for David Ferguson, who did whatever consular officials do and tracked Fitzgerald down. I suppose the tree, a huge banyan, had once been on a fancy piece of property. Now it overlooked a garage.

I found the *soi,* and then the house, by cutting through the grounds of a wat, or temple. It was amazingly peaceful in the temple grounds. Saffron monks' robes were drying on a line outside a row of houses, and a young woman persuaded me to buy a tiny sparrow in a bamboo cage from her, so that I could let it go and earn merit. The departing bird pooped on my shirt. Apparently this meant even more merit for me.

A gate in a hedge led to the house. The first thing I saw as I entered the grounds was a beautiful little spirit house. Most Thai houses have one, protection against the *chai,* or the spirits, who inhabit a place. They are ostensibly home to *Phra Phum,* or literally, the lord of the place. This one was a perfect Thai house in miniature. Incense sticks were burning, and the most beautiful little figures surrounded it: tiny horses, elephants, a carriage, baskets of fruit, sprays of flowers, all hand carved in wood down to the last detail. The workmanship practically took my breath away, so perfect was every last detail.

The rest of the place was not so enchanting. There were several signs posted about, in both Thai and English. I can't speak for the Thai, but the others were rather pointed. *Beware of Dog*, one said. *Trespassers Will Be Prosecuted*, went another. *Private Property. Keep Out*, the next one said.

The house, too, was equally unwelcoming, once I looked up and found it. Essentially, it was a large platform that wrapped around a huge banyan tree. It was supported by stilts, but I could see no easy way to get up there, only a long rope that reached almost to the ground. It didn't look strong enough to pull a person up, even if I were so inclined, which I wasn't, so I just tugged at it. Above me I heard a bell.

There was no sign of the dog, but I heard someone above me say something in Thai.

"Hello," I said. "Mr. Fitzgerald?"

"What do you want?" the voice in the leaves growled.

"It's Lara McClintoch," I said.

"So?" he said.

"So I phoned," I said. "It is Mr. Fitzgerald, isn't it?"

"I suppose you want to come up," the voice said.

"You can come down if you like," I said. Indeed, from my standpoint it would have been preferable, my tree climbing days long gone.

"I don't like," he said. There was a grinding of gears, and a set of stairs, much like a ship's gangway, which maybe they were, swung down toward me, stopping just high enough above the ground to be truly inhospitable.

"Well?" the voice said. "Haul yourself up." I hauled.

I found myself in a sala, a room open on all sides to the air, the ceiling the canopy of leaves above. The floor was beautifully burnished teak. I noticed a pair of shoes at the top of the stairs, and remembering the Thai custom, slipped out of mine. The floor felt smooth and wonderful under my bare feet. There was a dining room table and four chairs in teak and rattan, a sofa of bamboo, covered with cotton cushions in orange and pink, a coffee table in solid teak. The view, so prosaic from the ground, was at this height a pleasant vista over a *klong*. As I watched, a longtail boat swept by, causing the water to rock up and down either side of the narrow waterway. The place even smelled wonderful, the scent of flowers and freshly cut wood.

There was another spirit house, this one under construction, pieces of it scattered about the place. Dozens of tiny animals stood in neat rows on the coffee table. I leaned over to admire the workmanship, which was exquisite.

Mr. Fitzgerald, if that's who it was, was nowhere to be seen. I could tell right away, though, that this was not the Robert Fitzgerald of the portraits. Several paintings were on display. To my way of thinking, they were the kind of art that would be interesting to study in a gallery, but not the kind of art to have in your home. There was an underlying violence to it that I found quite upsetting. Some showed angry gashes of red across what would normally have been lovely scenes of rural Thailand. Another showed a Thai house that looked as if it was dripping with blood. A particularly disturbing one showed a pair of eyes looking out of a tree. One of the eyes had a knife stuck in it. I was clearly in the wrong place.

The sound of footsteps heralded the arrival of a man of about fifty, with reddish hair and mustache. He was way too thin, and furthermore, too young to have painted the portrait of Helen Ford. He didn't say anything, just looked at me.

"I'm afraid I may have come to the wrong Robert Fitzgerald," I said hesitantly. "I was looking for a portrait painter, someone much older than you."

"Then you are correct. You have come to the wrong place."

"Would you have any idea where I could find such a person?"

"No," he said.

"Then I'm sorry I've wasted your time," I said.

"I am, too." What a nice person Mr. Fitzgerald was.

"I guess I should be on my way then."

"I guess you should."

I turned to go, and as I did so, I had a feeling that the

one good eye in the painting with the knife was looking at me. I decided I was going to have to persevere.

"Who painted that?" I said, pointing to the canvas.

"My father," he said.

"And could I speak to him?"

"That would require a medium," he said.

"What?" I said.

"He's dead," he replied. "Two years ago."

"Did he paint portraits?"

"A long time ago."

"Do you have any of them left?"

"No."

"I don't suppose the name William Beauchamp means anything?" I said.

"Not particularly."

"Is that a yes or a no?" I said.

He didn't reply.

"Look, William Beauchamp is a former colleague of mine. He disappeared a few months ago, and I am trying to find him. He has a wife and a disabled child, and they need to know where he is."

"I can't help you," he said.

"Can't or won't?" I said.

He said nothing.

"Okay then, I'll be on my way."

He remained silent. I walked toward the stairs once again, but as I did so, a shaft of sunlight filtered through the leaves of the trees and made these lovely patterns on the floor of the house. I just paused for a moment and admired it, thinking how I'd take this tree house over the Chaiwong residence any day. I decided then and there that the person who lived there, and who had carved these wonderful houses and animals, couldn't be as bad as he sounded. "You have a wonderful place here," I said. "I'm glad that I got the chance to see it. And your carving is extraordinary. Now, about the dog. Is there one?"

"Dog?" he said.

"Dog. As in Beware of the," I said.

A faint hint of a smile touched the corner of his mouth. "Oh yes," he said. "But like most dogs, his bark is worse than his bite.

"In that case," I said. "How about some tea?"

"Tea?" He looked perplexed.

"Tea. You know, dried leaves you pour boiling water over to get a brownish-colored drink."

He paused for a moment, apparently baffled by my approach. "Would scotch do, as brownish liquids go?" he said at last.

"Absolutely," I said.

"Then come along." He led me down what I suppose one might call a hallway, with the tree trunk on the inside and wooden walls to the outside. This part of the house, unlike the sala, was enclosed in a manner of speaking with wooden walls and screened windows. It was still open to the air above, although I could see it was possible to pull canvas awnings across for protection. There was a tiny little kitchen, with a very small propane refrigerator and stove, and open shelves for dishes. Farther along there was a bathroom—I wasn't sure how it worked—and a room that looked as if it functioned as both bedroom and study. There was some electricity, strung from a pole out on the *soi,* and a cell phone rested on the kitchen counter.

"Do you live here or work here?" I said.

"Both," he said, taking down the bottle and a couple of glasses.

"How did you find it? Or did you build it yourself?"

"It was my father's studio," he said. I waited in vain for a detail or two. There weren't any. We took our drinks back to the sala and sat sipping them silently. I wondered which one of us would break down and say something. I was determined it wouldn't be me.

"Do you like my father's paintings?" he said finally.

"I'm not sure how to answer that," I said slowly. "He was an immensely talented artist, but I suppose I would have to say that I find them too disturbing to enjoy. What happened to him?"

"He died. I told you."

"No, I mean what changed him from a portrait painter to the person who saw such violent images?"

"I have wondered that myself," he said. "I don't know. He was certainly successful. His work is in many galleries. I, on the other hand, am a failure. I tried to be a painter—for years in fact—but never measured up. I have all his brushes and materials. I cannot part with them, but they are a daily reminder of my own inadequacy."

"Did you carve the spirit house?"

"I did. Oh, that reminds me," he said, going back out to the sala and peering over the side. "Just checking," he said, turning back. "You have to place them where the shadow of the house never falls on them. I studied everything very carefully before I placed it the other day, but you will understand with a tree house, there are certain challenges. I wouldn't want to offend the *chai*. Very bad luck indeed. I don't suppose you'd like one, a spirit house, I mean. Didn't you tell me when you phoned you have a shop?"

"It is very beautiful. I don't think there's a huge market for spirit houses where I come from, but your carving is exceptional. I might—"

"You don't have to say that," he said. "It doesn't matter. Sit down. Finish your scotch."

"I keep thinking chess sets," I said. "When I look at your work. All those rows of little animals and carts and everything. My partner Rob—he's a policeman—he loves to play chess. Do you think you could make a chess set, a distinctively Thai one?"

"I could do, I suppose," he said. He sat there for a minute. "Elephants," he said, finally. "I could use elephants for the knights. I would use two different colored woods, a red wood, and then black. Yes, I could do that. Are you saying you'd like one?"

"Yes," I said. "I might like more than one. I have a couple of customers who play chess, and others who would just appreciate the beauty of it, even if they don't play. You think about it."

"You asked a lot of questions before, but I'm not sure how I can help you," he said.

"I'm looking for William Beauchamp. He owned at least two portraits that were painted by your father."

"Three," he said.

"Three what?"

"Beauchamp bought three of my father's portraits. He bought all I had. All of the portraits, at least. What's left of his other work is here. There's a lot of it in galleries and such, as I believe I mentioned."

"So you did know Will Beauchamp," I said.

"Not really," he said. "He just came, bought some paintings, and left."

"And you have no idea where he might be at this moment?"

"Not this or any other moment," he said. "He paid cash. I didn't need to know anything more about him. He did give me his card. I suppose I could look for that. He owned an antique store, I believe."

"Fairfield Antiques off Silom Road."

"That sounds about right."

"Did you know who the portraits were of?"

"Two of them, I did. My father kept meticulous records. One was a Scot by the name of Cameron MacPherson. The other was his brother Duncan. Two well-to-do merchants who lived in Thailand after the war. I looked it up."

"And the third? Do you know who the woman in the third painting is?" I asked.

"Do you?"

"Yes."

"Are you going to tell me?" he said.

I was tempted to be as reticent as he was, but relented. "Helen Ford."

"Hmmm," he said.

"Do you know who that is?"

"No."

I debated about telling him his father had painted an axe murderer, but decided against it.

"I should," he said.

"You should what?"

"I should have known who it was. Baffling, really."

I had to agree with him.

"You see," he said, "it would appear that my father was an extremely well organized man. I didn't know him that well. He and my mother divorced when I was quite young, and she and I moved to England. I didn't come back here until he died. But the evidence is there. That's what made him so good at the portraits. He worked and worked at them until he had captured the essence of the person, not just their external appearance. I wish I had the talent. The artist gene seems to have passed me by."

"But your carving is wonderful. I've never seen anything like it." Fitzgerald Junior obviously had a serious inferiority complex. I don't know why I felt I had to keep reminding him about his talent, though. He just seemed terribly vulnerable, I suppose, and I couldn't resist mothering him.

"That's nice of you. The point I'm making, and I'll grant you I'm taking some time getting to it, is that my father kept the most careful records. I couldn't find anything that would indicate who that woman was. Come, I'll show you." Fitzgerald led me along to the other pavilion and to the room that looked both bedroom and office.

"My father, mother, and I lived in a big old house apparently. I can't recall it at all. I was just a baby when my mother took me to England. But he spent most of his days, and some of his nights, here," Fitzgerald said. "This is where he worked. He had his easel set up in the sala and painted there. My mother has told me that in the early days, many of his subjects came here to pose for him. Now, here is where he kept all his records. You see what I mean when I say he was a meticulous man."

He gestured toward a rather primitive teak desk with wooden drawers, one of which he pulled open. There were rows and rows of ruled cards, all sorted alphabetically by name, but also, I realized after I'd had a look, color-coded by date.

"The date on the back of the painting was January 1949.

I have looked all through 1949, 1950, and several years before," he said. "Now that you've given me a name, I'll check that, too. See," he said after a minute. "No Helen Ford."

"Try Chaiwong," I said. "Just as a test."

"Chaiwong," he said, rifling through. "Yes, here they are. Two portraits, one of Chaiwong, comma, Thaksin and Virat. This one was done in 1948. The other is Chaiwong, comma, Saratwadee and Sompom, age five. The date is 1949 for that one." He handed them to me.

"I've seen these two portraits. They're hanging in the Chaiwong family's living room. So your father's system works. I notice your father kept the dimensions of his paintings on the cards, too. Can you recall how big the portrait of Helen Ford was?"

"Maybe twenty inches wide by thirty," he said.

"So how do you think Will Beauchamp found you in the first place?"

"Not hard to do. I advertised in the *Bangkok Post* classifieds. Beauchamp seemed a pleasant fellow. It was a couple of years ago, right after I got here. He came to look at the portraits, because he said he was opening an antique store, and wondered what I might have. He took the three of them. I was able to tell him who the others were, but not this one. He said he really liked it, and he might keep it for himself and try to find out who it was. I shouldn't have let it go, really. It was one of the best paintings my father ever did. But I barely knew the man, remember him only vaguely. There were a few holiday visits with him, but that's about all. I found him to be a difficult man, on those few occasions I was sent out to spend time with him. I had no sentimental attachment to his work, is what I'm saying. However, it now seems to me that I didn't charge enough. You and Beauchamp are not the only people interested in that painting."

"Who else is interested?"

"I'm not sure I should say," he replied.

"I know Tatiana Tucker was interested in it. She's making a documentary."

"Tatiana? Right. Rather fetching young woman."

"Others are interested, too?"

"Yes. I've had a couple of calls about it, not mentioning the name the way you have, but describing it pretty clearly. And another person, an attractive Thai woman, also came looking for the painting and Beauchamp. Can't remember her name, though."

"You've been very helpful," I said.

"I don't know how I could have been," he said. "I don't have much to tell you. However, I haven't had a chance to look at my father's diaries yet. They're all those lovely leather volumes on the shelf there: one per year, pages and pages of very neat, tiny print. He did one every year from 1945 to 1949, then stopped, but took it up again in about 1960. I thought there might be something in them about who the woman was, but you know, once I'd sold it, there didn't seem to be much point. I did wonder, though, whether she was someone he was in love with. I wasn't sure how I'd feel about that, given she wasn't my mother, but the portrait was so beautiful. It touched me in some way. Now that I have a name, I'll look and see if there's anything that would give a clue. Tell me where I can reach you."

"You've been very generous with your time," I said, writing down the hotel number. "I'm quite envious of your home, and I loved seeing it. Thanks for the scotch and for showing it to me."

"Thank you," he said. "You can come again, if you like. I'll help you down."

"One more question," I said. "You said your father captured the essence of a person in his portraits. What was your impression of the essence of Helen Ford?"

"Interesting question," he said. "What would I say?" He hesitated for a moment. "Defiant," he said. "That's the best word I can think of for her."

I climbed down out of the tree rather depressed by my visit. Once again I hadn't learned much except that Robert Fitzgerald Junior was a man who lived in the shadow of a talented father he barely knew. I had to wonder why he'd come back to Bangkok in the first place, and even more why he'd choose to live in the studio of the man he envied so profoundly. I didn't think that there was anything I or anyone else could say that would make him feel the equal of his father.

Did Chat, I wondered, feel that way about his father, the hugely successful businessman? I knew Chat as a pleasant young man to meet and talk to, respectful of Jennifer, Rob, and me. From Jennifer I knew him to be solid, quiet, with a touch of *gravitas*, yet determined, with a very firm sense of what was right. Did he envy his father's success? Would Fatty, for that matter, grow up feeling inadequate because her mother was so extraordinarily accomplished?

And how, when it came right down to it, would Natalie cope with her daughter, Caitlin, never growing up at all? It was a thought that brought me to the most depressing fact of all. Despite all the buzzing around I was doing, I was nowhere nearer to finding Caitlin's dad.

When I got back to the hotel, there was another voice mail from Jennifer. "We're on our way back to Bangkok, apparently," she said. "I gather it's been a rather unsuccessful trip, although nobody is saying much. See you tomorrow."

Chapter 6

If defeat in our attempts to subdue Chiang Mai and Setthathirat was unfortunate, it was nothing compared to what was to follow.

I remember very well the fateful day on which everything in my life changed. While it ended most horribly, I recall the early hours with pleasure, as perhaps the last carefree day of my life.

That day, as we waited for the return of the king, I had taken Yot Fa and his younger brother, Si Sin, to see the royal elephants in their enclosure. They are magnificent beasts, elephants. I have always had a fondness for them. The light that day was preternaturally clear. There were storm clouds on the horizon, yet for us the sun shone.

"Soon I will ride with my father into battle on one of these elephants," Yot Fa said. "And you will be with me. I will be a great soldier, just like the king."

"You must learn to be more than a soldier," I told him, "if you are to follow in your father's footsteps."

We made our way back to the palace slowly, as boys that age do, generally making a nuisance of ourselves wherever we went. After the noise and heat of the elephant compound, the palace was strangely silent on our return. I heard, though, an ominous sound, what I took to be a distant wailing of women.

My mother rushed to greet us at the outer gate. "The king is dead," she said, tears streaming down her face. "What will become of us?"

I cannot recall the exact moment I became convinced Will Beauchamp was dead. And not merely dead, if one can use the word *mere* under the circumstances, but dispatched from this world by an unseen and malign hand. Certainly there was no blinding flash, no stunning revelation. Rather there was a growing sense that no matter who I talked to and what I asked, the answer was always the same. It was as if Will had held a Fourth of July party and then walked to the edge of a cliff, watched by numerous people who turned away the second before he went over the side. Except one of them had to have seen, had to have been complicit.

Perhaps the reason it took me so long to reach the inevitable conclusion was that I was two people while I was in Bangkok. As one, I was an antique dealer trying to find a fellow shopkeeper who'd decided to disappear. As the other, I was struggling to redefine my role in Jennifer's life, as someone who was perhaps a parental substitute. Unfortunately, I succeeded at neither. It was as if my right brain and left had been severed somehow, so that I was trying to be too rational on the one hand, too emotional on the other.

Both sides of the brain were functioning. The connections were not being made.

"Hi," a voice above me said. I turned down my newspaper. "It's me," Jennifer said quite unnecessarily. "I've come to help you find William Beauchamp."

Her nose was a little pink and her eyes rather puffy. "Have you had breakfast?" I said, signaling the waiter.

"I'm not very hungry," she said.

"You'd better eat anyway," I said. "Finding Will Beauchamp requires stamina. You have to climb trees and everything."

"What!" she said.

I told her about my visit with Robert Fitzgerald, and finally she smiled.

"Get something from the buffet and then tell me what happened," I said.

"Chat and I had a fight," she said. "A big fight. He isn't the same person when he's at home."

"Few of us are," I said.

"I know," she said. "It hasn't escaped my notice that I revert to being a little girl when I spend a lot of time with Dad. But there is something funny going on in that family. There is so much tension it gives me a headache, and I don't know why. You're going to tell me I'm crazy."

"No," I said. "I'm not. But what did you and Chat fight about? If you want to tell me, that is."

"I'd tell you if I knew, but it was one of those stupid things that aren't worth fighting over. He wanted to do one thing; I wanted to do another. We've always managed to work these things out before. But this time, it just blew up into a big argument, and I said something I shouldn't have. We all flew back to Bangkok first thing this morning. The rest of them have gone back to Ayutthaya. I came here. I hope that's okay." She looked as if she was going to cry again.

"Of course it is," I said in a soothing tone.

"I'm sure I wasn't being fair to Chat," she said. "There seems to be some big problem with one of the family businesses. Everyone was in a really foul mood. And Yutai! He tries to boss me around, tell me where to go, when to go. I'm not Fatty, you know. He can't run my life. He acts as if he owns the place. I really think there's something going on between Wongvipa and Yutai. Funny business, you know? I wasn't planning on mentioning it to Chat, but when we started arguing, I did. I shouldn't have. He got so mad. It was stupid of me to say that. It's his mother, after all. I must have been imagining it, mustn't I?"

"Not necessarily," I said. Of course she hadn't, but I didn't think it politic to say so.

"It doesn't much matter either way," she said. "I don't think I can go back."

"You haven't spent much time in Bangkok, have you?" I said.

"None," she said. "Chat and I were planning to do some sight-seeing, but with the trip to Chiang Mai, we never got around to it."

"So I think we set Mr. Beauchamp aside for a few hours and just do the town."

"Are you sure?" she said.

"Absolutely," I said. "Where is your stuff?"

"I have an overnight bag with me. I left it with the concierge. My big suitcase is still at Ayutthaya, unfortunately."

"We'll deal with that later. Now let's get going. By the way, if you're in Bangkok tomorrow, we have been invited to a very special party, a moving in party for a house, complete with blessing by priest."

"Sounds good to me," she said.

We had a really fine day, one I will always remember with fondness, despite how it ended. Far from the Chaiwongs, we reverted to our old relationship, sort of girlfriends, despite the difference in our ages. I think we both felt freer than we had since we'd arrived. We marveled at The Grand Palace with its Emerald Buddha, Wat Po with its huge reclining Buddha covered in gold, Wat Arun, or the temple of dawn, its every surface covered with decorations made from broken Chinese porcelain. We hired our very own longtail boat to tour the Chao Phyra and the *klongs*, stopping to see the magnificent royal barges that are still used by the king on ceremonial occasions, and watching the antics of children playing in the water.

We ate Thai green curry and sticky rice, served to us from a sampan on one of the *klongs,* the woman cooking it on a little burner right before our eyes. We had *gai yang,* or grilled chicken marinated in coconut milk, garlic, and coriander, at a food stall in a street market, along with *som tam,* a spicy green papaya salad. We had pork dumplings—*sakhoo sai moo*—further along the way. Then we finished it all up with *khao taen,* rice cakes rolled in palm sugar, for dessert. We laughed at our efforts to make ourselves understood, at the curious questions from minicab drivers—like "How much do you weigh?"—and we just enjoyed being tourists for several hours.

Our official Bangkok tour came to an end at Wat Mahathat, the largest and oldest wat in the city. As we exited the gate, we found ourselves on a really crammed little side street. There was a market on one side and across the way many shops selling everything from shoes to medicinal ingredients. On the sidewalk, several vendors were displaying small objects that were being very carefully considered by several people.

"What are those things?" Jennifer said to me. We went over for a closer look.

"I think they're amulets," I said, looking around. "You know, I think we have happened upon an amulet market." I took a couple of steps toward the place, already reaching into my handbag to get Will Beauchamp's amulets out. But then I stopped. *No*, I told myself. *This is Jennifer's day, not Will's. She needs to have fun, to forget the fight she's had with Chat, to just hang out.*

"What?" she said. I looked at her. "I know you're hesitating about something."

"No, I'm not," I said.

"Yes, you are. Tell me."

"It's nothing, really. Will Beauchamp sent two or three amulets to his wife, and the place made me think of that."

"So let's go," she said, heading into the market. "Do you have them with you?"

"We really don't have to do this now," I said. "Why don't we go for tea at the hotel or something?"

"Oh, come on," she said. "You know you want to. You've got them with you, haven't you?"

"Okay, yes. I'm looking for something resembling these," I said, showing them to her.

"It's hopeless," Jen said a few minutes later. "There must be hundreds of stalls here, millions of amulets. How would we ever know where these came from?" She was right. We were in a covered market that seemed to sprawl over at least a city block. Everywhere you looked, stalls were piled high with amulets. The aisles were crowded with people, even monks, carefully considering the amulets.

"I agree with you. It's hopeless," I said. "I have a picture of a monk, too, but every stall seems to have one of those. I guess it's the monk who blessed the amulets. I think *hopeless* is the word, all right."

"What you need amulet for?" a woman at the stall nearby said. "For stomach?" she said, rubbing hers. "Eyes? What you want?" She held out several amulets.

"Have you seen any like this?" I said, handing over Will's amulet. She looked at it for a moment.

"This no good," she said.

"What is not good about it?" I said.

"Bad," she said.

"Bad yes, but how bad?" I said, trying to make myself understand.

"Very bad," she said.

"Not how," I said. The woman looked perplexed. "What is wrong with this? Why do you say this is bad?"

"It is . . . I don't know English word," she said. "Buddha not do this."

"Do what?"

"Stand on world," she said. "Buddha for peace, not to stand on world." I looked at the amulet. It was true: the Buddha was standing on a globe.

"What about this one?" I said, taking the broken pieces and more or less fitting them together.

"Bad also," she said. "Buddha with alms bowl, not world." I peered at it. "Come," she said. "I show you." We went into her stall, and she went through piles of the amulets and placed a few on the table in front of us.

"Buddha has maybe sixty hands and feet," she said. "You understand me?"

"No," we said in unison.

"This is Buddha stop flood," she said, standing with both palms facing up and out, then pointing to an amulet that showed that. "This Buddha calling for rain," she said, standing with both arms down at her sides, palms against her thighs. "Buddha sit also, also lie down like this. She leaned sideways and put her right hand under her head. "This waiting for Nirvana. Stop fighting is Buddha sitting down, right hand like this," she said putting her right hand up with the index finger pointing down and the left hand flat. You understand?" she said. "Many different hands and feet of Buddha."

"I understand," I said.

"This one," she said, pointing to the broken one. "Like giving alms. Hands in front to hold bowl. See this one." I looked at the amulet she showed us. It did have Buddha standing with his hands cupped in front of him, holding a bowl. "Now you here," she said, pointing to mine. "Buddha holds world. You see?" I saw.

"Now this one," she said, pointing to the unbroken amulet, "Buddha standing on world. Buddha not stand on world. This is . . ." she paused. "No have English word."

"Blasphemy?" Jennifer said.

"Yes," she said, pointing to Jennifer. "That is word. Very bad. Where you get this?"

"I'm not sure," I said. "A friend had them."

"Bad for friend," she said.

"Perhaps it was," I said. "Thank you for helping me. Would you happen to know this monk?" The woman looked at the picture.

"Sure," she said. "Everybody here know."

"Can you tell me where I could find him?"

"Come," she said, beckoning us. "Come," she said again, as we hesitated. We followed her up and down the aisles until we were near the back. She stopped in front of a stall and called out. A rather large man, built like a wrestler, came out, spoke to her for a moment, and then led us into the back of his stall. A very elderly man sat there. I took a quick peek at the photo and then back to him, and I suppose it might have been the same person, but I really couldn't tell. If so, the photo had been taken a very long time ago.

"Is this the same person?" I asked the woman.

"No," she said. "His father."

"Now that I'm here, I don't know what to ask him," I whispered to Jennifer.

"I will translate," the woman said. "You ask me."

"Would you ask him where his son is?"

"I no ask," she said. "Son is dead. Two years."

"Oh, sorry," I said. "Then would you just ask him if he recognizes these amulets, the bad ones."

The woman took them and gave them to the old man. She had to move a light over so he could see them, talking away to him as she did so. Finally she turned to us. "He has seen these before. A man talked to him about them. A *farang*. He doesn't know him, has not seen him since. He told the *farang* what I have told you. These are very bad."

The man whose stall it was joined us and peered at the amulets, too. "I will take these," he said. "No good. I will give you in exchange two with much good power."

"Thank you," I said. "But I would like to keep these."

"Three, I give you three for these."

"That's okay," I said. "I think I'll just keep them."

"Very bad," the man said, reaching out for the amulets. For a moment I thought I was going to have to arm wrestle the man for them, but I got there first. I rather firmly put them in the plastic bag I'd brought them in and stuffed it in my shoulder bag.

"Thank you for your concern," I said. "But I'll take my chances."

"Where you staying?" the man said. "Hotel?"

"Yes," we said.

"Which hotel?" he asked.

"The—" Jennifer started to say. I nudged her.

"The Oriental," I said, interrupting her. "It's lovely." There was something about this man I didn't like, not his size, perhaps, but his attitude.

"What is your name?" he said. "I send very good amulet to your hotel for you."

"Helen Ford," I replied. "What's yours?"

"Goong," he said.

"Means shrimp. Very funny, yes?" the woman said. "Big man named shrimp." I wasn't finding him funny at all, frankly, but if the name I'd given meant anything to him, there was no indication of it.

As we left, the old man gave Jennifer a photo of the monk, the same one Will had sent Natalie. "Father very old now," the woman who'd brought us there said as we made our way back to her little stall. "Stays with his son during afternoon. He will die soon. His son has amulets, too, but not like this. Now you throw bad amulets away. Bad for you, too. I give you amulets for protection." She searched carefully through the pile on her table and solemnly handed us each one.

"Can I pay for this? I mean I would like to make a donation."

"No," she said. "I give to you. You need for protection."

"Thank you," we said.

"Better have a close look at those amulets Chat's mother gave us," Jennifer said. "See if she's trying to put a curse on us."

I laughed.

"Who is Helen Ford?"

"Just a name I made up," I said. "I didn't like the guy. He made me nervous." I also didn't see any point in telling Jennifer at this very moment about the woman who was supposed to have murdered her husband and child.

"What do you think that was all about?" she said. "Why would Will have had bad amulets?"

"I have no idea," I replied. "The only thing I can think of is that Will, for whatever reason, decided to collect anomalies. People do that, you know. For example, sometimes coins are issued with a mistake, postage stamps as well, and they very quickly become collectors' items. Perhaps Will was collecting the amulet equivalent of that, although if there is a market for such a thing, I haven't heard about it. Perhaps it was just a little idiosyncrasy of his. He may have found the monk the same way we did."

"I thought it was sort of scary," she said. "Nothing compared to what lies ahead, though."

"What might that be?" I said.

"I think I should go back to Ayutthaya and get my stuff. I don't suppose I could convince you to come with me for moral support. I would just pack my bag really fast, and tell whoever is there I'm moving, and then come right back with you."

"You could phone and tell them you're with me, and we could go and get your stuff tomorrow."

"I think I'd like to get it over with."

"Okay. If you're sure this is what you want to do, then of course, I'll come with you."

There was a voice mail message from Tatiana Tucker asking me to call her as soon as possible, but I decided that taking care of Jennifer was more important at that moment. We booked a car and driver from the Regent. I told the front desk I would be covering the bill from now on. I didn't feel right accepting the Chaiwong family's hospitality under the circumstances. The hotel was rather finer than one I would usually stay in, but I decided Jennifer and I could stay a few more days.

We saw only the doorman on our arrival. Jennifer still had her key for the elevator, and we went up to the guest floor. She packed quickly, as she had promised. "Do you think we could just leave without saying anything?" she said.

"No," I said.

"Well, could I leave a note?"

"Look, I'll go up with you. You have to thank them for their hospitality. If there's no one there, then you can leave a note. You shouldn't be intimidated by them. You are your own person, and you can do whatever you want. What they think about it doesn't matter in the slightest."

"Okay." She sighed. "I just hope I don't run into Chat. I can't bear to talk to him right now."

The family floor was very silent when we emerged from the elevator. We looked in the dining room. The table was set for dinner, but there was no one there. We went into the living room. Dusk had fallen, and the light was rather dim, with only one lamp lit. The room was absolutely silent.

"No one here, either," I said. "I don't know where else to

look. You may be right about leaving a note. Wait a minute! Now this is interesting," I said, walking over to the two Fitzgerald Senior portraits. I looked very closely at the one of the two brothers, Thaksin and Virat.

"Aunt Lara," Jennifer said.

"Look at this," I said. "The sword the younger brother is holding."

"Aunt Lara," she said again.

"You know, I think I own that sword," I said. It was identical, I was sure, to the one I'd bought at the auction: the same bone handle, the same silver decoration on the scabbard. "It's back in my room at the hotel! Come and see. I'll show it to you when we get back. There couldn't be two exactly the same, could there?"

"Aunt Lara, please!" Jennifer said. I turned to her at last. She was standing in front of one of the large wing chairs. She looked very, very pale. I went to stand beside her.

"I don't think he's breathing," she said.

Khun Thaksin sat propped up in the chair, his eyes wide open, head flopped to the side, his hands clasped in his lap. He hadn't been breathing for some time.

Chapter 7

The days and weeks following the death of the king are dangerous ones in Ayutthaya, particularly at this juncture, given that the dead king's wives had not produced an heir.

This meant that various factions were plotting for control. Spies were everywhere, and one had to take great care not to be heard supporting one candidate over another.

There were really only two contenders with blood ties to the king: the king's younger half brother, Prince Thianracha and Prince Yot Fa, now eleven years old.

Lady Si Sudachan, who heretofore had shown little interest in her sons' welfare, and was well known to have had various flirtations while the king was away at war, suddenly appeared the grieving lover and doting mother. Her hypocrisy was completely transparent to me and, of course, to my mother, but apparently to no one else. Or rather, it suited some in the palace to support the dissembling, no matter how false.

In the midst of all this intrigue, my mother fell desperately ill. Just before she died, she took my hand, and with tremendous effort, exacted a promise that I would look after Prince Yot Fa and Prince Si Sin. I have wondered since, given both my mother's robust health and the event that would follow, whether in fact she had been murdered. It is a bitter thought that coils around my heart like a cobra.

It was Prince Thianracha, finally, who resolved the issue of the kingship and brought the political turmoil to an end, at least for a time. Recognizing that our enemies would take advantage of a leaderless Ayutthaya, the good prince withdrew to a monastery to lead the exemplary life of a Buddhist monk. Invited to reign by the priests, astrologers, and government ministers, Yot Fa ascended the throne with great ceremony. Given that he had not reached the age of the cutting of the topknot, however, his mother, Lady Si Sudachan, became regent. At that time, in a most ominous way, an earthquake racked our city.

Sometimes I think that because there is a certain sameness to big cities everywhere—oh, there are differences, architectural details, setting, and so on, but essentially every metropolis shares something fundamental—those of us from the West who visit cities like Bangkok delude ourselves into believing we understand the place. Or worse yet, that we share a common understanding with those whose city it is, a belief that they view the universe from the same perspective we do.

It is a pitfall I try to avoid. Doing business around the world teaches you over and over again the folly of assumptions like these. But still I am lulled, only to be jolted out of my complacency, usually by the smallest of details, the patronizing comment of a fellow *farang,* or insignificant events, on the surface at least, that remind me just how ignorant I am.

"I'm so glad you've come," David Ferguson said. "And you must be Jennifer. Terrific! Please come in. The ceremony starts in about ten minutes."

"We won't be able to stay long," I said, taking him aside. "Jennifer's beau's father died yesterday. She's really upset, and I don't know how long she'll feel like staying. It's a little complicated. She had a fight with her boyfriend, and now this happened, and she isn't sure what to do."

"What happened to his father?" Ferguson said.

"Massive heart attack, apparently. Jennifer found him."

"Too bad," he said. "Let's hope this will take her mind off it. What's her beau's name, by the way?"

"Chat Chaiwong," I said.

"Not *the* Chaiwongs," he exclaimed. "Thaksin died. It was in all the papers."

"Those Chaiwongs," I said.

"Good lord," he said. "I didn't realize that. I suppose you never did mention their names. Why should you? That is quite the family your Jennifer has hooked up with."

"They're certainly wealthy," I said. "She finds it all a bit much. This may be academic, of course. As I said, she and Chat had a fight. I'm not sure whether it's a permanent rift or not."

"I do have dealings with Ayutthaya Trading on a fairly regular basis," Ferguson said. "They're regularly courted by U.S. companies trying to set up joint ventures here. I've visited them with our trade people. Rather fabulous offices."

"Speaking of fabulous," I said, looking around. "This place certainly qualifies." David's new home was an old one, on stilts, with a steeply peaked roof and wide, decorative barge poles that curved gracefully at the ends. To top it off, it was right on a *klong*, with a staircase that went down into the water, so that visitors could arrive by boat. At one time it had probably been home to a family of ten, but it was really quite small. The front half was veranda, screened in, and at the back was a very small kitchen, a bathroom only partly roughed in, and a small bedroom with an alcove off it that overlooked what I assumed would eventually be a tiny garden. The walls were all paneled, and the door thresholds raised so that you had to step up and over them.

"It is great, isn't it? I'm really pleased to have found it."

"The teak is wonderful. It will look really beautiful once it's been cleaned up. And I love the openness of it."

"I think so, too. The place is nowhere near finished yet, and it's small, I grant you, but I love it. It's the first house I've had since I left Nebraska. I feel truly at home in Thailand. I don't know why."

"Didn't you say you were born here?"

"Yes, but I left rather young. And even if I was born here, I'm a *farang*. You're always a *farang* if you're a white guy, even if you live here all your life. Still, this is where I want to stay."

"I almost forgot," I said. "This is for you," I said, handing him a bottle of scotch. "And this is for the house." I handed him a package wrapped in handmade mulberry paper.

"Thanks," he said. "You didn't need to do this, but I appreciate it. Aren't these great?" he said, as he opened the package. "They're for my spirit house, aren't they? The little cart and the elephants. These are extraordinary. Where did you find them?"

"Robert Fitzgerald," I said.

"You met him, did you? Was he the portrait painter?"

"No, his son, the wood-carver."

"Did you learn much from him?"

"Unfortunately not."

"Too bad. These are way too good for my spirit house. I just bought one in the local equivalent of a hardware store. I was informed that the decision had been made as to where it should go, and I wasn't ready. I bought the first one I could find."

"Well if you're ever in the market for a special one, go see Fitzgerald. His are amazing. Now where's Jennifer?"

"I think she's just sitting on the edge of veranda looking at the *klong*," he said. "We can't have her moping. I'll introduce her to some of my younger friends in a minute. Come and meet my aunts, would you?" he said to us both, guiding us over to two elderly woman seated in deck chairs. "This is Auntie Lil," he said, introducing me to one of them, a rather plump older woman of about eighty in a pretty blue dress. "And this is Auntie Nell," he said, indicating her companion, a slim and still pretty woman about the same age. "Aunt Lily and her best friend Nelly raised me. They made me the man I am today."

"Which is a shiftless wanderer who has finally got himself a home," a tall blond man said. "Something most of us do long before we turn fifty. Now if he'd just find himself a decent woman, he'd be all set. I'm Charles Benson. I work at the Embassy with Dave here."

"I'm Lara McClintoch," I said, shaking his hand. 'And this is my niece, Jennifer."

"Lara. Jennifer. Those are pretty names," Aunt Lily said. "Is this your first trip to Thailand?"

"Yes," Jennifer said. "But Aunt Lara has been here many times. Is it yours?"

"Oh no," she said. "I lived here for a number of years. It's Nell's first, though."

"Now don't you two be rushing down to the Pat Pong," Charles said. "You'd better stay out of trouble while you're here."

Lily giggled. Nell did not. I found Charles rather patronizing.

"When did you live here?" I asked.

"A long time ago," she said. "Just after the war. It's quite different now. Bangkok is just another big city, like New York."

"Ah," Charles said. "Here it is again: the glorious past to which the present never measures up."

I wished he'd just go away. I like stories about the past. It appeals to the antique dealer in me.

"It was very hot, then. No air-conditioning, can you imagine? And then there was the cholera every year. You had to boil and boil the water. The electricity was a bit on and off, too. You were never without candles. And you cooked on charcoal braziers. We didn't cook, of course. There were servants for that. Such good servants, too, and so nice. Everyone was nice. There was none of the resentment of foreigners you saw in other countries. I suppose it was because Thailand was never occupied by one of the imperial powers, so they didn't develop the hatred for Europeans that others did." As she spoke, Charles, already bored, wandered off.

"We had such lovely parties," she said. "You never go to parties like that anymore. Bangkok was ever so much smaller and friendlier than it is now. Everybody knew everybody. There weren't all that many *farang* in Bangkok. There was always a 'do' for some charitable venture or another, or a coming out party for one of the young women. I had a splendid coming out party, didn't I Nell?"

"I don't know, dear. I wasn't here," Nell said. Nell seemed to be a better shape than her friend, Lily. Her eyes were bright and intelligent.

"I forgot," she said. "It happens quite a bit these days. Pity, really. The best party of the year was the Fourth of July fete at the American ambassador's. I looked forward to it for weeks. I always had a new frock for the occasion. My friends did, too. Oh, it was lovely."

"When did you move back to the States?" Jennifer asked.

"I can't remember. Can you, Nell?"

"It was 1953, dear," Nell said. "That's when we met."

"That's right," she said. "Davie was just a toddler. There was a tram on New Road, but we loved to take *samlohs*. You know what those are, don't you dear? Pedicabs, you'd call them, on three wheels, pulled by Thais. They had bicycle bells, and they rang them all the time. For years, whenever I heard a bicycle bell, I was carried back to Bangkok. They were much nicer than those noisy, dirty motorized things we have now."

"I don't suppose you remember Helen Ford?" I said.

"Oh yes," Lily said. "I remember her. Very pretty girl. Something bad happened to her, didn't it?"

"She was accused of murdering her husband," I said.

"Yes," she said, vaguely. "Terrible thing to happen. We got to know the better Thais," she continued. Inwardly I cringed. "The well-educated ones," she said. "And rich, of course. Some of them actually came to our parties. You know, sometimes in the rainy season, you gave your beau your shoes, and you hitched up your long skirt and waded up to the house where the party was. It was rather fun, now that I think about it. Some of the parties you got to by boat. Most of us had homes either on the Chao Phyra or one of the *klongs.* They've filled in so many of the *klongs.* It's a shame. They've turned them into paved roads. It used to be such fun to go everywhere by boat. The tradesmen came by boat. The merchants delivered everything to your door that way."

"Now Lily," Nell said. "I'm sure that Lara and Jennifer have heard enough about the past. We should enjoy the party we're at. I think the ceremony is about to begin."

"I'm so glad Davie found this place and is having it all done properly," Lily said.

Two monks in saffron robes officiated. The house was wrapped in a cord of some kind, which I was told could not be taken off or the magic would evaporate. David had already put his little animals and people out at the spirit house, which had been placed in a corner by a little pool filled with lotus flowers. I could smell sandalwood, which I think was part of the ceremony. I couldn't understand a word, but it was very affecting, and I was happy for David.

Then the party got going in earnest. David, true to his word, introduced Jennifer to some younger people, and she seemed to be rallying. She'd been terribly shocked by Thaksin's death and our unpleasant task of finding the rest of the family and telling them. Wongvipa had betrayed no emotion whatsoever when I found her in her room. Dusit looked merely puzzled. Chat was clearly devastated by his father's death, but he did not seek solace with Jennifer. Instead, he stood by his mother and brother, without saying so much as a word to either of us, and watched as we drove away.

Jennifer cried all the way back to Bangkok and spent most of the next day in bed. I finally managed to get her up and to the party, something I think she did only to make me feel better.

At about ten in the evening, I noticed she looked very tired, and suggested we retire for the night. David walked us out to the main road and hailed us a minicab. "Thanks for coming," he said to me. "I'm sorry about your troubles, Jennifer. I hope everything works out okay."

"He's very nice," Jennifer said as we sank into the cab. "His aunties are cute, aren't they? I love the house, too. I'm glad we came. Maybe if Chat and I decide to live here part of the year, we could find ourselves a little house like that. Oh, what am I saying?" she said. "What a dope I am. This will never happen."

"I think you should just give this a little time," I said. "See how you feel in a day or two. Couples do have spats, you know. They aren't necessarily terminal." We sat in silence for a few minutes.

"You want to go shopping tomorrow?" the cabdriver said.

"I don't think so, thank you," I said.

"No pressure," he said. About twenty seconds went by. "I know very good places. Sapphires, rubies. Also good tailor for *farang* sizes."

"No thanks," I said.

"Okay. No pressure. I give you my card. You call tomorrow."

"Okay," I said.

"You could go shopping tonight. Some places still open. Very good."

"I think we'll go right back to the hotel," I said, but then I changed my mind. "Are you up for one more stop?" I said, as a familiar building appeared off to one side.

"Sure," she said. "You want to go shopping?"

"Not exactly," I said. "Information only."

I managed to convince the cabdriver to pull over, and we entered Will Beauchamp's apartment building. "I've been intending to come back here at night," I said. "But I've never really had the opportunity. I didn't want to come alone, for one thing. I'm trying to talk to one of Will's neighbors, and she doesn't seem to be here during the day."

There was light under one of the doors beside Will's. I knocked and heard footsteps, and someone, whom I couldn't see, opened the door only a little. The door was still held by the safety chain. "Are you Mrs. Praneet?" I said.

"Yes," she said.

"My name is Lara McClintoch, and this is my niece, Jennifer. I am a friend of Will Beauchamp's wife, and I'm trying to find him."

The door shut. I thought that was that, and turned to go away. But I heard the chain slide in the lock, and the door reopened. "Hello Lara, Jennifer," a woman's voice said. "Please come in."

"Nu?" I said. "It is Nu, isn't it? I'm delighted to find you, but I was looking for Mrs. Praneet." It was indeed Nu Chaiwong, daughter of Sompom and Wannee, granddaughter of Khun Thaksin.

"I am Praneet," she said. "Actually it is Dr. Praneet. I am a medical doctor. You perhaps don't understand our custom of nicknames. I am always called Nu by friends and family. Nu means Mouse. Many of us are named after animals. Would you like some tea, soft drinks?"

"We're really sorry about your grandfather," I said.

"Thank you," she said. "But please, sit down. I think you

want to talk to me about Mr. William. I did not know how to get in touch with you and couldn't ask Wongvipa. She doesn't like me very much, and she obviously did not want me to talk to you. I was wondering how to reach you without her knowing."

"I did come here a few times and knock on your door," I said. "Even if I didn't know it was you."

"I work at a hospital, and my hours are quite irregular, so it is sometimes difficult to reach me," she said. "You are here now, though, and I will tell you whatever I can."

"Give me a minute," I said. I went downstairs and tried to pay off the cabdriver, but he insisted upon waiting and charging me an hourly rate to do so. No pressure of course.

"Now what can I tell you about William?" she said, pouring us each a cup of jasmine tea. "I am very sad he is gone, but also angry."

"Angry?"

"Yes, that he should go away like that without telling me. Unfortunately, it seems that is the kind of man he is."

"What do you mean?" Jennifer said.

"He left his home in Canada, didn't he? He told me about his wife and daughter, his house, his store there. He also said that when he left to come to Asia, he intended to go back the way he always did. He didn't, though, did he? He just started all over again here."

"Is that, like, normal?" Jennifer asked.

"Are you asking me as a doctor?" she said. "No, of course it isn't. I wondered whether he had had a psychotic episode of some kind, a breakdown. And then having left like that, he couldn't go back. But when he just disappeared again, I thought this was a pattern for him. Perhaps he is just a wanderer, the kind of man who really cannot make a true commitment to anyone or any place. The other thought I had was that he owed money to his landlord, which you may or may not know, is Ayutthaya Trading. This has caused me some embarrassment, you will understand. I introduced him to the family, and they lent him money to start up the store. It was a kind of partnership arrangement between William and Wongvipa. Not only that, but they invited him to their home, both the apartment in Ayutthaya and their place in Chiang Mai. I was disappointed that he returned their hospitality and my friendship with such behavior."

"So you have assumed that he just up and left again."

"Didn't he?" she said.

"If I told you that he had enough money in the bank to pay them what he owed, but that the bank account hasn't been touched since July, would you feel differently about him?" I asked.

She paused for a moment. "I think I would."

"Can we start at the beginning?" I said. "How you met him, and what you knew about him while he was here?"

"Of course," she said. "I met him here. We were neighbors. We would see each other in the hallway, and after a time we talked a little. He invited me to a party he had, and we became friends, at least I thought we were. When I was working very long hours, sometimes he would make tea for me when I got home late. When he went away looking for antiques for a few days, I watered the plants on his balcony. He did the same for me when I went to Chiang Mai for a holiday."

"So when did you realize he wasn't there?"

"A few months ago," she said. "I had knocked on his door a few times. I have a key, just as he had a key to my place. I put a note under his door, but there was no answer. Finally

I went in. The place looked as it always did, except he wasn't there. My note was still on the floor inside the door. I looked around. All his clothes were there, so I assumed he would be coming back, but when he didn't, I decided . . . well, you know, what I thought. I feel dreadful now that I may have been wrong, that something terrible has happened to him, and I did nothing."

"When was the last time you saw him?"

"July, I think. He had a party to celebrate American Independence Day. I went to that. I don't recall having seen him since then."

"Did he have a lady friend? Or perhaps you. . . .

"No, I was not his lover," she said. "We were just friends. He did have women there from time to time, but I didn't have the impression there was anyone special. I think he still felt married."

"Tell me about that party. It seems to be the last time almost anyone saw him."

"I don't know what to tell you," she said.

"Who was there?"

"I didn't know a lot of the people. There was a very nice man from the American Embassy, David something, and another one, very blond and very sarcastic."

"Ferguson," I said. "The nice one, I mean. The other might have been Charles Benson."

"Yes, I think so. There was also a rather unpleasant man who said he was William's literary agent."

"Bent Rowland," I said.

"Something like that. Yutai was there. You met him at dinner, I think."

"Yutai!" I exclaimed. "When I asked him about William the other evening at dinner, he said he didn't recall the name. How could you come to someone's party and not remember them?"

"Perhaps he misunderstood you," Praneet said. "His English is not perfect. No one else from my family came. There was a young woman, a *farang*. Sorry, I shouldn't use that term. An American. Very pale, with a lot of blond hair."

"Tatiana Tucker. She said William was making a big play for her."

"What does this mean?" Praneet said.

"It means he was interested in her and was trying to seduce her," Jennifer said.

"Is that what she said?" Praneet replied. "I saw it differently. In my opinion, she was—what was that expression?—making a play for him. Very definitely. I don't think he was interested at first, but then, you know, the party went on, there was much American wine and beer for the occasion. They did disappear into the bathroom together and stayed there for some time. One makes certain assumptions about what they might have been doing in there. Still, I would have said that she was more interested in him than the other way around."

"Anybody else?"

"Some of the neighbors in the building stopped by. There was another man, I can't recall his name, but he was very interested in a painting that William had in the bedroom. He told me his father had painted it."

"Robert Fitzgerald," I said. "He seems to have forgotten being there, too." Apparently the rather grumpy woodcarver belonged to the ranks of those who had not been entirely forthcoming with me on the subject of Will Beauchamp.

"Perhaps that was his name," she said. "I really can't recall. I don't think we were introduced, but I did speak to him for a few minutes. He brought his mother with him. She was visiting from England."

"Do you know a Mr. Prasit, by any chance?"

"I know many Prasits. It is a very common name here. Can you narrow it down a little?"

"He's the assistant manager of the PPKK."

"What is that?"

"I was hoping you could tell me. He said he came and talked to you, asked you if you had seen Will."

"There was someone who came asking for Will. I told him I hadn't seen him in a long time. I have no idea who he was, and if he mentioned his name, I don't recall it."

"You implied Will and Wongvipa were in business together. Are you sure? That isn't the way she describes it."

"He certainly seemed to think so. He had cards printed up with some of her merchandise and sent it to his contacts. He even got an expression of interest from a couple of people. It seemed to me, though, that he worked hard at it for a while, but then lost interest. Instead, he started writing a book. I don't know how serious he was about it when he started, but as time went by, he spent more and more time working on it, and he finished it last spring, some time."

"Are you sure he finished it?" I said.

"He told me he had."

"Do you know what it was about?"

"He told me it was about a murder that occurred in Bangkok many years ago," she said. "He said he had happened upon the story quite by chance, but that the more he looked into it, the more interesting it got. That's all I know. He did not share any of it with me, so I can't tell you anything more."

"He was looking for a publisher," I said. "That horrible man Bent Rowland was his agent. He told me he was shopping it around in Singapore or something."

"William had a publisher. He had received, what do you call it in publishing, money before the book is published?"

"An advance."

"Yes. He was waiting to see if the publisher wanted any changes. He told me he had decided to throw the party to celebrate. The strange thing is, he didn't mention it at the party. I would have thought he would have made an announcement or something, but he didn't. He and Mr. Bent—is that his name?—had an argument about it at the party. They were in the kitchen with the door closed, and I was trying to help, so I went in with some of the plates, you know, that needed more food, not realizing they were in there having a private conversation. William was very upset about something, and Mr. Bent looked to me very, I don't know the right word, but like he was avoiding telling the truth."

"Evasive should about do it. Mr. Bent told me he was still looking for a publisher, and that William hadn't yet finished the book," I said. "Not quite the same story. Are you sure about the publisher?"

"Yes," she said. "William told me last spring some time, perhaps April or May. He showed me the check from that Mr. Bent. It had the name of the agency on it. It was for about two thousand U.S. dollars. William said that was for half of the advance, and he would get the other half when the publisher finished reading it. He joked about the name of his publisher. I didn't understand the joke, but he called them after a dessert you have in your country. It is a pie with limes in it, or something."

"Key lime pie?" Jennifer said.

"Exactly," she said. "That was not the name of the publisher, of course, but that is what William called them. I asked him if he was going to serve this at his party, and he said something about how it wasn't funny any longer, and he was going to have to have a serious discussion with Mr. Bent. I am certain they were having that serious discussion in the kitchen at the party."

"Did he say where this Key Lime Pie company was located?"

"I don't recall. I had the impression it was here in Bangkok."

"Where did Will work on his book?"

"Here, in his apartment. He had a laptop, and he worked on that. He also went away from time to time to work on it. I arranged for him to use the family home in Chiang Mai when he found he needed quiet."

"What did he do with the store when he went away to write?"

"He just closed it. I don't think the store was going to make him rich, but he thought the book might."

"Where is the book now, do you think?"

"I thought it was at the publisher."

"Do you think we could use your key and get in and see if we can find it?" I said in as casual a tone as possible. "A copy, perhaps. I can't help thinking this has something to do with his disappearance."

"I'm not sure. . . ." she hesitated. "Why not? If I didn't act when he first disappeared, I can act now, can't I? Let me get the key."

We looked up and down the hallway before we went to the door, unlocked it, and slipped inside. The place looked much as it had before, despite the fact the police had been over it.

"He worked here," Praneet said, pointing to a desk set up near the glass doors that led to the balcony. We went through it, but there was no manuscript.

"Where's the laptop?" Jennifer said.

"Good question," I said. "Where indeed?" We searched the room as carefully as we could. There was no laptop.

"Perhaps he did just go away," Praneet said.

"Perhaps he did," I agreed.

"Let's have a look in the bedroom," I said.

"It looks different," Praneet said. "I'm not sure why."

"The painting's gone," I said.

"That's right," she said. "The portrait of that lovely woman. But how did you know that?"

"A friend of Will's told me it was missing," I said. That was partly true. "Maybe we could just take a look around for the painting, too."

We did. It wasn't there. "I guess that's it," I said.

"Yes, I'm afraid it is. Now, come to my place again," Praneet said. "I want to give you my phone number at home and also the hospital, and perhaps you could tell me where to reach you as well."

We went back, had another cup of tea, and exchanged information. "And you, Jennifer?" she said. "Will I see you in Ayutthaya for the ceremony tomorrow?"

"I don't think so," Jennifer said, tearing up. "Chat and I had a fight."

Praneet looked at her for a moment or two. "Jennifer," she said. "Chat is under a lot of pressure. I don't know how to say this, but I suppose I should just tell you. William always told me that with *farang*, I should be more direct, clear in what I was saying, and not try to hide bad news. As blunt as this sounds, I think this is for the best. The Chaiwongs will never permit Chat to marry you. Even though my father is the eldest son, Chat is the heir to the family business. They may smile all the time and be very nice to you, but they are determined he will marry someone else."

"Who?" I said.

"Busakorn, of course."

"Of course," I said, thinking of the young woman dressed, like Wongvipa, to match the tablecloth. "Why Busakorn, in particular?"

"Two reasons: one is business. Busakorn's father, Mr. Wichai, is a business associate in Chiang Mai, head of a company called Busakorn Shipping, or in English, Blue Lotus Shipping. As you have noticed, he named the company after his daughter. Let's just say it would be mutually advantageous from a financial perspective if Busakorn and Chat were to wed. Secondly, the family will never allow Chat to marry a *farang*. I'm sorry, but that's the way it is.

"Thank you for your candor," I said. "I think it's time we went now, don't you Jennifer?" She could barely nod her head.

"I'm really sorry, Jennifer," Praneet said. "I tell you this because I know what they are like. As a family they can never be underestimated. I loved someone once they didn't approve of, a *farang*. They drove him away."

We had a very silent trip back to the hotel, punctuated from time to time with quiet little sobs from Jennifer. I just sat there beside her, ineffectually patting her arm. I was angry at the Chaiwongs and annoyed with myself for putting Jennifer through that, however inadvertently, in the name of finding Will Beauchamp.

When we walked into the lobby of the hotel, though, a man rose from his chair. "Hello, Jennifer. Hello, Aunt Lara," Chat said. Jennifer just stared at him. "I'm sorry, Jennifer," he said. "I'm not myself. My father . . . I have to run the company. My mother says that's what my father wanted. I don't know. I can't. I need you with me, Jen. Is there anything I could say or do to convince you to come back? I mean . . ."

"It's okay, Chat," Jennifer said. "I'm here."

Chapter 8

Once in power, King Yot Fa remained much as he had been. He was not well trained for kingship, but he was an intelligent boy and tried hard to emulate his father.

The regent, his mother, on the other hand, gloried in her position. She had the royal residence completely redone to her taste, at great expense to the kingdom, and moved ruthlessly to sweep away her detractors. Wives and concubines of the dead king were thrown out of the palace, and several of those who opposed her were sent away on missions of varying degrees of necessity and plausibility. Many did not return.

The regent tried to have me sent to the countryside as a laborer, but the young king would not allow it. Accordingly, she changed her tactics to try to drive a wedge between the two of us, a strategy that I unwittingly aided, just how it will soon become clear. I have no idea what poisonous things she had to say about me, but I could see, as the months wore on, that they were having an effect. The king began to view me with some suspicion, which usually, but not always, I was able to allay. Nonetheless, he continued to insist I remain in the palace, and indeed appointed me to a better position.

Shortly after the king's death and her appointment as regent, Lady Si Sudachan began a scandalous and completely inappropriate dalliance with a heretofore minor court official, Phan But Si Thep, the guard of the front image hall. Phan But Si Thep had always struck me as an ambitious man of little ability. The regent, however, clearly doted on him, and he was a slave to her every command.

The liaison was certainly to his benefit. Shortly after he succumbed to the lady's blandishments, for it was she who initiated the liaison, she appointed him Khun Chinnarat, guard of the inner image hall, demoting the former Khun Chinnarat to her lover's former title of Phan But Si Thep. That elevated position in the inner court made it possible for the two of them to be together, all the more so when the queen regent promoted him to an even more important post as Khun Worawongsa, in charge of the Office of Registration.

The queen regent obviously had no care as to how others in the palace would view her actions, because soon after that, she built Khun Worawongsa an official residence where palace officials were required to submit to his wishes. She then built him a second official residence at the Din Gate, after which Worawongsa began taking a much more direct interest in the affairs of the kingdom and appeared regularly at the regent's side.

There was talk, of course, but also fear of her wrath, and none objected, at least not in public. Indeed, all opposition to these measures was quickly quashed. One official, known to oppose Khun Worawongsa, was stabbed to death on leaving the residence at the Din Gate. It was increasingly clear that Lady Si Sudachan and her lover would brook no opposition; that to defy them meant, quite simply, death. Still, the gossip in the palace was, as you can imag-

ine, considerable when it became evident that the regent was expecting a child.

So there I was back in the bosom of the Chaiwong family, and not entirely happy about it. Nor was the family, with the exception of Chat, any more thrilled about my presence than I was. Certainly there was no one making an effort to make sure I felt at home. Indeed, my host, Wongvipa, made no secret of the fact she'd prefer I wasn't there. It was on the subject of my presence that Chat overruled his mother for the one and only time. He needed Jennifer to be near him, and she wasn't going anywhere without me. Whether Wongvipa or I liked it or not, I was there.

Not that Wongvipa made her feelings known to me face-to-face. Her instructions were never delivered in person, but rather by Yutai. Through him she had declared Chat head of the company in his father's place. According to Yutai, and as Chat had reported, Thaksin had made his views known to his wife before he died. No one argued, not even Sompom, who could be said to have a prior claim, given he was Thaksin's firstborn, and indeed had worked for several years in the company before escaping to the world of academe. It was experience Chat lacked.

A Buddhist of Thaksin Chaiwong's wealth and status might be expected to lie in state, as it were, for a considerable period, even months, but he was cremated three days after he died. His widow saw to that. Jennifer and I were not present at the cremation at Wongvipa's request. Busakorn, the chosen one, was.

There were other immediate changes about the place that signaled the new regime. The two Fitzgerald portraits, one of Thaksin and his brother, the other of Sompom as a child with his mother, disappeared from sight. In their place were portraits of Wongvipa and the two boys, and Wongvipa and Fatty. The official explanation was that it distressed Wongvipa to see her husband so young and well. Sompom, Wannee, and Praneet, regular guests at the family dinner table, were no longer invited.

"We've been banished," Praneet told me. "Our appearance is required at ceremonial occasions only."

"I think your mother and Wongvipa perhaps do not get along that well," I said, sympathetically.

"My mother feels that when my grandmother died, Wongvipa took advantage of Thaksin's grief and managed to insinuate herself into the family and his life. Certainly she got pregnant with Chat right away. They got married shortly thereafter. That's what I'm told, anyway. I was just a child."

"Still, Thaksin and Wongvipa were together a long time," I said. "Chat is what? Twenty-four or -five, I think."

"Yes," she said. "And I have a fair amount of sympathy for her. My mother was born into wealth and privilege, as I was. Wongvipa wasn't. She grew up in a village on the outskirts of Bangkok. I think she was very poor. It can't have been easy for her. She may have married well, but she is not without ability and charm. To tell you the truth, I'm just glad not to have to go to dinner there every week."

Still, the suddenness of all this surprised me. I would have thought the widow would have waited a decent length of time to dump the portraits and the relatives, but Wongvipa did not seem to care about such things. Nor did she make any effort to disguise her liking for Yutai. While I had tried to persuade myself that the intimate scene I had witnessed between them on my arrival in Ayutthaya had been my imagination, it was clear that it was not. Yutai could regularly be found at her side, rather more than mere business would call for, and from time to time, I caught her looking at him with a glance that was nothing short of smoldering. I, on the other hand, found he was often watching me, and not, I thought, with any affection. Having said that, it rather quickly became business as usual, and business took the family and therefore Jennifer and me, to Chiang Mai.

In a sense, to travel the more than four hundred miles north from Bangkok to Chiang Mai is to journey back through history, pushing against the tide of ethnically and linguistically linked peoples who, about a thousand years ago or so, began to move south out of China's Yunnan province into what was to become Thailand. It was a migration that was to take several centuries and to result in the formation of successive kingdoms, each a little farther south than the last. Chiang Mai was part of the earliest of five centers of power, the kingdom of Lan Na, which Thais consider to be the first of five Thai kingdoms. Lan Na was to be followed by Sukhothai, then Ayutthaya, then Thonburi, and finally Bangkok.

Now Chiang Mai is the principal city of Thailand's north. The Old City is still surrounded by walls and a moat, although the town has spread way beyond them, a bustling place, noisy with the whine of tuk-tuks that buzz around the city by the thousands, their sound competing with the crowing of roosters and the cries of street vendors. The markets are crowded and colorful, the stalls piled high with fish and exotic fruits and vegetables.

But in all the noise there are oases of calm, perhaps even silence. One of them was the summer residence of the Chaiwongs. It was built of wood on a platform above the Ping

River, and consisted of a main house with a huge veranda overlooking the river where the family took its meals, and off apart, a guest pavilion with three rooms and a sala that Jennifer and I shared.

If anything, I liked the place even more than the spectacular apartment in Ayutthaya. Here silk had been exchanged for cotton, gold and black lacquerware for exquisite old wood carving and painted columns, marble tile for a courtyard of laterite blocks.

It was here, I knew from Praneet, that Will Beauchamp had come on a reasonably regular basis to write. My bedroom had the desk I was certain he used, not because it was the only desk in the little house, although it was, but because it was the perfect place for contemplation and creation, with a view through an open window to sunlight filtering through the dark and luxurious tropical foliage that surrounded the grounds. I found his business card for Fairfield Antiques, one side in English, the other in Thai, stuck in the side of one of the drawers. In that same drawer I found red dust and some terra-cotta residue that made me think of the broken amulet. I looked in vain for more. If Will's ghost was there, I couldn't feel it. There was only the rustle of the breeze in the leaves, the rattle of bamboo, and the songs of birds. It was very close to paradise.

The guest pavilion also afforded me a view of the comings and goings at the main house. Khun Wichai visited, favoring me with his lovely smile and a wave as he went by. I hoped he would stay for dinner, especially given he'd not brought Busakorn, but he was there, apparently, on business. There were others who came and went, none of them familiar. I gathered that the business the family was there to discuss was Wongvipa's. She had a factory and kilns just outside the city where her terra-cotta products were made.

The other haven of silence was to be found in the temples, or wats. There were hundreds of them in the city, some of them so ancient they were essentially ruins, others more modern and vital. It was to one of these that I took myself one day, the piece of paper with its name written so laboriously by the woman in the amulet market in Bangkok clutched tightly in my hand. Wats are essentially composed of two areas, the quarters of the monks and the more public areas for worship. The residences tend to be rather austere, but the public areas are often a riot of color, and gold, and splendid carving. I presented myself at the wat in question, and asked to meet with an English-speaking priest. To my surprise, they obliged.

I was ushered into one of the public buildings, abandoning my shoes, and ascending a staircase lined with protective serpents, or *nagas*. I had been well instructed never to touch a monk but to kneel in his presence and bow, forehead to the floor on meeting him, to ensure that the bottom of my feet at no time pointed toward either the monk or, more importantly, the Buddha image. I was to call him *ajahn*, which I gather means teacher. I am not religious, I'm afraid, and I was so enchanted by the place, from the decaying frescoes in reds and blues that depicted scenes from the life of Buddha, to his gold image, so calm and majestic, and at least twelve or fifteen feet high and beautifully crafted, that I did not for a time notice the monk who was sitting on a platform, his legs crossed, watching me.

"Oh dear," I muttered and managed to get myself more or less in the right position. At the monk's command, I was able to sit up, but had to sit on the floor with my legs tucked to one side, a position that at my age is something of a trial.

I looked up to see a man, his head shaved, dressed in the orange robe of the monk, one shoulder bare in the Thai style. What I noticed most were his blue eyes.

"You're surprised," he said softly. "To see a white man here."

"I suppose I am," I said. "Where are you from, *ajahn*?"

"California, but I have been here many years." We talked about several things for a few minutes, the weather, how I liked Chiang Mai, his hometown of Fresno.

"Do you miss it?" I said.

"Fresno?" he replied with a slight smile. "California? My former life? Sex?"

That hadn't been what I'd meant.

"No," he said finally. But then he said, "You came here for a purpose."

"Yes. I am looking for a monk. May I?" I said, pointing to my bag. "I have a photograph. I'm told he is associated with this temple."

"Of course," he said. He barely looked at the photo before handing it back to me. "He is not here."

"But he was," I persisted. The monk did not reply.

"*Ajahn,* would you please tell me about him," I said. "I have no idea if it is relevant, but I do need to know if it is possible to talk to him. I am trying to find a man who abandoned his wife and disabled child in Canada, and I am following up every lead I have, which is not many."

The monk said nothing for quite a while. Then he said, so softly I wasn't sure I had heard him correctly, "In Buddhism, a cool heart is something to strive for."

"What?"

"You are very troubled about something."

I thought about that for a moment or two. "I don't think

so," I said. "Not any more than usual. Well, maybe I am. A little, anyway."

He didn't say anything.

I looked at the frescoes for a minute or two, admired the workmanship, the carved windows. Then suddenly I was just burbling away at this total stranger. I told him about Will and Natalie, about Jennifer and Chat, about my relationship with Rob. Part of me was horrified that I was going on like that, but the other was just relieved.

"You don't have children of your own, do you?" he said when I stopped for breath.

"No."

"Was that a mistake?"

"I don't know," I said. "Maybe. But I have no patience. If they wouldn't stop crying or something, I probably would have killed them." There was a perceptible pause. I was dimly aware of chanting off in the distance somewhere, and the ringing of bells, but they had a muffled quality. "Actually," I said. "That is not true. I would not have killed them. I would not have abandoned them. Will's daughter is mentally handicapped, but she has the most beautiful smile you have ever seen. How could he do what he did? And you know what? He came here and he started writing a book about a woman who chopped her husband into bits and murdered her child. At least everybody thinks she did. The child's body was never found. What would it take to make a mother murder her child? What possible conditions, other than utter madness, would have to prevail for that to happen? Surely it is our responsibility as adults to protect our children, our own, or somebody else's." I could hear my voice coming out in a croak as I spoke, and I realized that

I had had no idea I was this upset about everything. I thought I would choke on my bile.

"And you know what else?" I said. "Almost no one has told me the truth, Thais and whites alike, since I got here. They smile, they are polite, and they lie through their teeth. Or if they haven't lied, they have withheld information. And that includes you," I said, pointing at the photograph.

For a moment I thought I would be struck by lightning for speaking to a monk that way.

"I suppose all religious groups have their bad apples," he said after a minute. "He was one of them. He was a senior monk here, and he was found to have a rather spectacular home outside where he lived with a woman and drove a Mercedes. We thought he was retreating to meditate alone. The Ministry of Religious Affairs investigated—this was all done rather quietly, you understand—and he is no longer a monk."

"Is that it?"

"No. He obviously had a lot of money. It was thought he was taking money from the temple, but there was no evidence that he had. The police decided his money came from smuggling."

"Smuggling what?"

"Jewels, drugs, people. He is now in jail."

"Since when?"

"Two years ago."

"His father apparently says he is dead."

"Perhaps he is dead to him."

"Thank you," I said. "For telling me."

"You are quite welcome," he replied. "Now you should go back to taking care of the children."

"Could I ask one more question?"

"Yes."

"These amulets," I said, handing over my little plastic sandwich bag.

"These are—"

"Blasphemous, I know. But have you ever seen them before?"

"No," he said, handing them back. "Nor, in the interests of not withholding information, have I seen anything like them."

"Thank you," I said. "I feel better."

"I'm glad," he replied. "It must be difficult for you trying to be a mother to so many."

I opened my mouth to protest, to tell him I was childless by choice, that I had a wonderful life, a business that might not make me rich, but one I loved. I was going to tell him I owned a house, had very nice friends, got to travel all over the world, footloose and fancy-free. But I didn't say any of it. Instead, I bowed my forehead to the floor again, and by the time I looked up, he was gone.

I wandered around Chiang Mai for at least an hour after that, arguing with both the monk and myself in my head. I remembered Clive telling me that I was always flailing about helping people I barely knew, and I wondered if this is what the monk had meant. I supposed Clive was referring to people like Robert Fitzgerald. I'd told Robert I'd try to sell his spirit houses in my store. Spirit houses! And this in a neighborhood that leaned rather more to Armani and Chanel. If Fitzgerald had a problem with his father, was it up to me to try to fix it? Maybe Clive and the monk were right.

On the other hand, Clive could hardly be judgmental, could he? And the comment about people I barely knew was hardly fair. For example, why exactly had I taken him back as a business partner long after our divorce? You couldn't get much closer to home than that. I told myself it was because he was now my friend Moira's partner, but maybe it was because I sensed the vulnerability under his rather brash exterior, or maybe because I felt the marriage failed because of me. Certainly I knew that when he went into business in competition with me, and right across the road, that he wouldn't last long, particularly when he got dumped by his second wife, the rather wealthy Celeste. I could just have waited him out. He was no businessman, no matter how talented a designer.

And then there was William Beauchamp. Why had I ever said I would look for a man I didn't know very well, for a woman and a daughter I knew even less? Was that what the monk had been talking about?

Maybe the only person in my life I didn't feel responsible for was Rob. And maybe that was why I was so reluctant to move in with him. I thought our relationship would change, and I would not only be struggling with trying to be a mother to Jennifer, but he'd want me to mother him as well.

Deep in these thoughts, I was quite unaware of my surroundings, walking up and down lanes, barely noticing the buzz of the town around me. I will always think of Chiang Mai as a beehive because of the high-pitched hum of the tuk-tuks that must surely outnumber the cars. They whirred around corners and jostled for position at the intersections like annoying insects. At some point I found myself in the market off Moon Muang Road near the moat that surrounds the Old City. I barely noticed the piles of red, spiky rambutan fruit, the green papaya, the tubs of snakefish, the stacks of tofu and dried fish, the cries of the merchants.

Suddenly, though, I felt a tuk-tuk dangerously close to

me, and tried to move out of its way. I felt a hand grab at the bag on my shoulder and tug at it. I yelled and held on tight, but was thrown very hard against a fruit stand, dislodging a mound of jackfruit, and sliding to the ground. Two or three people nearby rushed to help me, and by the time I was able to look around, the tuk-tuk had disappeared in a haze of blue exhaust.

"You hurt?" the owner of the fruit stall said, helping me up.

"I don't think so," I said.

"Very bad man," one of the people who had come to my aid said, picking up the fruit and inspecting it before returning it to the pile.

"What happened?" I said.

"Young man on tuk-tuk," the woman said. "Tried to steal your bag. It is good you hold on tight to it. In day, too. Big risk, I think. No good," she added, pointing to a rather large bruise that was already forming on my arm. "He hurt you."

"Mai pen rai," I said. "I still have my bag, and I'm fine. It doesn't matter." So much for thinking too much, though. All it got you was a sore arm and a frayed strap on your bag. As a traveler I should have been paying more attention in a strange place. I resolved to avoid such introspection as much as possible.

I returned to the guest house rather shaken despite what I'd said, but not so much that I didn't notice that someone had been in my room. There was the maid, of course, as the most logical person, but the bed had been made up before I left. Will's business card was gone, as was the red dust in the drawer. I decided she had simply come back and cleaned some more, but I wasn't entirely sure. I kept thinking of the man in the amulet market who had tried so hard to separate me from the blasphemous ones. I carried them in my large shoulder bag at all times, so if someone had been looking for them, they would have been disappointed. But why would they? Could it have been the sword someone was after? That I'd left in Bangkok, determining rather sensibly that it wouldn't go in my suitcase, and I was unlikely to be allowed to carry it on to the airplane. I decided I was just being silly, that my imagination was expanding in the heat.

Too soon the interlude in Chiang Mai was over, and we all returned to the Chaiwong residence in Ayutthaya. The place was beginning to feel like a prison to me, no matter how splendid the setting. It was not as splendid as before, mind you. This time I was relegated to a room the size of a broom closet. A beautiful broom closet, of course—everything in the place was beautiful—but there was no doubt in my mind that I was now in the servants' wing. The lovely gold room was now occupied by Yutai. He had also moved into the largest office at Ayutthaya Trading, Jennifer told me, one with glass walls so that he could keep an eye on all goings-on. The man was rising through the ranks at Ayutthaya with breathtaking speed. It was too tempting to speculate why that might be.

Still, it got me back on the trail of Will Beauchamp. I had forgotten, in the chaos of the preceding days, my discovery of the portrait with my—it had come to be my—sword in it. I'd had the opportunity to study both the portrait of the two brothers and the sword very carefully, before the portrait disappeared, and there was no doubt in my mind that they were one and the same. I couldn't believe there would be two identical swords.

What, I wondered, had made Will think the sword had been used to hack up Helen Ford's husband? I went back and read the newspaper clipping that had been sent to Natalie very carefully, and there was no mention of it. I had only one clipping of what must have been many, given the nature of the crime in particular, and the propensity of newspapers in general to keep a good story going as long as possible. Still, given the way newspapers summarize an ongoing story every time they add to it, I would have thought the use of a sixteenth-century silver sword as a murder weapon would have been worth a mention at least some of the time.

So, assuming the story about chopping up Mr. Ford was untrue, if Will had happened upon the sword somehow in the course of a buying expedition, what did he do? Did he try to sell it to the Chaiwongs? That's what you'd do, after all, if you were a dealer—unless you were my kind of dealer, which is to say I fall in love with things I purchase and then can hardly bear to part with them.

But assuming he wasn't my kind of dealer, if he recognized the sword as the one in the portrait, then he would offer to sell it. If you were the Chaiwongs, given money was no object, surely you'd buy it for sentimental reasons, or just for the novelty of it.

Or, then again, perhaps Will purchased it from the Chaiwongs. It had been in the family at some point in the last half century or so. But why would they sell in the first place? They didn't need the money. Which brought me back to the possibility that maybe they'd disposed of it because it had been used to hack up a body.

Still, that was just so implausible. It was much more likely that Will had just made up the story on the spur of the moment to impress Tatiana. If Praneet was right, though, he didn't need to do that. Tatiana was the one on the prowl, not him. Was it possible that it was not Will but Tatiana herself, with an eye to a career in film, who had invented this story as a way to help sell her idea?

I decided the only thing to do was to pay her a visit. In fact, I was going to pay all of them—Fitzgerald, Rowland, and Tatiana—a surprise visit to see if their memories had improved since last we'd talked. But first I had to have a chat with the people at Keene Lyon Press, the company I was betting was also known, in Will Beauchamp's world, as Key Lime Pie.

The distinguishing feature of the office, the defining motif, was fish. There were photos of fish, drawings of fish. There were fish with teeth, pretty ones with gorgeous coloring, scary ones that peeked out from behind rocks under the sea. A rather large aquarium built into the wall featured the live version, in contrast with the stuffed ones mounted on the side table. In a corner, a video ran on a loop. It showed, what else? Fish. There were magazines about fish, a fisherman's newsletter, and even a fish cookbook—at least that is what it looked like—on the coffee table. The fish in the aquarium were very soothing to watch, but why, I had to ask myself, so many fish? I was not to wonder for long.

I was greeted within a few minutes by a pleasant young man called Mr. Nimit, who told me he was the senior editor. He ushered me into the back office where he sat at a desk piled high with papers. Two other workers, both women, were working at their desks, one of them with slides on a light table, which she used a magnifying glass to look at from time to time, the other with what looked to be galley proofs. There were a lot of fish photographs on the walls in here, too.

"I see you are admiring our photographs," he said, after the formalities had been taken care of. "We take great pride in them. These are from our books," he said. "Given you are here, you no doubt know all about our books."

"I'm afraid I don't," I said.

"We are the largest publisher of fish books in Bangkok," he said proudly. "It is a very big business now. Our founder, Mr. Lyon," Mr. Nimit said, indicating a framed photo above his desk, "was very smart. He knew this would be a very good selling item for us. Mr. Lyon died a few years ago, and unfortunately did not know how successful his company would become. It is now Thai-owned, of course. By my family," he added just a little smugly.

"What other kind of books do you do?" I said, on the assumption that Will didn't know any more than I did on the subject of fish.

"No other books," he said. "We work all year on fish books. We do a newsletter, we have a web site, all about fish. Now, how can I be of service?"

"I'm trying to get in touch with one of your authors," I said. I was starting to have a bad feeling about this. "William Beauchamp."

Mr. Nimit looked startled, then wary. "We do not have an author by that name."

"But I think you know the name," I said with just a touch of irritation in my voice. I was getting really tired of people not telling me things, despite my therapy session with the monk in Chiang Mai. But in Thailand, showing your irritation is a bad idea that gets you nowhere fast. "I'm sorry," I said. "I do apologize. Mr. Beauchamp is a colleague of mine from Toronto. He has not been seen for several weeks, if not months. His wife is worried about him. I was told you were his publisher."

"Mr. William was here," Mr. Nimit said, somewhat mollified. "He came to introduce himself. He said he was one of our authors. We were all very surprised. I showed him the books we publish. You are also most welcome to look. I believe Mr. William was very upset. We were sorry we could not help him. He said his agent had given him an advance for this book. He showed me a photocopy of the check, but it was from an agent, not from us. Perhaps a colleague was making a joke of some kind, but if so, it was not in good taste, was it? Not very funny."

"No, it was not very funny at all," I agreed. "Now when was this that Mr. William came in?"

The man thought about it for a moment, and then spoke in Thai to the two women, who were pretending to work while they listened to our conversation. One of them replied.

"We believe it was exactly July two," Mr. Nimit said. "It is the birthday of Miss Peroontip," he said, gesturing to the woman who had spoken. "She remembers the day exactly therefore."

"And you didn't see him again?"

"No," he said. "There was no reason. Mr. William said his book was not about fish."

"You've been very helpful," I said.

"Please," he said. "A copy of our newsletter, and a catalog of our books. We also offer videotapes."

"Thank you so much," I said. It had been a discouraging conversation for me, but not nearly as bad as it would have been for Will. Bent Rowland was apparently even more of a sleaze than I thought. He and I would be having a chat shortly, but on the way, there was Tatiana Tucker to be seen.

"It's too late," she said, as I walked through the agency door.

"Too late for what?" I said.

"To return my call," she said.

"Oh," I said. "I am so sorry. I completely forgot!"

"Well," she said. "At least you didn't say you didn't receive my message."

"Thaksin Chaiwong died," I said, trying to explain.

"Who's Thaksin Chaiwong?" she said. "And what has this got to do with returning phone calls?"

"A very wealthy man," I said. "Jennifer and I found him. Dead, I mean. It rather put other things out of my mind."

"Oh," she said. "I guess finding a corpse will do that for you. But it's still too late. I've unfortunately lost the papers you were looking for."

"The m—?" I said. She shook her head almost imperceptibly. I stopped midword. The two other women in the office tried to look as if they weren't listening.

"I'm going home, by the way," she said.

"Home?" I said.

"The States," she said.

"For good, you mean?"

"Yes."

"When?"

"Tomorrow morning. I'm just here to clear out my desk."

"Isn't this rather sudden?"

"I'm like that," she said. "I make decisions, and I act on them." She hadn't looked at me once during this conversation. The other women in the office were assiduously pretending to work.

"Please let me buy you lunch, a drink, a coffee, whatever

you have time for," I said. "As a send-off. And as an apology for not returning your phone call."

"That's not necessary," she said.

"Please," I said. "I feel terrible."

I could see she was thinking about it, and in the end her better nature gained the upper hand. "Okay," she said. "I could use a drink."

"You lost the manuscript!" I exclaimed as soon as we sat down at a table in a nearby bar.

"Shh!" she said, looking about her carefully and speaking in virtually a whisper. "I didn't lose it. I destroyed it. And it wasn't the whole manuscript anyway. It was just the introduction."

"But why?" I said. "What happened to the movie?"

"It didn't pan out," she said, but I could tell she was lying.

"That's too bad," I said, trying to keep my irritation and curiosity out of my voice. "It sounded interesting. I guess that means you don't need the sword anymore. Too bad. I spoke to the soon-to-be owner, and he seemed interested. There'd have to be insurance and everything, but he was willing to at least discuss it." If there was a contest on to tell more lies than anyone else in Thailand, I intended to be part of it.

"That was nice of you," she said. "So few people these days do what they say they will."

I felt like a worm.

"I think you should just forget about what I told you about the sword," she said. "It was pure fabrication."

"Did you invent the story?" I said. "You obviously have a vivid imagination. No wonder you work in film."

"Too vivid," she said.

I said nothing.

"I've been getting phone calls," she said. "Nasty ones. Telling me to go home."

"From whom?" I said.

"Don't know," she said. "But they are really scary. Obviously I've stirred up something with this movie idea. I wish I hadn't. Probably they're watching me right now. They said they were. You shouldn't even be here with me."

"There's nobody in here but us," I said, looking around. "It's too early for anybody else."

"They seem to know what I'm doing. They said if I went back to the States right away, nothing would happen to me. That's what I'm doing. If I were you, I'd go back home, too."

"And you're convinced these calls have something to do with the film about Helen Ford?" I said.

"Of course they do," she said. "I work for a travel agency, for God's sake. Do you think people call in death threats because the airline I booked them on ran out of the chicken entrée before they got to them? What else would it be?" Her hands were shaking badly as she spoke.

"These were death threats? Really?"

"Yes," she said. "They started out as 'Go home, you don't belong here,' to 'If you stay around, you could get hurt,' then on to 'If you don't leave you'll die.' "

"These calls," I said. "Man? Woman? Thai? English?"

"Man," she said. "They're in English, or I wouldn't understand them, I don't think. My Thai isn't that great, yet."

"But do you think it's a Thai man calling you?"

"Maybe," she said. "Not sure. I'll bet they follow me right to the airport and see I get on the plane."

"It's a big airport," I said. "And that's hard to do these days."

"You think this is a joke!" she said.

"No, I don't, but I like to think these are idle threats. Have you thought about calling the police?"

"No," she said. "I'm going home. I don't know whatever made me think I belonged here."

"I'm sorry," I said. I meant it. "Look, could you at least tell me what it said, the manuscript, I mean?"

"That's the ridiculous thing about this," she said. "There was nothing in it that you couldn't read in the *Bangkok Herald* archives. Helen Ford killed her husband, or had him killed, depending on which version you prefer, then his body was chopped up and disposed of. The torso was buried near the Chao Phyra, the head and limbs were burned. Her child was never found, but there was an assumption he, too, was killed. Helen was charged, convicted, sentenced to die, appealed, won the appeal, and then disappeared."

"Nothing about corruption, scandal?"

"No," she said. "Scandal, of course. The whole story is scandalous, but other than that, there were only hints of corruption in high places. Nothing specific. It ends with something about this being the story they didn't want you to know. All rather melodramatic, but not very exciting when it came right down to it."

"Who is they?"

"No idea."

"When you spoke to Will, did you get the impression he'd finished writing the book?"

"Yes," she said. "Or just about, anyway. He said he might have more work to do on it, that the more he looked into it, the more he learned, and that in a way, it would never really be finished. But yes, I got the impression that at least the first draft was done."

"So why do you think that someone would be threatening you over something everyone could read in the archives?"

"Good question. I don't plan to hang around to find out."

"Did you invent the story about the sword and Helen Ford?" I asked her again.

"No," she said. "I didn't. Will told me."

Robert Fitzgerald was next on my list. The first thing that struck me as I cut through the hole in the hedge was how untidy the grounds around the tree had become. On the previous visits, the grass and gardens had been immaculate. Now there was litter everywhere. A breeze caught a piece of paper, and it swirled across the yard. The tree house itself looked a little more welcoming than it had the first time: the stairs were down. That might have meant he was expecting someone, but he certainly hadn't felt the need to make me feel welcome the first time I came. Still, when I'd come back to purchase the carvings for David Ferguson's spirit house, he'd left them down for me. Nothing like being a paying customer to improve relations with someone, even someone as crusty as Fitzgerald. The stairs also might mean he already had a visitor, which, if so, was going to put a crimp in my line of questioning. Still, I decided to haul myself up, to use his expression.

I called out his name a couple of times as I ascended, but again there was no reply. That left a third option, which was that he had gone out and left the stairs down for his return. That certainly seemed to be the case. The sala was empty, but I could see he was working on the chess set, which warmed my heart. I stopped for a moment or two to admire them. He'd done one complete set of pieces in a black wood. The little pieces were really lovely, and he'd used tiny Thai houses for the castles. The king and queen were in traditional Thai dress, seated on elephants. Rob was going to be thrilled.

It was then I heard the faintest of sounds. It was difficult to identify, a wounded animal perhaps, a moan. It could have been the wind in the leaves of the trees, or the house merely creaking. Still, I felt I couldn't ignore it. I tiptoed along the passageway to the other side of the house. There was no one in the kitchen, but the hall was littered with books and papers. I heard the moan again.

Cautiously I peered into the studio/bedroom. Fitzgerald sat on the floor, propped up against the side of the bed, legs straight out in front of him like a large rag doll. There was blood pouring from a wound on his head. His father's diaries were everywhere, scattered about the room.

"Are you all right?" I exclaimed, kneeling beside him. It was a stupid question.

"You're late," he barked.

"What happened?" I said. "And how could I be late if you didn't know I was coming?"

"Yes, I did," he said. "Someone told me. That's why I put the stairs down."

"Who?"

He looked baffled for a moment. "I don't seem to recall," he said, after a pause. "They didn't get it, though."

"What?"

"Whatever it was they wanted." He took a handkerchief out of his shirt pocket and wiped blood from his face. "I don't suppose you could go to the kitchen and get me some of that brownish liquid we fancy? Straight up. You can skip the ice. I feel rather strange."

"I'm going to get help," I said. "Don't move."

He grasped my hand as I tried to stand up. "I think we need to talk to my mother," he said. "The spirit house." Then he passed out.

It was much later in the day when I went to see Bent Rowland. I was dreading seeing the odious man again, but there was nothing more I could do for Fitzgerald. The doctors at the hospital told me he had a severe concussion and was in serious condition. The police had been called. They said they'd try to find his mother. Robbery was their official position.

The stairs up to Rowland's office were dark and smelly. Rowland was sitting in his chair with his back to the door, looking out the small window on to the alleyway just as he had done when he'd contemplated the masterpiece I was writing. The smell in the room was even worse than the last time, the pungent reek of perspiration rather sickening. Rowland had been suffering from the heat and something more, some stronger emotion like fear. There was some other smell there, too, which I thought I might identify if I had time to think about it. However, I had questions for Bent Rowland. I'd ask them as fast as I could and get out of there.

"Mr. Rowland," I said. "I've come to talk to you about my manuscript. This time I'd prefer truth to fantasy."

Rowland didn't move. I thought perhaps he'd fallen asleep, and then, given his lack of response that, overweight as he was, he'd had a heart attack in the heat. I suppose in a way he had. The knife through his heart would have done that, no doubt.

Chapter 9

I see now, looking back, the signs that should have warned me that danger lurked in the palace. Soon after Yot Fa was anointed king and his mother queen regent, as I have already recounted, an earthquake rocked the city. If that in itself was not sign enough, later a truly terrible event occurred. King Yot Fa was entertained by spectacle of various kinds, and shortly after he became king, declared that the chief royal elephant would engage in a duel with another. Many, including me, accompanied the king in the procession to the elephant kraal for the fight.

A gasp went up from the crowd when the second elephant's tusk was broken in three pieces. Even more horrifying, later that night, the royal elephant mourned, making the sound of human crying, and one of the city gates groaned in sympathy. It was a bad omen indeed and perhaps signaled the events that were to follow. But I was distracted and perhaps did not fully understand the significance of the events around me.

It was about this time that a very pretty young woman of the court, a servant to Lady Si Sudachan, caught my attention. I should confess that I was by then well past the age that I should have taken a wife or two, but perhaps because of my close attachment to my mother or the precariousness of my position, I had not done so.

Now I was smitten. I found the young woman's dark eyes mesmerizing. Everything about her, even the rustle of her garments as she walked made me feverish. To my surprise, she made it clear that she, too, was interested in me. I was flattered beyond all reason. She was the most desirable creature, and I was almost delirious with her attentions.

I will not reveal to you the delights we shared, except to say that for a period of many weeks I was distracted by her presence. I saw less and less of the young king, and the two of us became rather distant. I had hoped he would share my joy in the relationship, but he did not and in fact was quite petulant about it, perhaps because his mother was so obviously besotted by the object of her affections at the same time I was with mine.

If anyone lived the life I had imagined for Will Beauchamp when I'd first heard about his disappearance—it seemed so long ago—it was Bent Rowland. His home was a small but pretty little house with a pleasant neglected garden in a reasonably decent neighborhood, according to David Ferguson, who took me there.

The door was opened by a girl I at first thought must be Rowland's daughter, given she couldn't have been a day over fifteen, but I soon realized was his lover. And not just that, but the mother of the sweetest little baby tucked into a bassinette in one corner of the kitchen. The girl, whose name, apparently, was Parichat, wore the shortest of shorts and a tight cotton T-shirt, her long, skinny legs thrust into very high-heeled sandals. She looked terribly young and vulnerable. There are those who have said with some cynicism that the pudgy foreigner and the small-boned Thai woman with delicate features are the quintessential couple of Thailand, but the thought of her and Bent Rowland together made me nauseous.

As she and David spoke, I looked around. The kitchen, while small, had every conceivable gadget and appliance, from a refrigerator with icemaker, to a microwave, to a very trendy looking blender. Everything looked absolutely brand-new. The living room furnishings, while chosen with questionable taste, were also spanking new. A pile of boxes was stacked in one corner of the room.

"Is she moving already?" I asked David, in a lull in the conversation, as she went to tend to the infant who had begun to wail.

He asked her the question. "No, just moved in a couple of months ago. With the birth of the baby, she hasn't had time to unpack everything. The usual story," he added in a quieter tone. "She's from a village up north. Came to the big city to make her fortune. Ended up in prostitution. Met Rowland in a bar. He bought her from her pimp. Lovely story, isn't it? This is the dark side of Bangkok. Her parents think she's working in a store and is engaged to a nice Thai boy. There are way too many stories like hers, unfortunately. She thinks she's got it made here, though, and it's not a bad spot. Apparently they were living in a tiny little apartment until recently. Rowland must have been a successful literary agent, even if I'd never heard of him."

"Not judging from his office," I said. "Nor his attitude. He oozed failure from every pore."

"According to police, he's been depositing rather large

sums of money every week since the spring sometime, five thousand dollars, always in cash," David said. "The deposits add up to about eighty thousand. The last one was a week before he died. He was getting money somewhere. I suppose it's possible he got a big advance for Will's book and only gave him two thousand dollars of it, and hasn't been paying him his royalties either, although one could argue that's because he couldn't find him."

"Have you read any good books about Helen Ford lately?" I said.

"What? Oh, I see what you mean. No book, no royalties."

"Exactly. Looks to me as if he was being paid for something else. His silence, for example."

"Blackmail? You didn't take to this guy, did you?"

"No, I didn't. I thought right from the start he was a sleaze and a con artist. Nothing I've seen here today has changed my mind. The timing's right. Will finished his book on Helen Ford in the spring and gave it to Rowland, who presumably read the whole manuscript. Then he told Will he'd find a publisher, which he hadn't, at least not the one he told Will about. And suddenly a guy who has been eking out his existence as a literary agent is depositing rather a lot of cash. What if somebody was paying Rowland to keep Will's book from getting published? Then when Will disappeared, died, whatever, Rowland was suddenly dispensable, too."

"Are you angling around to saying there's an eighty-year-old axe murderer out there somewhere still chopping up her victims?"

"I know it sounds ridiculous. I don't suppose you could just do a little checking of Embassy records, though, to see if there's anything on what happened to Ford? She was an American."

"I did already. I confess you got me curious. There's nothing that I could find. Sorry."

"Too bad. What's going to happen to this girl?" I said. The girl in question returned to the room, still holding the child, and started speaking quickly and in a heated manner to David, who kept shaking his head.

When she hesitated for a moment, I said, "Ask her, will you, when you get a chance, if she knows Will?"

He did, and said, "She says she met Will. He once visited them at their former home. She said her husband was representing Will, and had sold his book for a lot of money last spring. Maybe I'm right about Rowland keeping the money. Anyway, let's get out of here. There's only so much of this kind of situation I can stand."

"You didn't answer my question about what will happen to her," I said as we drove away.

"I went to discuss with her the fact that Rowland's sister in Atlanta wants us to help with the formalities of having his body shipped back to the States. That's what started that tirade. Parichat wants to go to the States. She says she married an American, her kid is American—the kid's name is Bent Rowland Junior, poor little tyke—and she thinks she's entitled to citizenship."

"And is she?"

"I doubt she's really married to him," he said. "Let's just say that complicates matters. And he is dead now, after all. I'll see what I can do about the kid. I sure hope she has some of that cash still stashed somewhere."

"Why?"

"Because he left all his money, everything he has, to his sister," David said.

"Oh no!" I said.

"Exactly. She'll be back on the street in no time. Some days I really hate my job," he added. "So where do you want to go now?"

"I need to go and pick up something," I said. "Robert Fitzgerald suggested I get it." That was more or less true, although, granted, the man had barely been conscious when he'd said it.

"You mean you want to go now?" he said.

"Yes," I replied. "Before others get there."

"What others?"

"I wish I knew. It's at his house, whatever it is."

"Neat place," he said as he looked around the tree house. "I've never seen anything like it. Look at these chess pieces, will you? They're fabulous. Now, what are we looking for here?"

"I don't know. Fitzgerald told me they, whoever they are, and I assumed it was the people who bashed him and made such a mess of this place, didn't get what they wanted. He also said we had to go and see his mother. Maybe you could help me find her. Now, what does this look like to you?" I said, gesturing about the place.

"Other than a mess, you mean? People were looking for something, obviously. I have no idea what, but, come to think about it, these shelves are interesting. One of them has been emptied, the others not even touched. Do we know what was on this one shelf?

"Diaries," I said.

"Hmm," he said. "In that case, they were looking for diaries for the years between about 1945 and 1960. The others aren't touched. If that is the case, they didn't find what they wanted, because they went on to go through all the drawers, check under the bed, searching through the kitchen cupboards, that sort of thing, or maybe it was something else they wanted. This is right off the top of my head, but that's what it looks like to me."

"Me, too, and some of those dates are about right," I said.

"For what?"

"The murder Will Beauchamp was writing about."

"The fifty-year-old crime again: Helen Ford," he said. "So you really don't think Rowland got the money from the publisher? That's how it works, doesn't it? The publisher pays the agent who takes his commission and passes the rest of the money along to the author?"

"I think so," I said.

"There are other options here, you know. Didn't you say Bent gave Will a couple of thousand dollars as an advance? Maybe Rowland did manage to get Will a small advance, took his cut, and passed the rest along, and the money he's been depositing is from some other source. I suppose the trouble with that is, why lie about the publisher if there really is one? So, maybe you're right and he's dishonest, got a lot of money from some other publisher, and didn't pay Will. Or he just gave Will a couple of thousand of his own money to give the impression that he had sold the book. Maybe the guy was just an abject loser who was trying to play in the big leagues, or at least give the impression he was."

"You're right. It could be any of the above. But it is still possible somebody paid him not to find a publisher, and he was just playing for time with Will."

"Why wouldn't he just tell Will he couldn't find a publisher for it?"

"Because Will would get himself another agent. End of payments for Rowland."

"Will was bound to find out—did find out, as a matter of fact. This ploy was only a temporary solution."

"My point exactly."

"You're saying that Will is dead, and not just dead, but murdered."

"I'm coming to believe this is the only possible conclusion."

"Realistically, who would kill over a book?

"If I had the book, I might know the answer to that question. But it wasn't in Will's apartment. I looked. I doubt it will be in Rowland's office, either. Now let's keep looking here for whatever I'm supposed to find. Fitzgerald said 'spirit house.' There was one he was working on in the living room, and another, the one protecting the house, is outside."

"It didn't do a very good job, did it?" David said. "Protecting the place, or him, I mean. I'll go check the spirit houses. This one looks perfectly normal," he said.

"I'll go down and check the one outside. I'm hoping not to disturb whoever it is lives in these things."

"I'm sure they'll forgive us," I said.

He returned in a minute or two. "Nothing again, I'm afraid."

"There has to be something," I said. I picked up the unfinished spirit house, the one I'd promised to buy for my store, and turned it over carefully. I could see where one piece of its floor was not perfectly fitted together, not up to the standard of the rest of Fitzgerald's work. I gave it a careful tug, then a harder one, and the floor came away to reveal a hollow in which was stuffed two slim leather diaries. "Got it," I said.

"Good for you," he said. "Let's see? Diaries for 1948 and '49. We should turn them over to the police," he said. "They might be relevant."

"First, we read them," I said, taking them out of his hands and slapping them into my bag. "Let's get out of here." What I wanted to do, indeed what I would have done if I'd been there by myself, was to sit down and read through them on the spot. I knew, though, that with David there that was impossible.

Difficult as it might be to think that a crime that had taken place fifty years earlier had anything in particular to do with the present time, the inescapable conclusion now seemed to be that Will Beauchamp's disappearance was definitely connected with the book he was writing on Helen Ford. Anybody who knew anything about the book he was supposed to have written had had something very bad happen to them, from threats to injury to murder. The only course of action it now seemed logical to pursue was to find out more about Helen Ford.

But for a while, I didn't, distracted as I was by a visit from Chat. "What are you doing in this room?" Chat said that evening when I opened the door to his knock.

"This is the room I was assigned," I said. "It's very cozy."

"But you are supposed to be in the gold room," Chat said.

"I believe Yutai is now in the gold room," I said.

"Yutai!" he exclaimed. "On whose authority?"

"I expect it's your mother's."

"I will see to this," he said. "But I have a favor to ask of you, Aunt Lara. I am wondering if you can help me with a business matter. I am not, as Jen has probably told you, very inclined to business. I do not have a head for it. I have no wish to manage my father's company, but I realize in the short term it is necessary for me to do so. You know about business," he said. "And I am hoping you will give me some advice."

"Chat, I will help you any way I can, but I own a little antique store. I know nothing about big business like Ayutthaya."

"But you can read financial statements, can't you?"

"Well, yes," I said. "But . . ."

"You know so much more than I do," he said. "I studied the arts, political science. I did not take commerce or finance."

"I didn't either," I said.

"Please," he said.

"Okay," I replied. "Is there something you want me to read?"

"I would like you to come to the offices on the main floor," he said.

"Now?"

"No. Tonight. Late. When everyone has gone home. Perhaps midnight?"

Midnight? "Okay," I said. "I'll meet you at the glass doors at midnight."

Chat was waiting for me when I arrived, having just finished moving back into the gold room. I was once again living in luxury, while Yutai, now my bitter enemy, I was sure, was elsewhere.

I smiled as pleasantly as possible at the chauffeur who was doubling as a security guard in the lobby, and went in. Chat might be trying to do this secretly, but I didn't think much went unreported in that place.

We sat down at a computer, Chat pulled up some financial charts, and asked me to have a look through.

"The spreadsheets are in English," I said. "But you may have to translate some of the notes."

"I will," he said.

"So what do you think?" he said, after awhile.

"I think Ayutthaya acquired a new partner last spring sometime."

"Busakorn Shipping," Chat said. "Blue Lotus, in English."

"Khun Wichai's company?"

"Yes," Chat said. "It is Khun Wichai's company. He named it after his daughter. His wife is dead. His daughter is everything he has."

"Then you have a new partner in the form of Khun Wichai."

"I'm not sure this is something I would want. Khun Wichai is . . . I'm not sure about him. I've always had a sense he was in businesses one is better off not to ask about. I told my father that, and we had a fight. He said I'm not very practical, not very skilled in the ways of the world. I told him he was exploiting people. I am very sorry about that now, as you can imagine, but I remain convinced Khun Wichai is not the kind of man we want to be in business with."

"It looks to me as if this is now academic," I said. "I think he's a partner, or at least a minority shareholder, already. What else have you got there?"

"Figures for my mother's business," he said.

"She's doing awfully well, isn't she?" I said. "Good for her. She's in partnership with Busakorn again."

"Now take a look at these," he said.

"These are financials for . . ." I didn't know what to say.

"Tell me," he said.

"They are financials for the same company, but they're different. In this second set . . . where did you find these?"

"Dusit found them. He was just fooling around. My little brother is rather good with computers. Now tell me."

"It just looks as if there are two sets of books for your mother's business," I said.

"That's what I thought," he said. "Would there be a good reason for that?"

"I'm not sure," I said, but I was thinking, *Not likely.* I couldn't imagine what a reason might be, at least not one either Chat or I wanted to hear. "And by the way, a couple of others have or have had a small share in the company as well."

"I noticed. William Beauchamp is one," he said.

"Could I help you, Mr. Chat?" a voice said.

"And here is the other," he murmured. "I was just showing Ms. Lara our computers," Chat said aloud. I gave him a questioning look, and he nodded. Yutai, apparently, was the shareholder in question.

"I'm very impressed," I said. "By your computers, I mean."

Yutai looked at his watch. "It is very late," he said.

"We didn't want to bother people when they were hard at work," I said.

Chat said something to Yutai in Thai, and after a very slight hesitation, the man turned and left. "We'd better go," I said. "Let's just print a copy of these financial statements, and I'll have a closer look at the numbers," I said.

"Thank you. I believe I may have to go to Chiang Mai

and pay a visit to my proposed father-in-law."

"I know I shouldn't ask," I said. "But what are you planning to do about that? I'd prefer you not string Jennifer along if you have other plans."

"I would not do that, Aunt Lara," he said, looking wounded.

"I'm sorry," I said. "I shouldn't have said that. It's just that . . ."

"You love her," he said. "I do, too."

The next morning I looked at the two diaries, and then at the pile of financial statements, trying to decide where to start. "Diaries or numbers," I muttered to myself. My hand hovered over first one, then the other. In the end, Will Beauchamp won. Why did I, after all, have to be the one to tell Chat his mother was cooking the books, no doubt with the help of her lover, the guy Chat thought was a secretary? It wasn't going to help his relationship with Jennifer if I was the one to bring some unsavory facts to his attention. Praise be to whatever guardian spirit was looking out for me that I had not agreed to do business with that woman, only to make enquiries.

If my views on Wongvipa and company were crystallizing, my image of Will was not. He remained an enigma to me, a man who had deserted his wife and child, but had not succumbed, like Bent Rowland, to the sensual enticements of Bangkok. He'd started a business much like the one he had at home, lived what seemed to be a relatively quiet life in a nice but not luxurious apartment, was a pleasant enough neighbor, held a party every now and then and went to bars on occasion, but didn't seem to have done anything too awful. Perhaps, as Praneet had suggested, he hadn't been able to handle the pressure of a disabled child anymore and just flipped out temporarily. Maybe all it would have taken was one phone call from his wife to have him fly back home, but it never came. It was sad to think of Natalie and Will as two lonely people who loved each other, thousands of miles apart and both unable to make the smallest of gestures toward the other.

Presumably too, if Will had asked the mysterious Mr. Prasit to send that envelope to Natalie when he hadn't heard from him in awhile, worthless though the contents might be, he must have had an intimation of his own mortality. The note he'd sent to Natalie personally could be said to have an impending sense of doom. Perhaps Will thought writing about Helen Ford was a dangerous thing to do. Maybe it was.

I turned back to the diaries. They were written in a small, tight script. I figured it would take days to work my way through them, even if I worked steadily, but I started into them anyway, and soon I was hooked.

They were a fascinating account of life in Bangkok after the war, but they were also personal, Fitzgerald writing about his painting, the people he met, the meals he had eaten. It was during this period that he had begun to build the tree house studio and to work there. Two of the first people to sit for their portraits were Mr. Thaksin and Mr. Virat, obviously the two Chaiwong brothers of the portrait in the living room. According to this account, the two men had come to see Fitzgerald Senior, but he had gone to Thaksin's home to do the portrait of Thaksin's first wife, Somchai, and little Sompom. While these four names were quite clear, some of the people referred to were only initials. I had no way to be certain why that would be. Perhaps it was for reasons of discretion, if not secrecy, or it was simply that these were people he knew very well and therefore did not need to write out their names.

Early in the diaries there were several references to Helen. I didn't know whether this was Helen Ford, of course, but there were at least a dozen references to her sitting for her portrait and of other more domestic activities: "*Helen and I went shopping today to find her a frock. She told me I was the only person in the world who was completely honest with her, and would not let her buy something which made her look like a fat pig. Not that she could ever look that way.*" Or another: "*The rains were terrible today making it almost impossible to go out at all. Helen and I sat and read, but soon Helen was bored, and started inventing word games for us to play. I really just wanted to paint, but I had left all my brushes at the studio, careless man that I am, although all were carefully wrapped against the rain. I decided not to venture forth, as it would be folly to do so. Helen, much braver than I, went visiting. She is not happy anymore, just being with me. I ask her where she goes, but she won't tell me. Whom does she see? What do they do? I wish to know, but part of me dreads the answer.*"

At some point in the narrative *Helen* disappeared, to be replaced with references to merely *H.* "*H has confided in me. I am horrified by what she has told me, but somehow not surprised. I had thought the trip to Singapore five years ago was the end of it. What will become of her? . . .*

"*H was here today with W,*" one entry said. "*She looked so beautiful, radiant really, that my fears for her vanished, if only for an hour or two. I am happy that she has confided in me, but I worry so about what might come of this.*" Or later: "*This cannot end well for H or the other two, but it is H I care about. How I wish I could convince her to take another path.*

"*H's marriage is a mistake. What if he finds out about W? I have beseeched her time and time again to go back home and forget all of this. I have told her how much I love her, how I would do anything for her, that she must listen to what I say. She is adamant!"*

Toward the end of that diary, there was this terse statement: *"What I most feared for H has happened. I am too much of a coward to help her. I can only help with W and B. I cannot write any more. God help us all."* The entry was in September of 1949. There were no further entries that year, only blank pages. The newspaper clipping said Helen Ford's husband's dismembered body was found in October of that year. If what his son had told me was true, Robert Fitzgerald Senior didn't write another word in his diaries until 1960.

This is just too hard, I thought, suddenly. *I don't want to try to figure this out anymore. This was supposed to be a bit of a holiday. I can say in all honesty to Natalie Beauchamp that I tried to find her husband, and I just didn't succeed. End of story.*

I could, though, I thought, call David Ferguson and ask him more about Khun Wichai. There! I'd managed to assuage my guilt at not doing Chat's financial statements for him. I was doing something for him, anyway. As I reached for the telephone, I noticed the sword was not in the place I thought I'd left it. *How did it get over here, I wonder?* I said to myself. *I'm sure I left it over by the cupboard.* I looked it over carefully but could see absolutely nothing wrong with it. *The lady who cleans,* I thought. There was no harm done. Still, I did continue to have the feeling that someone was going through my belongings.

"Come to think of it," I said right out loud. "Who told Robert Fitzgerald I was coming to visit?"

Robert Fitzgerald had said I was late. Surely that meant he'd been expecting me. He had a bad concussion, and I suppose one is not expected to be coherent when you've been hit on the head. But still, it was something else to think about later. I picked up the phone and dialed.

"I'm glad you called," David said. "I've been meaning to ask you if you'd like to go out to dinner tomorrow night after the performance."

"Sure," I said. "But tell me a little about what we're going to see. I know Sompom is an expert in it, and the performance tomorrow is dedicated to the memory of Thaksin, who was a patron of the theater. I also know Chat would really like us to go, but I'm not entirely sure what to expect."

"A performance of Khon. It's a very ancient form of masked dance and theater, brought to Thailand from the Khmer empire in Cambodia, and it tells the story of the Ramayama, or in Thailand, the Ramakien. The Thai version was probably developed in the Royal Palace of Ayutthaya several hundred years ago. It was lost when Ayutthaya fell to the Burmese, but it has been revived since. The National Theater puts on performances of it. To do the whole thing would take weeks of continuous performance, so we'll just see an episode or two. The costumes are really quite wonderful. I think you'll enjoy it."

"I'm sure I will. Now, what can you tell me about Khun Wichai?"

"Where will I begin?" David said. "He gets mixed reviews. He's smart, can be very charming, obviously good at business—he's rich. He's a poor boy from the boonies, in this case Chiang Mai, who has made good. For a guy who started out with a couple of rice barges, he's built quite a transportation empire. He ships all over the world. Companies line up to do business with him. He is rich, but he isn't part of the upper crust, if you understand me. He probably lacks a little finesse, that's all."

"He wants his daughter to marry Chat," I said.

"That would take care of the social standing, wouldn't it? That's unlikely I think. Isn't Chat sweet on Jennifer still, or again, whichever it is? They'd just had a fight when I met her."

"They're back together, and yes, he is sweet on her. But you said Khun Wichai gets mixed reviews. Is just his social standing on the downside? Chat seemed a little nervous about him, or at least about doing business with him."

"There are rumors," he said. "Nothing substantiated. In a word, drugs."

"He uses them, or he ships them?"

"Maybe both. I repeat there is absolutely no proof. When any of his ships are searched, they're clean as a whistle. The authorities do search boats at sea and find them loaded with drugs—there was one a couple of years ago, boarded in the Andaman Sea between Thailand and Myanmar, Burma, just loaded with the stuff. Heroin and crystal meth. You might know that as ice. Millions of tablets and bags of the other stuff. But are these boats ever linked in any way to Wichai? Absolutely not. He sits up there in Chiang Mai looking much like a warlord, with his cadre of followers who are intensely loyal. But there's nothing anyone can prove against him."

"Anything else?"

"There's a sense that his opposition tends to disappear."

"Disappear?"

"As in disappear like our friend Will Beauchamp. They're never heard from again."

Chapter 10

Indeed the young king had every reason to be out of sorts, and not just with me. Lady Si Sudachan, now the mother of a daughter by Khun Worawongsa, went to her chief ministers and suggested that, given Yot Fa had still not reached the age of the cutting of the topknot, that is thirteen years, and because he was, according to his mother, although I would not agree, still uninterested in affairs of state, the enemies of Ayutthaya might try to turn this state of affairs to their advantage. The solution, she said, was that the ministers should invite Khun Worawongsa to administer the kingdom until Yot Fa was of age.

The chief ministers, some, no doubt thoroughly intimidated, others under the lady's spell, agreed, and to the sound of trumpets, Khun Worawongsa was escorted into the inner palace on the royal palanquin and proclaimed king with great ceremony.

From this moment on, the affairs of the kingdom altered drastically. Worawongsa's brother was appointed uparat, *or heir ap-*

parent and viceroy, and the governors of all our northern provinces were recalled to Ayutthaya and then dismissed, men loyal to the queen regent and Khun Worawongsa appointed in their places. But that was not the end of it.

Next, the queen regent and the usurper, Khun Worawongsa, determined that Yot Fa should spend some time in a monastery, something that many young men did, and it was arranged that he go to the Khòk Phraya Monastery.

It is customary, before a young man enters the monastery, for a great celebration to be held, and on the evening before he was to go, Yot Fa commanded a performance of a masked dance. All the court was invited to the event, including me.

It was a most spectacular occasion. The middle court was lit with hundreds of torches as we arrived, and great delicacies were served before the performance. The royal party ate as usual from bowls of delicate celadon porcelain, because, as it is well known, celadon will crack if it is touched by poison.

Soon the dance began. It was a most edifying production, telling the story of how Phra Ram and his brother Phra Lak, supported by an army of monkeys led by Hanuman, fought Thosokanth and his demon army.

All the roles in the drama are performed by men, even the female roles, such strenuous activity being, of course, too much for women. The costumes of the dancers, brocade encrusted with stones, glittered in the torchlight. The masks of the demons were truly terrifying, and the battles between good and evil most ably performed.

What made the evening most wonderful for me, though, was the presence of my beloved beside me. We had found a place toward the back of the crowd where we could see everything but not be overlooked by anyone. Her hand rested lightly on mine when we were certain no one was watching us.

At the point in the drama where the evil Tosokanth appears, I noticed a court official approach Khun Worawongsa. That in itself would not necessarily be unusual, but there was something about the way they both looked about them, as if to ensure no one was looking, that intrigued me. As I strained to see, Worawongsa took something from under his garment, a vial, I think, and handed it to the man, who then slipped into the crowd and away.

I was puzzled, but turned back to the performance. As I did so, I saw the queen regent watching me. I was terrified by her glance. I knew I had seen something I was not supposed to, even if I didn't understand it. But then I saw my sweet love's smile, and in a moment I forgot.

"There seems to be a little tension in the air," I said to Jennifer, as we stood in the lobby of the National Theater, waiting for the doors to open for the performance. "Between Chat and Yutai, I mean." Around us the rest of the Chaiwong family was holding court. A number of dignitaries had come to pay their respects, and there was much *wei*-ing on everybody's part. Chat was doing his best to help his mother with the hosting, even though it was clear he wasn't in his element. He was a shy man, like his half brother more at home in the academic world, but he took his family responsibilities seriously. From time to time he'd look to see where Jennifer was, and a smile would light up his face when he found her in the crowd.

"I'm afraid so," Jennifer said. "Between Chat and his mother, too. Chat went and had a long conversation with her about the business. He wasn't too happy about her bringing Khun Wichai into it without telling anybody, and I gather, given what you've learned from David, he's right. She has responded by telling Chat that she understands that he doesn't really want to be involved, and she has therefore appointed Yutai as chief operating officer. To top it off, Yutai's brother, Eakrit, has been brought in as chief financial officer. Chat is to remain as president, but really, the day-to-day will now be taken care of by Yutai and his brother. Poor Chat." She sighed. "He really doesn't want to run the business, but I think he is completely disconcerted by this latest move of his mother's. And Yutai! He is just reveling in it. He even bosses Chat around. Personally, I think we should just leave them to it and get on with our trip, and then live in the States or Canada. If we get married—"

"Has he asked you?"

"He has. I said yes, too. Don't tell Dad if you're talking to him, will you. Chat wants to formally ask for my hand in marriage, can you believe it? He's bought me the most astonishingly beautiful ring. I can't wear it right now, of course, not until it's official, but I'll show you later. Anyway, when we get married, Chat can certainly stay in Canada."

"I'm really happy for you," I said. "If you're sure this is what you want."

"I'm sure," she said. "I really love him, Aunt Lara. This trip together was to see if we were meant to be together, and given all that's happened, I think we must be. I know it will work for any number of reasons, not the least of which is that he has become my best friend."

"One more question," I said. I felt a lump in my throat. "Has he told his family?"

"He's going to tell them tonight. Wish both of us luck. Now here we go. I think they're opening the doors."

I turned to look for the others. As I did so, I had a blinding flash of insight that left me stunned. Standing over to one side were Wongvipa and with her, Fatty. As I watched them, Yutai came over to speak to Wongvipa, and for a moment the three of them stood together in front of a portrait of Thaksin that had been placed on the wall of the lobby for the occasion. I suddenly knew that I was looking at a family. But it was not Thaksin's. It was Yutai's. Little Fatty had the same cheekbones and slightly flattened nose as Yutai, and bore no resemblance that I could see to the man in the portrait behind them. I would stake my life on it: Fatty was Yutai's daughter.

As I tried to digest this information, I saw Yutai move away and speak to the chauffeur cum security guard, the same one who had called him when Chat and I had gone looking for financial statements, and to two other men, one of whom looked familiar, although I couldn't see him very well, and couldn't place him. After first looking about him carefully, Yutai took something from the man who looked familiar and handed it to the chauffeur, who nodded, then quickly slipped into the crowd and out the door. Yutai looked back at Chat, and the most awful smile appeared on his face. It was only there for a split second, but I felt the mask had slipped for a moment, and the man's true feelings were revealed. It made me feel slightly ill, and I turned away. When I turned back, Yutai was gone, but Wongvipa was looking straight at me. I didn't like the way she looked at me, either. Something was wrong. Perhaps Chat was going to be drummed out of the company completely. I smiled and waved at Wongvipa as if I hadn't seen a thing. She didn't smile back.

The crowd started moving forward toward the doors into the theater, and I found myself caught in something of a crush. As I stood there, trapped, I heard a hoarse voice behind me and very close to my ear. "Go home," the voice said. "You don't belong here." I tried to turn but couldn't, and by the time I did, no one I knew was that close to me.

A minute or two later David Ferguson caught up to me in the aisle. "Do you know that fantastic-looking woman over there?" he said. "The one in the green dress?"

"That's Praneet," I said. "Praneet Chaiwong. She is fantastic looking, and she's also a doctor."

"I don't suppose you'd introduce me," he said. "Maybe we could invite her to dinner."

"Sure," I said.

"You're a pal," he said.

I found myself seated next to Khun Wichai. His daughter, Busakorn, was, as usual, supposed to be with Chat, but Chat was changing seats to sit with Jennifer.

"I see you and I are rivals of a sort," Wichai said, as we watched the musical chairs. He looked amused and not at all the rather intimidating person David had described to me. Two large men, however, were sitting in the row behind us, one to either side. I assumed they were Wichai's bodyguards, two of the cadre of loyal followers David had mentioned.

"I suppose we are," I agreed with a smile. "I have a feeling that no matter what, though, we will have nothing whatsoever to say regarding the final decision."

"Alas," he said. "Times have changed since I was young. My wife was picked out for me when I was a mere boy. Still, we got along well enough. Your Jennifer is so, well, Western."

"Please don't say she'll never fit in here," I said. My tone was light, but I was starting to wonder whether the hoarse voice had belonged to Mr. Wichai.

"I wouldn't dream of it," he said. "I have done rather well, speaking personally, from globalization. May it flourish. And now I think the performance is about to begin."

He's not such a bad sort, I thought, as the lights went down. *For a man whose rivals simply disappear.* I looked around for Yutai. I couldn't see him, but I could see the other man I recognized. *Who* **is** *that?* I wondered. *I know him from somewhere.*

The Khon performance was an interesting one. Masked dancers told a story from the Ramakien, Thailand's rather more secular version of the Hindu Ramayama. There was live music played on the traditional Thai instruments: *klong tadt* and *klong kak* drums, the sacred *tapone*, the two-faced drum that Thai dancers pay homage to before the performance so they will dance well, and *ranad-ek* and *ranad-thum*, both xylophone type instruments, and assorted cymbals and gongs. The dancing was highly stylized, the costumes and masks spectacular, and I really wished I was able to enjoy it more.

The Khon depicted the battle between good and evil, and I had a feeling, somehow, that it was being played out in real life, right in front of my eyes. It was as if everything I had seen in the theater lobby had been almost as choreographed as the performance I was now watching. The masks of the demons on the stage were the smiles of the people I had met. The vision of Yutai and Wongvipa, and the looks on their faces, haunted me. *Shrimp,* I thought suddenly. *The brother of the monk who was now in jail for smuggling, the big man in the amulet market who told me his name was Shrimp, and who had seemed determined to take the bad amulets off my hands. That's who was talking to Yutai.* The way I saw it, the meeting was neither a coincidence nor casual.

At the end of the performance I found David Ferguson.

"Come with us," I said to Jennifer and Chat. "It will be fun." In truth I just wanted to keep them both near me, to keep them safe.

"You go, Jennifer," Chat said. "I have a really bad headache. I think I'll just go home."

"I'll go with you," she said loyally.

"No, really," he said, squeezing her arm. "I'm just going to take something for this headache and go to bed. I'll see you in the morning."

"If you're sure," she said.

"I'm sure. I'll have the car pick you up at the Skytrain around what? Eleven, eleven-thirty?"

We spent a very pleasant evening with David. I made the introductions with Praneet, but she was on her way back to the hospital and couldn't join us, much to David's disappointment. As promised, he took us to a restaurant where we were the only *farang*. I had no idea where we were, but the food was fabulous. Jennifer enjoyed herself, too, although I could see she was thinking about Chat a lot of the time.

It was a busy night in Bangkok, and after dinner we got stuck in traffic that barely crawled along. At some point we found ourselves in what I suppose might euphemistically be called an entertainment district, all flashing neon and crowded sidewalks.

"This is Pat Pong, as you've no doubt already surmised," David said.

"Stop the car," I said.

"That shouldn't be difficult. We're barely moving."

"Pull over," I said.

"Are you going to be sick or something?"

"We have to find a parking spot."

"A parking spot!" he exclaimed. "Here? You've got to be kidding."

"I'm getting out," I said. "I'll see you later."

"Lara!" David exclaimed. "Where are you going?"

"I'm coming, too," Jennifer said. "Wherever it is we're going."

"Hold it! You're not going anywhere without me," Ferguson said. "Just give me a minute to park. Now what is this all about?" he grumbled a few minutes later, as we abandoned the car in an alley. I pointed to a bright neon sign on top of one of the buildings and the arrow that pointed down the street.

"You have a sudden urge to go to something called the Pink Pussy Kat Klub?"

"PPKK," I said. "We're going to have a chat with Mr. Prasit, the assistant manager."

"Okay, here we go." Ferguson sighed. "Hold on to your wallets. There are pickpockets everywhere."

The Pat Pong may be tame now, compared to its heyday, when American servicemen fighting in Vietnam went there for a little R and R. But it was still racy enough for me. Neon signs flash out Kiss Me Club, Dream Boys, and Super Pussy. VIP-service rooms to rent on a short-term basis are advertised everywhere. There's a massage parlor every few yards. In the midst of all this, there's a night market the locals disdain for its cheap merchandise and high prices, and for something of a contrast, a few well-known fast-food and coffee chains.

At night most people come for the alcohol and titillation, not for the burgers. From the *soi*, it is easy to see inside to the table dancers, young and not so young men and women scantily clad, gyrating to the loud and persistent music.

Outside are the hustlers, trying to lure you in. Sometimes these are men with suggestive photos of what is inside. In other cases there are women in long, formal gowns, with numbers pinned to their dresses, shouting at unaccompanied men to get their attention.

The Pink Pussy Kat Klub was, if anything, among the worst. Outside, very young Thai girls were dressed in school uniforms, of all things, with oxfords and kneesocks, navy pleated skirts and ties, white shirts, and blazers. In keeping with the theme, the kneesocks and blazers were pink. I felt a pang as they reminded me of Bent Rowland's Parichat, and indeed maybe she'd been one of them until Rowland took her away, at least temporarily, from it all. Inside, the music was so loud I could feel it in my bones, and flashing strobes made me dizzy. The place smelled of stale booze, perspiration, and cheap perfume. Rather lithe young women in extremely brief bikinis, pink, it perhaps goes without saying, were contorting themselves into positions middle-aged women like me can't even think about without hurting ourselves. I yelled my question about where to find the assistant manager to David, who in turn shouted in Thai to the bartender, who waved us in the direction of the back. We pushed our way through a throng of men, mostly white, overweight, and badly dressed, who were sweating from heat and excitement, as young Thai women pressed themselves against them. It was, in a word, revolting.

"Yuck," Jennifer said.

Being in this place made me think of Rob, Rob the policeman, that is. He'd have had the place closed down in ten minutes. We passed a particularly young girl—she couldn't possibly have been more than twelve—sitting on the lap of an overweight American in a Hawaiian shirt who was fondling her as she murmured, "You my darling," or words to that effect. *Make that five minutes,* I thought. Rob would have been absolutely horrified.

Mr. Prasit's office was at the top of the dark stairway. He shared it with another young man. The room had a small window on the inside, presumably so that he could keep an eye on the goings-on downstairs, a small desk, and a computer. His job, I could see, was to keep the accounts. Even up there, the noise was painful and the heat almost unbearable. He looked surprised to see us.

"My name is Lara McClintoch, and these are my friends Jennifer and David Ferguson," I said. "I'm here at the request of Natalie Beauchamp, Mr. William's wife. I am hoping you can spare a few minutes to talk to me, and perhaps have something for me to take back to Mrs. Natalie."

"Not here," he said, looking terribly embarrassed, which I would have been, too, if I'd been him, dressed in his bright pink shirt in such a place. "Please to follow me." He spoke in Thai to the other resident of the office, who nodded. We made our way out the back—I was happy not to have to press my way through the throng in the bar again—and down an alley that I wouldn't want to be in alone. A block or two away from the hubbub we mounted a staircase to a second-floor flat. Prasit's apartment was tiny and smelled of cooking from the restaurant below. He shared it with his wife, Sarigarn, who was out at work at that time, he told us, his mother, and two children of about five and two. I found it hard to reconcile his home and his job, and apparently he did, too.

"You will please not to mention my children about my job, okay?" he had said just before we went in.

"Okay," we agreed in unison.

"Please sit," he said. "My mother bring tea. Cannot rest here so long. Must go to club very soon. I have for Mrs. Natalie package. Please wait here."

He disappeared into another room as his mother poured tea into chipped cups—David had to stand because there weren't enough seats—and reappeared a minute or two later with a large package wrapped in brown paper. "Sorry not send Mrs. Natalie. Very expensive for mailing. I am for saving money to send it."

"That's okay," I said. "I'll make sure she gets it." But not without opening it first. "How do you know Mr. William?" I asked.

Prasit pondered the question. "I think one year," he said.

"Why don't I translate?" David said. "It'll go faster." The two spoke for a moment or two, while I smiled at Prasit's mother and his two kids.

"Prasit's wife works for a cleaning company that has the contract for the building Fairfield Antiques is in," David said finally. "She works at night. During the time Will had the antique business, Mr. Prasit had a day job, and he would take his wife there so they could have a little more time together. Mr. William would talk to him while he waited for her to finish up. He says Mr. William was very kind and gave his wife extra money for special cleaning, and also helped to get him medicine for his mother, who has what I think is arthritis. Occasionally Will came to the Pink Pussy Kat Klub, but I gather from Prasit he was not a regular and only stopped by for a drink. He says he thinks Will was a bit lonely and wanted to talk. He also practiced his Thai on Prasit, and Prasit did the same with English."

"Can you ask him when he saw Mr. William last?"

"I already did. He saw him early in July. Same time as

just about everybody else. It was about that time that he got the night job, so he didn't take his wife in anymore. She went in and cleaned for several weeks without seeing Will, but that was not necessarily unusual. She only saw him when he worked late. He had often left by the time she got there. Finally, of course, the landlord came, and the store was closed."

"And how did he get this stuff of Will's? The envelope with the clippings and this big package."

Ferguson and Prasit spoke for a minute or two. "He says Will gave it to him shortly before the last time he saw him. He said Will just told him if he didn't see him for awhile he was to send it to Natalie. He feels badly, I think, that he took so long to send it. He said that he didn't realize at first that Will wasn't coming back. His wife didn't say much, and when the store was closed down, he realized he had to send the stuff. He knew where Will lived. I gather his wife made extra money from time to time doing some special cleaning there, and he knew there was a Mrs. Praneet next door with a key, and so he checked for Will there. He says he has to go back now, or he'll lose his job. I think we should let him go. I'll give him my card, and if he thinks of anything else, I'll ask him to call me."

Jennifer was rather silent the rest of the way back, especially as we sank into the back of the Chaiwong limousine. "You're thinking about the conditions under which Mr. Prasit and his family live," I said.

"I am," she said. "It is quite a contrast to Ayutthaya, isn't it? I suppose I have trouble reconciling the two, but I can see why Chat thinks things could be better for people here. What is it, do you think?" she said, changing the subject and pointing to my package.

"We'll have to wait and see," I said.

I knew what the package contained, but I didn't open it until I was back in my room at the Chaiwongs. I didn't want the driver to see it. After Yutai's conversation with the security guard, I decided I didn't trust any of them. It was the painting, of course, the one by Robert Fitzgerald that had hung in Will's bedroom. I unwrapped it carefully and stood it up against the back of a chair.

A young woman stood there staring straight at me. She was in her mid- to late twenties, with dark hair and pale, flawless skin, dressed in a celery green suit and white blouse. She was standing behind a small table on which was placed, to her right, a stone head of Buddha. Her left hand seemed to be reaching for the Buddha, although she wasn't looking at it; the right hand was at her side. She was very beautiful, but there was, indeed, a touch of defiance in her gray eyes, as Robert Fitzgerald had said. Behind her was a mirror in which could be seen, only faintly, a dark shadow.

"She's lovely," Jennifer said. "Who is she?"

"Her name is Helen Ford, and it's a long story, not necessarily a lovely one. I'll tell you tomorrow."

"Okay," she said. "I'll look forward to that. It's late. I think I'll just leave Chat to sleep. I won't wake him. He'll feel better in the morning. I'll show you the you-know-what then, too," she added, pointing at her ring finger. I watched her go down the hall, wondering whether I should tell her about Fatty. I decided I'd see how I felt in the morning.

Chapter 11

It is a solemn but also a joyous occasion when one is admitted to the monkhood. Once across the river, Yot Fa was carried on the shoulders of two courtiers to the Khòk Phraya Monastery, to the sound of drums and gongs, and accompanied by his friends, including me. There the head abbot directed the young king to kneel, and after prayers, cut a lock of the young man's hair. Then his head and eyebrows were shaved, he was undressed and wrapped in the simple robe of the monk, then water was poured over him to wash away the world. As I watched him rub his bare head and smile, I thought how both prince and poor man were alike, somehow, in the robe of the monk. Like the others, Yot Fa would go out at dawn to beg for food, would spend his days in contemplation and prayer. It was an unsettling experience for me. As I looked at him, I felt the world shift beneath my feet. "You can join me as a monk," he said to me, but I could see nothing but my beloved's face and turned back to the city. It was a terrible mistake.

One night, shortly after Yot Fa had entered the monastery, I awoke from a terrible dream. I heard footsteps running, and a courtier was soon shaking me. "Come," he said. "Quickly. The young king asks for you." The man was shaking so much he could hardly speak.

It was a long trip across the river in the dark, to Khòk Phraya. The courtier would tell me nothing. Part of me thought the young king was just being, well, kingly, and wanted his friend with him. The other trembled at the thought that something terrible had happened. By the time I had arrived, however, I had persuaded myself it was the former and was annoyed with the young man for not having the fortitude for the monastic life and for disturbing my sleep.

A monk met me at the gates of the temple. "I fear you are too late," he said. I did not comprehend what he was saying, did not do so, until I entered the tiny cell where the Prince slept. He was dead, his face and body contorted, still, in agony. On the floor beside the humble cot a wooden cup lay empty. The monk who had greeted me picked it up and sniffed it. "Poison," he said. I fled.

By morning, Chat was dead.

What I remember most is the wrenching cry of pain from Jennifer when she found him, not so much a scream as a primitive groan of grief. It will stay with me forever, even more than the sight of his body, curled up like a baby, except for the head that was thrown back in a horrible grimace of agony.

I also remember Wongvipa, standing over the body of her dead son, looking from him to Yutai, who stood in the doorway. On her face was an expression of what? Surprise? Complicity? I couldn't tell. I tried to comfort Jennifer, but the words wouldn't come.

"She's asleep now," Praneet said. She looked exhausted, but more than that, older, as if she'd aged overnight. Maybe she had. Maybe we all had. "I have given her something. She shouldn't wake for at least eight or ten hours. I'm so sorry," she said, touching my shoulder. "Try to remember she's young, she's resilient. She'll get over this eventually. Have you called her father?"

I nodded.

"Would you like me to give you something to help you sleep as well?"

"No," I said. "I want to feel every bit of this. I want it to hurt very much. This is my fault. It happened because I wasn't paying attention."

"No, please, Lara," she said. "Don't do this to yourself. As painful as it may be to realize this, Chat took street drugs. I know you liked him, Lara," she said. "We all did. And you want to think the best of him. But he took recreational drugs. Crystal meth, ice. It is horribly addictive. If Jennifer didn't notice, how could you?"

"He doesn't do drugs," I said. "Jennifer said so. I don't care what you say, she would know. I'm sure he thought he was taking painkillers." Inside my head a voice was screaming and screaming and wouldn't stop. Somebody had killed Chat. I knew it was Yutai, maybe with the tacit approval of Chat's mother. Yes, I was accusing Wongvipa of the worst crime a woman could commit, that of killing her child. Worse still, I knew I would never be able to prove it.

"Thank you for everything you've done," I said to Praneet in as normal a voice as I could muster.

"Are you sure you're all right?" she said as she left.

"Yes," I said. But I wasn't. I was convinced this was my fault, and nothing anyone could say would make me feel better. I had spent my time looking for someone I knew only casually, while evil was swirling right under my nose. Will Beauchamp's wife and daughter were worthy of some effort, yes, but not at the expense of Chat and most especially my Jennifer. I was responsible in some very fundamental way for her happiness, and I had failed her. Chat had seen something bad happening at Ayutthaya, and he'd come to me for advice. And what had I done? I'd gone off to read some diaries of a dead painter! I hadn't been paying attention to what mattered most.

I was so angry at myself I thought I'd lose my mind. I grabbed Will's bubble envelope full of junk and dumped it on the desk. I tore the clipping and the letter from Prasit into a million little pieces. Then I took one of the unbroken amulets and smashed it against the side of the desk. When that didn't work, I dropped it on the floor and stomped on it. Then I took the portrait and shook it. I wanted to cut it to shreds, but I couldn't think what I had that would do that. Then I remembered the sword and went for that.

I was poised to slash the painting when I noticed a computer floppy disk that must have fallen out of the back of the painting when I'd shaken it. I was about to grind that beneath my heel when I saw something else: a red eye winking at me from the dust that had been the amulet. I knelt down and found six rubies, beautiful ones, stunningly perfect, in the remains. I took the second amulet and broke it, to find six blue sapphires in the dust. And I realized then that the carefully wrapped pieces of broken amulet in the envelope were a message from Will. He was telling Natalie that a broken amulet meant something. No wonder the horrible man in the amulet market had wanted them back and someone had been searching my luggage. And didn't it just explain why someone had risked trying to snatch my purse in a crowded marketplace! The computer disk, too, was a message from Will. I picked it up, went downstairs and through the etched glass doors of Ayutthaya Trading, and spoke to the first person I came to. He introduced himself as Eakrit, the new CFO. I told the little worm I wanted a computer with a printer with lots of paper in it, and I wanted it right now.

Paradise Lost
The Untold Story of Helen Ford
Copyright William Beauchamp
C/O The Bent Rowland Agency, Bangkok, Thailand

In November of 1949, as Loi Krathong celebrations to mark the end of the rainy season got under way, revelers floating their lotus flower–shaped boats on the Chao Phyra just north of Bangkok made a grisly discovery. The torso of a farang, *a white foreigner, was found near the edge of the river. With no head nor limbs to help with identification, it seemed the murder, which clearly it was, would go unsolved.*

But within weeks, through a fortuitous discovery of bone fragments and teeth in the ashes of a large fire, the body was identified as that of Thomas "Tex" Ford, an appliance salesman from the U.S. living in Bangkok. Shortly thereafter, in February of 1950, his widow, Helen Ford, was charged with his murder.

The lurid case caused a sensation in the expatriate community in Bangkok. The beautiful Mrs. Ford had been a fixture on the social scene, and many hearts had been broken when she married Ford. Some said a jealous former suitor had murdered him in the hope of marrying his widow. Others said Tex Ford had gotten involved in some shady business dealings with Thai traders and had paid with his life. Helen Ford herself said that she had thought that Ford, whom she claimed had been abusive, had deserted her, taking with him their young son. His death, she claimed, had come as a complete surprise to her.

It was clear to everyone that love, if there had ever been any between Tex and Helen, was long gone by the time he died, just over a year after they married, and four months after the birth of their son. Helen had resumed her social schedule almost immediately, and if she mourned the loss of either her husband or her child, she didn't show it. She told everyone she planned to return to the U.S. as soon as she was permitted to do so, to start her life over.

But before she could do that, she was charged with murder and sentenced to die.

This is Helen Ford's story. It is a tale of passion, lust, and greed. It is the story of justice perverted, of love poisoned by prejudice, of the dark side of high society.

This is the story they didn't want you to know.

There was more, of course, 267 pages of it, to be precise. Even discounting a rather derivative title and the supermarket tabloid elements, it was a riveting tale. Helen Ford, née Helen Fitzgerald, and her brother Robert had come to Bangkok with their parents right after the war. The father, who had been a member of U.S. special forces, had been stationed in Bangkok during the war, and succumbing to the lure of the East, moved his family there. He died shortly after, however, of wounds he had received in combat in the Pacific. The mother, too, died not much later.

There had been some money in the family, although not

a lot of it, and it was important that Helen marry well. She was seen at all the best parties and apparently had a succession of suitors. But she loved someone else, someone unsuitable. In the mid-1940s, she began a liaison with a young Thai from a well-to-do family. They met clandestinely for at least two years. In a remarkable twist, given the times, it was not Helen's family who objected to the relationship. It was his.

At some point, the man told his family he was going to marry Helen. They were horrified and would have none of it, considering Helen to be after his money. The family tried to pay Helen off, and needing money and perhaps seeing the hopelessness of her situation, she apparently accepted. The young man's engagement to a Thai woman was announced a few months later. Shortly after that, Helen married Tom Ford. It was clearly a marriage of convenience. They had a son born eight months after the wedding. Ford was a drunk and a philanderer, according to Will. He may also have been a wife beater.

What seems clear is that Helen and her Thai lover continued to see each other. Will's hypothesis was that Tom Ford caught them in their little love nest, a tree house in Bangkok that belonged to her brother, or that the Thai came upon Tom beating Helen. Whatever the reason for the meeting, at the end of it, Helen's lover lay mortally wounded. He died from a stab wound before Helen could get help.

After that, Will's story sinks into speculation. According to his account, Helen went berserk and did, indeed, stab her husband. Then, in an effort to ensure his body couldn't be identified, probably with the help of her brother Robert, she hacked the body to pieces. She then killed her infant son. That body has never been found.

The story then enters the realm of public knowledge. Helen was tried, convicted, sentenced to die, appealed, won, and was instead jailed for about six years. She then disappeared from public view. It was a fascinating story at any time, but for me, at that moment it was a revelation. Because while at no time in the public record was either her lover nor, indeed, any other member of his family mentioned, Will Beauchamp felt no such compunction, naming Virat Chaiwong, Thaksin's brother, the second young man in the family portrait, as the lover. Even then, the Chaiwong family's power and influence must have been insurmountable. If the murder of Virat had been part of Helen's defense, she might have gotten off with the lesser sentence right away, the justifiable homicide idea. But Will had combed the records, what there were, anyway, and could find nothing.

So there it was. If I'd thought that finding Will was a separate issue from Jennifer and the Chaiwongs, then clearly I'd been wrong. But what did it mean? The picture of Will that was emerging was contradictory at best. He had been in business with Wongvipa, a business that required two sets of financial statements for some reason, and it couldn't be good. At the same time, or at least soon after, he wrote a book that was a damning indictment of Wongvipa's family. The obvious conclusion was the Chaiwongs were trying to stop publication of the book and were prepared to murder Will to do it. But what about Chat? Was Helen Ford still out there somewhere, determined to take her revenge on the family through the next generation?

I went back to look at the portrait. I swear I stared at it for an hour: Helen Ford in her lovely celery suit standing behind a table on which was placed a stone Buddha, her hand seeming to reach out for it. She stared directly at me. Then I tried not looking at her, but my eyes kept coming back, not to her, but to the Buddha on the table.

"There's something wrong with this painting," I said aloud. It was something about the hands. She looked a bit as if she was reaching for the Buddha image, but the hands were not quite right if that was what she was doing. To me it looked more like a protective gesture of some kind, but why protect the Buddha? I picked up the phone and called David Ferguson.

"I heard about Chat," he said. "What a terrible thing to happen. Is Jennifer all right?"

"She will be with time," I said.

"And her dad? Have you talked to him? And you? What happened?"

"Drugs," I said. "There must have been some mix-up. He thought he was taking painkillers for his headache." I could almost hear his brain ticking over. He was thinking what everybody else was thinking, that Chat was a drug addict. It seemed Jennifer and I were in a very exclusive group that saw it differently. And I had no way of proving otherwise, not yet anyway.

"Look, David, I can't talk long, and I'm nervous about using the telephone here, and yes, this is an unusual request under the circumstances, but I must know what the stuff on Will Beauchamp's wall was. The stuff we thought might be blood. Someone must know."

"Lara, why are you worrying about this now? You must be in shock or something."

"Please, David," I said.

"I'll call you back," he replied.

* * *

"Oil paint," he said about an hour later. "The kind artists use. There's some red pigment as well, and a thinner. The lab guy said he might have been cleaning brushes and managed to spatter it on the wall. That mean anything to you?"

"It does," I said. "Thanks." I grabbed the painting, had the security man call me a car, and headed into Bangkok.

"Oh, it's you," Robert Fitzgerald said, peering over the top of the railing. He was very pale, and his head was still bandaged, but he was home. "Come up," he said. "I see you've found the painting."

"Do you feel up to a little project?" I said.

"I think so," he said. "As long as it doesn't require running a marathon or anything."

"I want to clean this area of the painting," I said.

"The whole painting could use a little cleaning."

"I want you to remove the Buddha," I said, pointing. "Start right about here."

"I don't know that I should do that," he said. "It's a wonderful painting, and the artist is, after all, my father."

"Just look at that painting for a minute," I said. "Your father was an exceptional craftsman. His perspective was perfect. This is not perfect. Someone, maybe him, maybe somebody else, has changed this painting. Will Beauchamp thought so, too. He was starting to clean it when he was killed. See, if you look closely, you can see where he started."

"Killed!" he said. "You didn't say anything about him being killed. I know who Helen Ford is, by the way. I looked her up. A murderess. Why would I want to get involved in this?"

"How about because she was your father's sister?" I said.

"What!" he exclaimed. His pallor grew more noticeable, and he lurched back on the sofa. He seemed to be wheezing. I didn't care.

"I'm afraid so. Now, about the painting—"

"Oh my," he said. I suddenly realized that for all his bluster, Fitzgerald at the best of times was a rather fragile individual, and these were hardly the best of times. "Could you hand me that puffer?" he said, gesturing weakly to the device on the table. "My asthma—"

"Robert," I said, handing him the puffer but not waiting until he inhaled the medication. "This is really important, or I wouldn't be here. I'll explain about your aunt as we go, but you have got to get going on this."

Breathing restored, he peered at the portrait carefully for a few minutes. "You may be right," he conceded. "It could well be that someone painted over the original."

"Can you do it?" I asked.

"I think so. Just give me a minute to get some materials." He limped to the back while I sat in an agony of anticipation.

The face emerged slowly over the next several hours: dark hair, almond-colored eyes, tawny skin, and a gaze that matched that of the women whose hand was stretched out protectively toward it. "My God," Fitzgerald said. "It's a child, and it has to be hers."

"Is your mother still in town?" I said.

"Yes," he said.

"Let's go and see her," I said.

"Can you do that without me?" he said. "I'm feeling rather strange." He didn't look well at all. The pallor he'd exhibited when I'd arrived had in the meantime acquired a tinge of green.

"I'm sorry," I said. "This is too much when you're not well. Just point me in the right direction."

* * *

"Hello, dear," Edna Thomas said. She was a tidy little woman with gray hair and blue eyes. Her hands were gnarled with arthritis. "You're the nice girl who found Bobby and got the doctor, aren't you?" she said. "Of course I will help you any way I can." She spoke with that rather indeterminate accent many Americans acquire after they've spent many years in England. I found her in what could charitably be called a tourist-class hotel. The room was clean but rather depressingly spare. If her former husband had made money with his paintings, she did not appear to have benefited from them.

"I need to know about Helen Ford. Specifically, I need to know about her children."

"Mercy!" she exclaimed. "I'm not sure . . . what children?"

"Mrs. Thomas, please," I said. "People are dying over this. Your son could have been one of them if I hadn't found him. This is what I know." I told her everything I'd read in Will's manuscript, and then I told her about the painting.

"He should have destroyed it," she said. "I told him to. He couldn't bring himself to do it, though. That painting was all he had left of his sister, whom he adored. In order to be able to keep it, he painted over the child with that Buddha."

"The children," I repeated. "I must know about them."

"There were two," she said. "One by her husband, one by Virat Chaiwong. She was single, of course, when she got pregnant the first time. Both times, come to think about it. That first time, she was sent off to Singapore. That's what girls did then. They just said they were going back to the States or whatever for a few months. Then they came back looking much like before. Most of them came back empty-handed. Not Helen, although I didn't know it at first. Robert knew, but he didn't tell me right away. I confess I was shocked when I saw him. I know I shouldn't say this, but you have to think of the times. I was horrified. His father was obviously Thai. They are beautiful, though, the children of mixed race. The boy was one of the most beautiful children I have ever seen. It didn't matter what I thought, of course. This was her love child, and she wasn't giving him up. She was a stubborn one. She didn't give two hoots what people thought. The child was cared for by a Thai family. They knew the child was Helen's but not who the father was. She visited the child every day. There weren't many places she could meet with the boy, other than the home she'd placed him in. She used to take him to Robert's studio. They'd sometimes meet Virat there.

"When she killed her husband—and she did, believe me: it was shortly after the birth of Bobby, and I've often wondered if it was a really severe postpartum depression. These days she might have got off, with a good lawyer. . . ." She seemed to be fading a little.

"Did she kill the children?" I said, rather brusquely, I'm afraid. I felt I had to keep her focused, or I wasn't going to find out what I needed. "I must know whether or not she murdered her children."

"Of course not! How could anybody think that a mother would do such a thing. She told Robert and me to get the children away, that nobody was to know where they were, and no one was to know that Virat's boy even existed. That's why Robert painted him out of the portrait. I took the other boy to England. You won't tell Bobby, will you? I have brought him up as my own son, loved him as my own son."

"I won't. If you think he should know, I'll leave that to

you, I promise." It was tempting to tell her that a large part of Robert Junior's problem was due to the feeling that he would never be as good an artist as his father, and that he might well feel better knowing he wasn't the great painter's son. But this was not the time for that.

"I'll never tell him," she said. "He's rather gruff, but he's a sensitive soul underneath. This would be too difficult for him. He had a nervous breakdown a year ago. I sometimes wonder if he takes after his mother way too much. She was always what we used to call high strung."

"And the other child?"

"Thaksin Chaiwong found out about the relationship between Helen and Virat—I don't know how—and that was the end of it. He was furious. Thaksin was the younger brother, but he took the part of family leader pretty quickly when he found out. He was already settled at that time, with a wife and small child of his own. He demanded that Virat cut all ties with Helen, and for a while, at least, he did. Helen was heartbroken, but she didn't abandon the child, and as far as I know, Thaksin never knew about the child, couldn't have known. Virat's engagement to a Thai girl was announced, and Helen married that dreadful fellow Tom Ford—I could never bring myself to call him Tex—just as you said. It was doomed right from the start. She was pregnant again, and I guess she saw no option this time. Then I think that Helen and Virat started seeing each other again.

"I'm not exactly sure what happened the night Virat was killed, although I do know that it was Tom who killed him. It's what happened to Ford after that I'm not certain about. But we knew what we had to do to protect the children. Robert, my husband then, sent the Thai family who were looking after the Chaiwong boy, who was about five, to Chiang Mai. We gave them as much money as we could so they could look after him. We didn't have a lot. We were sure that the Chaiwongs would kill the boy if they found him. They were awful people. At least Helen thought so. They weren't for having complications where inheritance and such were concerned."

"Will Beauchamp thought she'd used an antique sword that belonged to the Chaiwongs to do the, you know, chopping," I said.

"That's a silly notion. The sword was my husband's, not Virat's. Robert acquired a lot of interesting things to use as props: that sword, the stone head of Buddha in Helen's portrait. You could find things like that in those days, buy them for next to nothing. He used to let his subjects choose a prop for their portrait if they wished. He said it relaxed them, but that it also told him something about them. That's a laugh, isn't it? Virat Chaiwong, the swordsman. A rather poor joke, I suppose. I have no idea what she used that night or what weapon killed Virat. But the sword was in my possession that night.

"It ended our marriage, you know. Robert and I went to England, but he had to come back here. I wouldn't go. It had all been too much, and I was afraid they'd take Bobby away from me. We divorced a few years later. My second husband, Ed, was such a fine man. He adored Bobby. He, too, thought he was my son. Bobby took after his mother's side of the family, and therefore he looked like Robert. He has his uncle's hands and talent. No one thought anything of it. You could get away with those kinds of things if you knew the right people in Bangkok in those days. I left with papers that said he was my son.

"I've worried about the other boy, you know, over the years. Robert sent money when he could. He stopped painting for a while, though, so it was tight. He didn't start again for ten years, and then he painted those awful things—grotesque, I thought they were. But at least he started to make money again. There are people who like to have horrifying art in their living rooms, I suppose. Perhaps it's the shock value. Who knows? My interpretation of them was that Robert had something to do with what happened to Ford, the body being carved up and everything, although if he did, he never told me about it.

"I don't know if Robert continued to send money to the family in Chiang Mai. By this time, we were divorced, I'd remarried, and in addition to Bobby had a little girl. I live with my daughter and her family now. I see I needn't have worried about the boy, though. He seems to be doing just fine. The Chaiwong talent for making money, I expect, runs in his veins."

"How do you know this?" I said.

"I saw him in the paper, didn't I? The *Bangkok Herald*. Christening some big ship or other. Wichai Promthip," she said. "That's his name now."

My God, I thought. "And Helen?" I said. "Do you know what became of her?"

"She changed her name, her identity, and went back to the States," she said. "She vowed never to see the children again. She thought to do so might put them at risk, and anyway, how could she ever explain what happened? She created some kind of life for herself. She was that kind of determined, but I'm not sure she was ever really happy."

"How did she avoid being—"

"Executed? I'm not sure. She appealed, of course. I'm sure

Thaksin and the rest of the Chaiwongs would have been thrilled if she'd died, but she hired a very aggressive lawyer for her appeal, and I expect she made sure the Chaiwongs knew that she'd drag the family down with her if she didn't get off. Thaksin thought it was better just to get her out of the country. I have often wondered if in the end he helped her get a reduced sentence and then disappear. She was the kind of person who would have demanded it. In many ways she was fearless. Perhaps this was the price of her silence, I don't know. I hear Thaksin has died. I suppose we'll never know. She did spend time in jail, and it was horrible, I'm sure, but I'd left by this time. All I know is that there was a lot going on behind the scenes."

"Are you going to tell me where she is and what her new name is?"

"No," she said.

"Please," I said. "Chat Chaiwong has been murdered. He was a very good person, and engaged to my niece. I keep wondering if it has something to do with this."

"If you're thinking she did it, taking revenge on the Chaiwongs, then you'll have to think again. I'm not saying she wouldn't be capable of it. Maybe she was, and maybe she wasn't. But she's dead. I think it should all die with her."

"Would you tell me she was dead even if she wasn't?"

"Yes, I would," she said. "There have been a lot of people looking for her over the years, reporters and the like. Even that man William Beauchamp. He had the details, everything except the children, but I wasn't helping with that. He just wanted to know where Helen went. I didn't tell him, and I won't tell you. In over fifty years, I've never told anyone where she went. I'm not about to start now."

Chapter 12

What agony I *have endured. I cannot find words to express the rage and self-loathing I felt at the young king's death, emotions so strong that I thought I would die. I had betrayed my mother, my king, and indeed Ayutthaya.*

My horror at what had happened was made worse by a fear about my personal situation. Terrified, I presented myself at Ratchapraditsathan Monastery where, prostrating myself before the chief abbott, I begged to be accepted for training as a monk. He refused my request, but perhaps seeing my distress, granted me a few days' sanctuary at the temple. My fear and guilt soon manifested themselves as an illness. Racked with fever, I tossed and turned, at times delirious, I am certain.

My illness did not respond to the care and treatment of the monks, and eventually the abbot came and sat with me. "Your thoughts are like a poison in your body," he said. "I have seen you racked with despair. I have heard you cry out in the night. What is this poison that destroys you?"

It was several days before I was able to tell him what I had seen that night by torchlight, as the dancers performed, and what I thought it had meant. He was right, however. The next day, though still weak, I was able to take some food for the first time in many days.

The next evening the abbot led me to a room guarded by monks. In the room were four men and another priest. To my surprise, it was the priest who spoke.

"Do you know who I am?" he said.

"I do not," I replied.

"Look more closely," he said. "Beyond the robe and the shaved head."

I gasped. "You are Prince Thianracha, the dead prince's uncle, brother to his father, King Chairacha." I prostrated myself before him.

"That is so. Please, rise. Do you know these men?" he said, gesturing to four who were with him.

"I have seen them in the palace," I said. I was trembling in the presence of such power. My life, it seemed to me, hung in the balance.

"Do not be afraid," the prince said. "This is Khun Phirenthòrep." The man looked straight at me, and I had to look away. "And this is Khun Inthòrep," the prince went on. "Mun Rachasena, and Luang Si Yot. These good men have come to tell me about the state of affairs in the royal court of Ayutthaya, and the abbot has suggested you have information that would be of use to me."

At the prompting of the abbot, I told my story again, brought to tears with the retelling of the death of my god-king and friend.

"You see, it is as we told you," Khun Phirenthòrep said. "Something must be done about this usurper and his deadly queen."

"We are agreed," the prince said. "Let us retire to Pa Kaeo Monastery to practice candle divination before an image of Lord Buddha to ascertain our chances of success in these endeavors."

We, all of us, went to Pa Kaeo to make obeisance to the image of Lord Buddha and to light two candles, one for the prince, the other for Khun Worawongsa. For a time it looked to be that the prince's candle would be the first to die, thus indicating that Khun Worawongsa's cause was more just, but then, most extraordinarily, the usurper's candle was suddenly extinguished.

"The day is yours," the abbot said to the prince. "The candle divination is proof that you have sufficient merit that you will be successful in what you plan."

"I accept the result, though I do not ask for it," the prince said. "Now all will return to our posts to make plans and await an opportunity to act. Your bravery in telling us this story will not go unrewarded," he said, turning to me. "Now go to the palace and await word."

The first time I'd journeyed to Chiang Mai, I'd found a peace of sorts in the rhythm of the river and the tranquillity of the wats. This time I was not there to try to re-create the calm I'd felt in the temple. That had been revealed as an illusion, or at best a temporary respite from the poison that seemed to seep around everything I saw and did. I had not come back to find comfort. I had come for revenge.

The headquarters of Busakorn Shipping was just outside of town, located in what looked to be an abandoned hotel. To one side of what had once been the lobby was an empty swimming pool. To the other, a two-story white stucco structure surrounded a courtyard in which an empty fountain sat in a sea of brown grass. Dragonflies flitted about the courtyard, and the air shimmered from the heat. There was a guard right inside the door who, after looking me up and down suspiciously, agreed to call Khun Wichai's office.

"Tell him it's Lara McClintoch. We are acquainted through the Chaiwongs. I have something I'm sure he will be interested in," I said.

To the guard's surprise, and in a way to mine, I was permitted to enter. Intimidating though it was, anger and guilt carried me across the courtyard past a number of young men, all of whom watched me closely. They nodded pleasantly enough, however, and directed me through a breezeway at the back and then on to a warehouse beyond.

The warehouse was lined with shelving on which sat terra-cotta Buddhas by the hundreds, if not thousands. Khun Wichai's office was at the back. Before I was allowed to enter it, a young woman searched me. She was polite but thorough. Two very large men stood outside the office door. They didn't *wei,* perhaps because it would have taken their hands too far away from their guns. "Come in, Ms. Lara," Wichai said at last. "Sit down, please. Tea? Or perhaps something stronger. Whiskey?" A man who looked capable of picking me up and wringing my neck like a chicken at the smallest of provocations stood in one corner.

"No, thank you. This is not a social visit. I'm here for what I hope will be a mutually beneficial exchange of information," I said. "I have a number of questions, or rather, I need to test some hypotheses, and I hope you can help me. I've brought you a gift, something I thought you might like to have. A remembrance of things past." I handed him a large package wrapped in brown paper.

The guard stepped forward and seemed about to whip the package away, but he was stopped by an impatient gesture on the part of my host, who after a few moments' hesitation, opened it.

"You'll perhaps want to have it fully restored," I said. "This was just a first effort. It will clean up very well, though, don't you think? If you're looking for someone to do it, I'd suggest Robert Fitzgerald. You and he have a lot in common."

"Where did you find this?" he said. His voice was even, but I could see he was wrestling with strong emotion.

"A man named William Beauchamp bought it from the artist's son. It came to me through a series of circumstances."

"Do you know her name?"

"Yes, I do."

A slight smile crossed his face. "Then perhaps you should ask your first question, test one of your hypotheses."

"Thank you. I am trying to confirm some details of the death, perhaps I should say *murder,* of William Beauchamp. Did you kill him?"

The guard, who apparently understood English, stepped forward in a rather menacing way. Wichai said something in Thai, and the man left the room, obviously reluctantly.

"There. That's better, isn't it?" Wichai said. "You are either brave or foolhardy, I'm not yet sure which." Actually, I was desperate, but I didn't say so. "But, to your question: the answer is no."

"What about Bent Rowland, his agent?"

"I realize I have something of a reputation, but again, no. Perhaps at some point in this conversation you might tell me why you think I would be responsible for these deaths."

"William was writing a book that somebody didn't want published, and given it reflects rather badly on the Chaiwongs, I naturally think it must be one of them, or possibly one of their friends, concerned that its publication might reflect badly on certain business interests they have in common. Bent Rowland, Beauchamp's agent, was, I believe, being paid by the Chaiwongs to make sure the book never got published, and died for the same reason Will did."

"I haven't killed anyone in connection with this at all yet." There was just the slightest emphasis on *yet.* "Nor do I know with any certainty who did it. I could, however, speculate." Up to this moment he had been looking around the room, or out the window, or on a spot just above my head. But suddenly he looked right at me. He had the most extraordinary eyes, almond in both shape and color, flecked with green.

"Helen Ford," I said.

He looked out the window for a minute before replying. "I had occasion to introduce someone I assume was representing the Chaiwong family—they spoke to me through an intermediary, you understand—to an associate of mine who would be the sort of person who would undertake such an activity. The family was in some distress about the situation, and as their friend, and as you have hinted, a business associate, one who has plans for the company, naturally I felt obliged to help them."

"Naturally," I said.

"Speaking as a dispassionate observer, I must say it was all rather ineptly handled. I believe in killing someone only as a last resort. I would have thought large sums of money would have been effective, and if that failed, then intimidation. How could they have thought he wouldn't find out about the false contract?"

"I see you know a fair amount about this matter. I have obviously come to the right place. Money worked with Bent

Rowland, at least it did until he either became frightened or expendable. And certainly, given the fact that Will chose to move some of his belongings, including this portrait, to a safe place would indicate he was frightened. But I have more questions. Was this intermediary you spoke of Mr. Yutai?"

"Possibly."

"And this colleague of yours you introduced him to? Would he have a stall in the amulet market?"

"That, too, is possible."

"And I suppose that once the connection had been made, the two men might continue their business relationship on other related projects: intimidation, a little roughing up, and so on."

"I suppose that, too, is possible, although I have to tell you I have no direct knowledge. I am only a dispassionate observer."

"What if I told you the book was actually about her?" I said, pointing to the portrait. *Still dispassionate?* I thought.

"Was it?" He seemed momentarily disconcerted. "Then I regret my involvement, no matter how peripheral."

"Your English is impeccable," I said.

"Thank you," he said. "It is a skill I acquired in my very early years as a purveyor of various commodities to American troops enjoying a respite, well deserved I'm sure, from the hostilities in Vietnam. My parents both died when I was quite young, and I was forced to support myself. I found I was rather adept at it. This book: is there a copy? No, of course not. That was the point, wasn't it?"

"That was the point, yes," I agreed.

"If there were," he said. "I would very much like to see it."

"I would be interested in knowing, if you'd care to share them, those plans you mentioned for Ayutthaya Trading," I said.

He chuckled. "You Western women really are very amusing. In keeping with the rapport we seem to be establishing here—you'll notice I have found a smattering of French useful for my interests on the other side of the border with Vietnam, or should I say Indochine?—I will tell you. I plan to take over the company. My whole life I've looked at the Chaiwongs and aspired to be like them, wealthy and socially acceptable. I plan to acquire that wealth and acceptance. One way or another, I might add. I had hopes for a marriage union. But so far that has not worked out. I rather liked young Chat. I would have been happy to have him as a son-in-law. But he apparently loved another. That is not your Miss Jennifer's fault. I know that. She has nothing to fear from me. There is still Dusit, but I love my daughter, and I think he is not the sort of young man I would choose for her. He is spoiled and will never amount to anything. That leaves me the business option."

"The marriage idea wouldn't have been a good one, anyway. Your daughter would have been marrying her cousin."

Several long seconds went by, a lifetime almost. I thought I heard a plane overhead, and the buzz of an insect somewhere. Outside the door, I could hear the low murmur of the guards.

"Is that right?" he said at last.

"I believe so," I said.

"You surprise me," he said. "I am not often surprised. I have tried to ensure I can't be. I knew the minute I saw that painting in the living room, the one with the sword, there had to be a connection. It took me back to my childhood in a flash. I was allowed to play with it, you know. In the scabbard, of course, and never when I was alone. But I never dreamt . . . There was a man there, in my memory. His face is a blur. You are going to tell me he was my father."

"Virat. Thaksin's older brother. Your father."

"Is that right?" he repeated. There was another long pause. "So I am the bastard son shipped off to the north and forgotten, am I?"

"I think it was for your protection," I said. "People who actually cared about you."

"And who might these people be?"

"Your mother and her family. Your mother felt that if Thaksin knew of your existence, you would not survive. I have no idea whether that is true or not. Perhaps if they had known, they would have killed you. On the other hand, perhaps they would have welcomed you into the family, and you would have had the life of luxury and social acceptability you wish."

"Knowing what I do of the family, I have no doubts as to which of those two options they would have chosen," he said. His eyes turned very dark.

"Your aunt has worried about you over the years," I said. "She's Robert Fitzgerald's widow, the man who painted the portrait, and mother . . ." I hesitated for a second, but I'd made a promise, even if it meant depriving this man of a brother. "Mother," I repeated, "of another Robert Fitzgerald, the one who started cleaning up the painting. If you're interested in meeting them."

"I will have to think about that," he said. "And *my* mother?"

"Her former sister-in-law says she's dead, that she went back to the U.S. under an assumed name."

"Do you believe her?"

"I don't know. Your mother would be almost eighty. I'll have to leave that one to you."

"Yes," he said.

"Now to get back to your plans for Ayutthaya Trading," I said.

"If anything, you have strengthened my resolve," he said. "While I have not yet read this book, should I find myself with a copy, I am reasonably sure I will not be happy with what it says, enlightening though it may be."

"You aren't in it. It was only the portrait that put me on to you. But, as for Ayutthaya, I take it you plan to have-Busakorn Shipping take over Ayutthaya Trading," I said.

"Exactly."

"What do you ship, Khun Wichai?" I said.

"Whatever my customers need me to ship," he said. 'I am a mere cog in the international service industry."

"Things like these amulets?" I said, setting a plastic bag filled with the broken shards in front of him. "Sapphires and rubies?"

He didn't even look at them. "I am as surprised as you are, of course," he said with the hint of a smile.

"And all those Buddhas out there in your warehouse. The blasphemous ones, with Buddha holding the world like an alms bowl. I assume that's how one goes about identifying the, shall we say, special ones, is it? What would be in those? Rather large for sapphires and rubies. What about plastic bags filled with white powder? Heroin out of Burma by way of Chiang Mai? Or pills? Ice, for example? You could ship a lot of pills in those things."

"As I said, I ship whatever my customers want me to. Some things I ship officially. Others I ship unofficially. You are treading on dangerous ground here, Ms. Lara."

"And Wongvipa would be one of the latter kind of customer?" I went on, ignoring him.

"Possibly," he said. "She has expensive tastes. I could marry the widow, I suppose—my wife died two years ago—but I would not be able to sleep for fear of my life." He laughed at the thought. "But tell me, why would you think that?"

"Because of the book, actually. The information in it would have been embarrassing, certainly, to the family. The events in it, though, took place half a century ago. One could easily shrug them off, in a way. But the book would have been a sensation, and it would focus attention on the family and its businesses, some of which might not stand up very well to intense scrutiny."

"I see."

"Wongvipa was seeking my assistance in developing the North American market for whatever it is she is actually selling."

"I expect you find that offensive," he said.

"She also engaged the assistance of William Beauchamp. I expect when he figured it out, he was offended, too."

"You are implying, I think, that he wrote the book as a way of trying to stop her, by focusing attention on the family and their business interests. That is possible, I suppose, but a dangerous strategy. He was perhaps out of his depth. You will forgive me, I hope, for saying that those among us with scruples are at a disadvantage in these situations. As to your discomfort with her unofficial business dealings, perhaps you had a more privileged upbringing than either she or I had."

"You are saying that I can afford to do the right thing,

and that is true," I said. "But so now can Wongvipa." And so, of course, could he.

"Some people never have enough," he said. "Their childhood experiences color their lives forever. Perhaps this sounds as if I am speaking of myself. My personal code, if you are wondering, is that I deal honorably with those who deal honorably with me."

"You are in business with Wongvipa," I said. "You should take a good look at the financial statements."

"I see them every month," he replied.

"To use your terminology, there are official financial statements, and unofficial ones."

"She's skimming, is she?"

"Possibly," I said.

"All the more reason to take over," he said. "But to go back to something you mentioned a minute ago: perhaps your reference to the contents of the Buddhas, should there be any such contents, is your way of accusing me of giving young Chat the pills that killed him. I did not do that. I was less than amused to find that the young man I had in mind for my daughter did drugs. I do not, nor does anyone in my employ. If they do, they are sent into rehab. If that does not work, then they are disposed of. As I have already told you, my plans to take over the company involved either marriage or a takeover."

"You have competition, Khun Wichai," I said, softly. "And no, I am not accusing you of killing Chat. I know who did that. Let's just say that someone without your scruples gave the pills to him, someone whose ambition is, if anything, greater than yours, someone whose greed is insatiable. Chat had a headache, and thought he was taking painkillers. The person who did that wants to own the company, too. Like you, he is prepared to consider marriage, in this case to Wongvipa, and if that doesn't work, then he'll try something else. Murder, apparently, is one option he is rather partial to."

"Yutai!" Wichai said.

"Fatty is his daughter, by the way, by Wongvipa."

"Ah," he said. "The power of love. Interesting, indeed. Can you prove it? That Yutai gave Chat the pills?"

"No. But I know what I saw."

"And about Yutai and Fatty?"

"No, but just take a good look," I said.

"And are you saying that what Yutai has done, he did with the approval, or at least the acquiescence, of Wongvipa?"

"I am."

"Even so far as the murder of her own child?" His voice sounded as if someone had put a rope around his neck and was slowly tightening it.

I took a deep breath before I replied. "I don't know," I said. "Maybe. Yes. I didn't see her try to stop it."

"I see. I can't say I ever really loved my wife," Wichai said. "But I have always loved my daughter. You are a fierce adversary, Ms. Lara. I am glad that we are not on opposite sides of this issue. I have found this conversation a most enlightening one. These are perhaps not the kind of people I would be able to do business with at all. Now I think you should go home, don't you, to Canada? You should take Miss Jennifer with you."

"That is exactly what I plan to do, Khun Wichai," I said.

"Good. Thank you for the information, and for the painting," he said, rising from his chair. "It means a very great deal to me. I remember her a little. Sometimes I still dream about her. Now I think this is good-bye. I believe you and I have reached an understanding here. I don't anticipate we will ever have the pleasure of meeting again. One of my colleagues will see you safely back to the airport."

"I have a couple more things," I said. He remained standing. "It would be very helpful if this colleague of yours could be persuaded to tell someone where William Beauchamp is buried. His daughter requires a great deal of medical attention, and she and her mother would benefit from the life insurance, assuming Beauchamp is proven dead."

"And the second thing?" he said. His voice was very quiet.

"If you look behind the painting, you'll find a small package containing a floppy disk taped to the back. It is the only disk I know of, and my paper copy has been destroyed."

"Good-bye, Ms. Lara," he said with an almost imperceptible nod.

"Good-bye, Khun Wichai," I replied. We did not shake hands.

Epilogue

The opportunity to *save Ayutthaya from the evil usurper came only two weeks later and was acted upon with considerable speed and the utmost coordination. When the usurper ordered his officials to move out to capture a large male elephant, the four conspirators, joined now by the Phraya of Phichai and the Phraya of Sawankhalok, moved quickly and assertively. Mun Ratchasena was dispatched to the Sua Landing to wait for Khun Worawongsa's brother, the upstart* uparat. *The others took to their boats and went to the Pla Mò Canal to wait in ambush.*

That day, Mun Ratchasena, who had hidden himself at the landing, shot the uparat *off his elephant, whereupon the man died. The other conspirators with their supporters, myself among them, rowed their boats right up to the royal barge, upon which rested Khun Worawongsa, Lady Si Sudachan, the daughter of their union, and Prince Si Sin, younger brother of Yot Fa. All were to die. "Save the Prince Si Sin," I begged them, remembering my mother's words. Moments later the usurper, the lady, and their daughter were all dead. Prince Si Sin, alone, was spared.*

The victorious conspirators then entered the great city and secured the royal palace before taking the Chai Suphannahong Royal Barge to Ratchapraditsathan Monastery to ask Prince Thianracha to leave the monkhood and to accept the throne. The prince agreed, and casting aside his simple monk's robe, assumed the trappings of majesty. The barge, with the peacock umbrella, fans, and golden shades, and accompanied by vast numbers of subjects, carried the prince to the palace landing, where he was invited to enter the royal palace.

On an auspicious day soon after, with all due ceremony, in the presence of all chief ministers, patriarchs, astrologers, poets and counselors, abbots and monks, Prince Thianracha ascended the throne, taking the royal title of King Chakkraphat.

Those of us who assisted the great prince have been well rewarded, the ministers with positions of great authority, the right and left gold trays of rank, land, and royal ladies and concubines for their wives. I, a lowly commoner, have been given a government post, the hand of my beloved in marriage, and many gifts, among them my most cherished possession. It is a sword, given to me by the king, sharp in its silver scabbard, its bone handle smooth in my hand.

I fear I will have much cause to use it, and indeed have already done so. Our enemies lurk, always poised to take advantage of the slightest sign of weakness. Already there is discontent and intrigue brewing within the cadre of nobles, Prince Si Sin, though he was adopted by our most compassionate king, among them. And sometimes, in the night, I look back on the past with some regret and to the future with much foreboding.

I've done a lot of thinking since I got home, most of it in the middle of the night, about whether or not I should have done what I did. In the end I believe justice was done, but at a price I am only just beginning to understand.

I have this idea that there's a concept in law that has to do with the notion of the reasonable person. It's a test, really. Could a reasonable person be expected to know something or other? Would a reasonable person act in a certain way? Because that, surely, is the question that haunts my sleep. Could I reasonably have anticipated what would happen next?

This question has cast a shadow on my relationship with Rob. He feels it, too, although he doesn't understand it. He says he thinks there must be things we need to talk through. I wish I could, but at the end of the day, how could I possibly tell a policeman what I've done?

I would dearly like to discuss it with someone. Moira, perhaps, who is my best friend, even if she took up with my ex-husband. She's smart, and best of all, very down to earth. Or even Clive, who beneath that rather cavalier exterior is actually an intelligent, thoughtful, man. The person I would most like to talk to about this is Jennifer, young as she is, but that's a long way off. She is, as all have said, resilient, but she still has a way to go. She's decided to finish up her university studies in Toronto. She can't bear to go back to California right now.

There are others I remember with real affection from that time: David Ferguson, who was a generous friend, and most especially, Praneet. She has more or less moved into the tiny teak house on the *klong* with David. So far there has not been so much as a peep out of her family about the fact that David is (a) white, and (b) twenty years older than she is. Real life has caught up with some of the Chaiwongs at last.

Then there's Robert Fitzgerald. His chess sets just fly out of the store. We can't keep them in stock. Even spirit houses are selling reasonably well. You wouldn't think there'd be a market in Toronto for spirit houses, but when Clive puts his mind to it, he can sell anything. Be warned. I think of the rather delicate wood-carver every time I sell something he created.

But ask any of these people the question? No. That leaves the demons of the night, some who rush to justify, others who hasten to condemn.

I wanted most of all to avenge Chat Chaiwong, you understand, a fine young man who had the potential to do great things. I also thought a child was entitled to know who his parents were, and perhaps more importantly, to know he was loved. I also wanted to put a stop to it, to strike a blow against the death and destruction those who sell drugs wreak. There is nothing wrong with any of that. The question, however, remains.

About a month after I got home, a plain envelope, with no return address but postmarked Thailand, slid through my mail slot. It contained a clipping from the *Bangkok Herald*, nothing more. According to the reporter's account, tragedy continued to dog the Chaiwong family. In the most recent event, there had been a terrible boating accident on the Chao Phyra near Ayutthaya, in which Khun Wongvipa, widow of the late industrialist Thaksin Chaiwong and vice president of Ayutthaya Trading and Property, had lost her life. The body of a senior official with the same company, Chief Operating Officer Yutai Boonlong, was found the next day, floating in the river. The only survivor of the accident was Dusit, younger son of Wongvipa, unable at that time to recall anything that had happened. Another child, a daughter, Prapapan, was most fortunately staying with a friend of the family, Busakorn Promthip, at the time of the accident.

Police were trying to determine how an accident of this magnitude could possibly have happened. They cited inexperience as a possible cause, Mr. Yutai having purchased the boat, valued at close to U.S. $100,000 only recently. In a separate and apparently unrelated incident, Mr. Yutai's brother, Eakrit, was also killed in a car accident as, upon hearing of the boating accident, he raced to the scene.

The article concluded with a statement by a spokesman for Ayutthaya Trading and Property that reassured customers and suppliers of the company that the affairs of the company were in good hands. Khun Sompom Chaiwong, son of Thaksin by his first wife, and one of the few remaining family members, had acted decisively to ensure continuity at the company. A minority shareholder, Khun Wichai Promthip, well known as founder and president of the extremely successful transportation company, Busakorn Shipping, had been persuaded to take the helm.

A couple of weeks later, Natalie Beauchamp called me. "I heard from the Bangkok police," she said. "They've asked me to help arrange to have William's dental records shipped to them. A body has been found, and they seem pretty sure it's his. I thought you'd like to know, given how hard you tried to find him."

"I'm sorry, Natalie," I said. "But I guess in a way this is good news."

"Yes," she said. "The life insurance will make a big difference. Those gemstones did, too. I know William sent them to me originally, but it was you who figured out they were there. I would have left those amulets just lying in a drawer somewhere, or I might even have thrown them out. It would have been thousands of dollars down the drain. I suppose the gems were Will's way of making amends?"

"I'm sure they were," I said.

"At least this dentist business will bring closure, if it works out. That's the most important thing. I feel as if I can get on with my life, and my daughter, in her own way, can, too. I've already made inquiries about special programs for her."

"That's terrific," I said.

"The police told me some anonymous person phoned in a tip as to the location of the body. After all this time!" she said. "Don't you think that's amazing?"

"Amazing," I said.